DEAD SPACES

DEAD SPACES

A DRUNKARD'S JOURNEY

PART II: BLOOD AND MADNESS

MARTIN GIBBS

Dead Spaces

By Martin D. Gibbs

This is a work of fiction.

ISBN: 978-0-9887121-9-5

Also By Martin Gibbs

The Untying: A Drunkard's Journey Part I
We Three Kings (republished by Ellechor Press
November 2014: Formerly known as *Following
Yonder Star*)

With Arthur Graham:

*Voltaire's Adventures Before Candide (and Other
Improbable Tales)*
*Voltaire's Excellent Adventure: The Broken
Boarder*

To Dori, Aidan, and Sam
My whole life would be dead space without you

Contents

Map

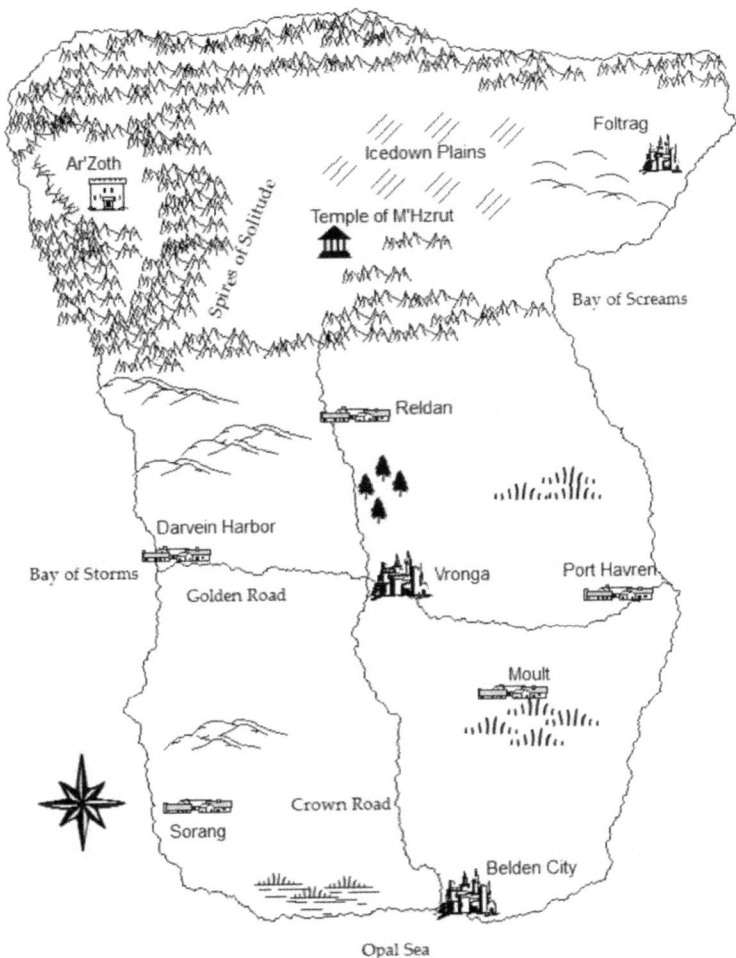

Foltrag

Icedown Plains

Ar'Zoth

Spires of Solitude

Temple of M'Hzrut

Bay of Screams

Reldan

Darvein Harbor

Bay of Storms

Vronga

Port Havren

Golden Road

Moult

Crown Road

Belden City

Sorang

Opal Sea

Prologue

Madness consumed all. Where once there were flickers of madness between the spaces of sanity, now the slivers of sanity were only speckles in the black void of madness.

Her voice.

HER voice! Her *VOICE!*

It grated. It charred. Like a fire, it burned me, then froze me as if I were being dangled out over the ramparts, left to flounder as a greater, unseen hand clutched my tail.

The horde called, the horde beckoned. It willed out. Without any direction it clawed closer and closer to the surface. What would happen if they reached the surface without my direction—without my control? What would happen to *me?* Would they kill me? Tear me limb from limb in their ecstasy of murderous rage? I was a prisoner, trapped inside of myself, trapped by the woman I had killed. Why? Why?

I was Ar'Zoth! I had mercilessly slaughtered anything that remained of Bimb. Bimb? Who was Bimb? Why was that name familiar? Had I killed someone already? No, wait! I do remember that name... it was a name that was forced upon me, a name that forever doomed me to a life of idiocy and despair. That is, until Ar'Zoth saved me from myself. Memories, perspectives, understandings, even music, was put to the flame. Bimb was dead. Ar'Zoth remained. Ar'Zoth and madness. Madness and demons.

Let us out.

"I will," I promised with a strained whisper. Magical spells, once forgotten, came back to the fore, but each time I began to take action, her voice would grate and grovel and beg and plead and cry and cry and cry and cry and CRY and CRY!

STOP! I tried to will the voice to stop, but was greeted only by pain and torment.

I will stop you, the voice whispered after an hour-long fit of rage.

"You will never," I panted. "I will find a way. Ar'Zoth will find a way!"

No, you will be stopped, Bimb.

Bimb! That name again. No, no, NO! Bimb was dead!

"Bimb is dead—Mother."

Then Bimb will have to die again.

$\oint$

"So where is he?"

"He's in the North, hopefully dispatching a dangerous warlock."

"Why?"

He spread his large hands. "It had to be done. No one else would believe the truth."

"Possibly because it was a lie all along?" the stranger sneered, balling a fist. "You sent him to his—"

"He's a strong man and will survive... he has aid. A little mage, a very powerful mage, is helping them. And again, I didn't send—"

"How...?"

"I have connections to the Counsel Guard and to the Archives. I know a thing or two." He paused, glanced around, and nervously continued, "This is far bigger than any of us, and we are better now that he has journeyed. And yes, it was my doing."

"But why?"

"It had to be done," he repeated flatly.

A huge fist slammed down on the pine surface, rattling glasses and sending various liquids into the air. "But he—he was a like a son to me, and you sent him..."

"I didn't send him anywhere," he replied, bristling. "He went of his own accord. And trust me; it was for the betterment of everyone. *Everyone.*"

"He could be..."

"No, we still stand here. This building and this city are still here. It would be much worse had he failed."

The rough hand pounded the bar again, this time with less force. "If I find out that he is dead, you will—"

"I will what? Answer to you? Go to the restraining house?" He chuckled deeply and shook his head. "If he dies, he will die a hero. Do you understand? You will wake up in the morning because of the sacrifice. Remember that."

A once-proud head hung low for a moment, then rose up, eyes glistening in the odd flashes of firelight. "Aye. I will try."

"I would like to speak no more of this," the man replied, lowering his voice. "Thank you for sharing your concern, but things must continue."

The stranger turned and walked to the door. He paused for a moment and looked back at the rough man. And for a mere moment, his lips broke into a smile before curling back into a frown. He carefully shut the door behind him.

Chapter 1
A Swirling in the Inner Depths

Do you stop for a wayward soul? For he who is lost? For the traveler who has wandered afar? If you choose to stop, or if you choose to continue, you create for yourself additional knots. Which is better? It cannot be known. Each may create for you a dangerous future.

Prophet Zhera, IV Age

Blinding sunlight hammered his skull. Fierce and unforgiving beams knifed into the backs of his eyes, sending tears flowing to protect against the onslaught. Even with lids tightly shut and an arm draped across his face, the intensity of the sun was enough to push him to his knees, sobbing. His knees screamed in throbbing pain as they smashed into the crumbling stone porch, but the brutality of the light was enough to quickly wipe away the sudden shock. With an arm outstretched in pleading, he moaned, "Who are you?"

A gruff voice in the sun-splashed street cursed something, and feet shuffled noisily on the stones. With his eyes covered, his sense of hearing seemed to explode into heightened sensitivity—he distinctly heard a sprig of dried clover crushed underfoot. The strange voice cursed again, and Zhy thought he recognized the voice. With extreme effort, he cracked his lids open ever so slightly and peered out. The figure was terribly familiar, and he recognized it at once—or did he? A flash of a memory passed before his eyes and then vanished. For a scant second, he was sure he had seen these men before, or men like them. But where?

The snow is too bright, he thought, then caught himself. Snow? There was no snow. Not here.

I don't want to go anywhere. I want to lie down and die. "Where?" he croaked. *Where are we going?*

"You know the answer to that question, Zhy. We're not finished. It is not finished. And no, you did not dream it. You were dead. Perhaps you still are. Come." The man spat and turned away.

Zhy rose slowly to his feet. Or at least he tried to. His knees buckled again and he collapsed, every nerve ending aflame with soreness and searing pain, his head throbbing as if smashed between two stones. He needed his arms free to push himself up, but the brightness of the snow—sun?— snow?—forced him back, face-down on the stone.

"You better get up, Zhyfrael," came a rough voice.

He swore, but it was nothing but a squeak. Zhy forced his lids shut, pushed his trembling hands against the porch and heaved himself to a standing position. As soon as he was upright, however, he took one step and wobbled, shooting an arm out to support himself against the crumbling doorframe. The strangers muttered to themselves. He was the subject of their conversation, but the pounding of blood in his head drowned everything.

"Zhy...?"

"I'm coming," he thought he heard himself say, but the words were a jumbled and garbled gurgle. It took a few moments, but he finally took a steady step forward and then another. His legs, as if lined with a thick syrup, did not feel solid, and his arms dangled oddly at his sides. Zhy's chest felt collapsed and efforts to pull air into his lungs brought only scorching anguish. A few more steps and he gained a little confidence, and ten paces later, he found himself staring at the brown, fuzzy fur of a massive horse.

The gruff stranger's voice bored into Zhy's ear, and Zhy grimaced as the stranger barked at him. "Zhyfrael, you can take that horse." He squinted fiercely against the late autumn sun, a sun which by all accounts should be muted and dusty with winter clouds. Instead, the southern reaches of Belden were sweltering in an extended duration of so-called dog days; the weather would eventually turn cooler, but snow was rarely seen this far south. Seagulls squawked in the distance, and he could hear the faint roar of the surf, only a few miles from where he wobbled. A smell of salt filled the air, but it was dulled and tarnished, as if the sea itself were slowly trying to bed down for a long winter.

"Zhy," he muttered his own name with a cracked voice. The sun seemed to gain in intensity, and he flung his arm over his eyes once more. *I have done this before*, he thought for an instant, but the gruff man was already grumbling about a need to start moving.

"Eh?"

"Call me—" He let out a hacking cough. "Call me Zhy." Finally, he let his arm fall away from his face and forced his eyes to adjust to the brightness. His face was pinched as he examined the—*strangers?* No, they were not strangers. There was something too familiar about these men, a presence that at once made them known companions, but also feared enemies. A vision of flashing steel and spraying blood passed briefly through his mind's eye. *I should not have opened my door.* Even if he hadn't, would they have simply burst in and hauled him away bodily?

The two men were of medium build and dressed in black. Their faces were almost shock-white, as if something had covered their faces. *Yes, where are their cloth masks?* Zhy wondered, then caught himself. How could he possibly know that? Where had the thought come from? The ill-tempered man was easily identifiable by his constant scowl, and his companion had a smoother, "easier" face, as Zhy would describe it. His glimpses at the strangers were brief, as he kept squinting his burning eyes. *The snow makes it worse.* Snow? No, there was no snow here. Why did he continue to think about snow?

"Zhyfrael, get on the horse."

The other started to speak, but shook his head briefly and gave his companion a quick, stern look.

"You can call me Zhy," he heard himself repeat. He had hoped to sound forceful, but his voice was a whimper. He approached the horse and stopped. As bright as the sun was, a murky fog seemed to cover everything like a tattered blanket. He put a knuckle in his back and the joints cracked loudly. An image of rock and snow—and falling. There had been endless falling before... *before what?* he wondered. He shook his head, every fiber throbbing in a dull ache. "Am I dead?"

The one looked at the other, as if to question whether his query deserved an answer. "No, you are not dead," the leader replied. "She said you had been dead for years before you truly died, but you are no longer dead. That is what she said. That is what she said," he repeated, scratching his head. "She said it would be like you had woken from a dream."

"She didn't say anything, and you know it," his companion admonished him. "It was written down."

"What is the Sacuan-blessed difference?"

"Plus, you added to that—she never said anything about him being dead. Where's that coming from?"

"Who are you talking about?" Zhy asked and thumbed his earlobe. He finally let his arm drop. The older man was already on his horse. He looked like a gargoyle sitting there—clad in black, hunched in his saddle, his rounded face a dour mask.

The nicer man—as nice as a caged and ravenous dog could be—flashed a brief smile and then glanced at the horses with a wisp of irritation. He had a longer face and had recently shaved off a mustache, Zhy noticed. His eyes were round pools of slate. Long eyelashes that would make a tavern maid blush blinked against the sun. "Some woman. She is dead. Really dead. I will explain on the way. We ride hard for Vronga." His voice was a little more soothing and patient. Though he sounded hurried and under stress, he still took the effort to provide Zhy with information. Useless information at this point.

"But how could she know me?" It was the first question of a dozen that leapt from his lips. A dead woman? *I never knew any women, at least that I can remember. Certainly not a dead—*

"That is unknown," the calm stranger replied, breaking up his thought. His companion scowled in silence. "Like I said, I have no idea how this works. The writing was so faint and so hard to read, I was convinced she had written it after death, though that is not possible." He gestured to the horse with irritation. "Mount up," he clipped. "Now. We can talk on the way." And he was already fifty paces ahead before Zhy coaxed his body into mounting the horse. His legs popped and creaked as he forced them up and over the body of the horse. The animal seemed to know what to do, for as soon as it felt Zhy's weight on its back, it launched forward to catch up with the others.

He had a fleeting memory of a long horse ride. Weeks, no... months, had gone by. Then the fog rolled through his mind and smothered the thought. *Why did I get on the horse?* he wondered. He should have remained in his home; he should have told the men to leave. He should have— *what? What does a dead man do when he wakes up?*

Zhy shook his head sadly. Everything around him was brown and gray. The leaves had fallen, and every tree was full of spindly, cragged, and bare fingers. As they swayed in a light breeze, Zhy swore they called out to him, *Come back, come back, little one. We are not done.* "Not done," he whispered.

He tried stretching his back again, but the bouncing and jarring along the cobblestones only worsened the pain. As soon as they had set a pace for the horses, the leader kicked his into a dead run. Likewise, the other two mounts shot forward, and Zhy lurched in the saddle, his body screaming in protest. At this pace, there would be no opportunity to talk. Every muscle cried out in agony. *Like I fell off a cliff. Like I fell off a—*

"Cliff!" he barked out loud. "I fell off a cliff!"

They were moving too fast for his companions to hear. *At least, this time, we're leaving the city at a much faster pace,* he remarked with an edge of cynicism. Then again, last time, he had left with a mountain of equipment—hadn't he? This group was traveling quite light. The horses were very large and bred for speed... where could they be going with such little gear? Certainly not very far. Not like last time, with gear loaded high, and a long trek before them, what with—

Wait! Where...? The vision was clear, but only for an instant. He had seen horses piled with equipment, and a burly man clad in leather, standing in a bright sun. It had been warm, then, as well. *Have I missed an entire year?* he wondered. No, no it could just be a very long autumn this year... a vision of snow flashed before his eyes once again, and his back screamed in agony, nearly sending him flying from the saddle. Panicked, he grabbed the pommel with an aching hand and kept his head lowered.

He had died. A tiny voice in his head whispered, *Death, is not always death*, and was then silent. Had he died? He shut his eyes tightly and tried to remember. *Falling. A cliff. I remember a man, standing...wind rushing through my hair— and a sudden darkness.* His eyes snapped open. *I died!*

"And I am dead!" he screamed, his eyes all whites, hair flowing in wild, unkempt curls. This time he yelled loud enough for a seagull far back on the shore to hear. A passing horseman glanced briefly at him, then quickly turned his gaze southward. "I am DEAD!" he screamed even louder.

"You are not dead!" the leader shouted back, without turning in his saddle. He too was hunched over his pommel, his eyes wide and his jaw set. Only the gruff leader sat erect; his round face was stern, his lips set in a flat line. He paid no heed to the small bugs that were colliding with his face, though he would spit now and again.

He's going to run these horses to death.

A stray bug flew into Zhy's mouth and he spat it out. Wanting to offer up a question, he instead grimaced at the metallic taste in his mouth and kept his head down as they raced along. A maple tree marked a curve in the road. Only the topmost branches sported any leaves, but by now they were a dull brown. When they careened around the corner, the leader suddenly barked and pulled the reins hard. The horses stopped willingly.

"No need to kill these ladies yet."

"I was wondering when you would stop—we've ridden too far, too fast already," the other man said, putting words to Zhy's concern.

As a response, the man swore as he dismounted and took the reins of the horse. He directed the others to do so.

"We will walk for a mile or so before riding again, Zhy," the other man said quietly.

Zhy followed and looked at the forest. Everything seemed duller somehow and not only with the aura of an oncoming winter. His memories were cloudy whirls and bubbles that refused to coalesce into anything solid. Faces and events were grainy and distorted—there was a cliff. A long, seemingly endless fall. And a shattering end. Death. Blackness. *Was that a voice? Right at the very end? A woman's voice?* No, wouldn't have been possible. A dusty inn swirled and slowly gained focus, but then spun off into the void. Two figures, one bulky, the other small, danced on the edges of his mind, but then vanished. Snow filled his mind. Snow and rocks. And a cliff. More memories tried to inch forward, but all were replaced with the rocks and the cliff. And a nauseating fall with a sudden, crushing stop. Again he shook his head against the protestation of his violent headache.

What is going on?

In an effort to increase their speed, but still save the horses, the leader of the strange trio developed a pattern. They would gallop the horses for seven or so miles and then stop to walk the horses for a mile or two. Next, they would push at a full run for two miles and then walk again. The cycle repeated once, but the leader finally spat something about "losing time" and kicked the horses into a gallop and kept them at that pace. They were killing the animals by doing that, even with the frequent walking. Perhaps they would get new ones in Forshen.

Forshen? Forshen... that was a name he remembered. Had he stopped there before? Why would he think that they would stop there?

No, I didn't miss a year, Zhy remarked as the pace slowed. The temperature was much cooler this far from Belden City, and the wind had definitely shifted—there was no longer a warm sea breeze to provide the feel of summer. Instead, the icy breeze, although still warm for the time of year, blew dead leaves across the cobblestones and off of roof tiles.

The men had sweat nearly as much as the horses as they hung on to their horses with a grim determination, every so often whipping their reins. And when they finally stopped, the icy north wind nearly froze the sweat to their faces.

φ

They arrived in Forshen, men and beast alike covered in a thick sheen of quickly-freezing sweat. The temperature had dropped almost twenty degrees along their northward trek. Given the distance they had traveled, it was obvious the men had ridden the animals to near-death in a frantic attempt to reach wherever it was they were going.

The leader dismounted in front of a seemingly reputable inn. But what constituted a reputable inn? "Take a bath. We will rest here, but not sleep. Fresh horses will be ordered, and we will continue as far as we can with the little amount of daylight left. Right now we all need food." He turned and went into the inn.

Zhy dismounted and stood, staring at the inn. Something was familiar, but yet very foreign about the place. The common room seemed like a room he had entered countless times, with its blinking fire and smattering of guests. The smell of ale was present, but not overpowering, and a burly innkeeper moved with a purposeful slowness. Zhy moved through the haze and toward the man, asking about the bath with a voice that was detached and hollow.

φ

The scalding bath water eased his aching muscles, and slowly, the pain ebbed. He groaned at even the thought of mounting a horse again, but for now the soothing, warm water was welcome. The fire that someone had thoughtfully set roared in a corner of the room. Coupled with the hot water of the bath, fatigue and cold seemed to melt away. Physical pain all but vanished, while his mind still was coated in a murky and deep fog.

What really happened?

He tried to piece together events, but there were still only pieces of memories and snatches of images. The only solid and distinctive memory was that of bright white snow and a cliff. And that fall. He jerked in the tub as his body remembered the jolt of hitting the bottom of the canyon.

I was dead! Am I still dead? he asked himself for the millionth time. By now, he should have awoken if was only a dream. Furthermore, the current events were too sharp and real to be a delusion. But he still felt as if he were moving through a fog—the morning fog seen in those hours before first light. Tea would help wake him, he thought.

The leader burst in suddenly, fully dressed. He set a mug of something on the stool next to the door. He then flung a bundle of clothes onto a small rack next to the stool. "Almost time to go," he snapped. Then he worked his mouth into what could almost pass as a smile. "Feeling better?"

"A little," he said, rubbing his head. "I still don't know what is going on. I must still be dreaming—or dead."

"Stop saying that. You are neither dead nor dreaming. Well, not anymore. You were dead. I'm sure. She must have been right." He scratched his head. Zhy started to speak, but the older man held up an impatient hand. "I am sorry it has to be like this... she made it sound very bad. We do not have much time, so relax there a little longer and I will explain what I can. We ride too fast to talk and will ride into the night if we have to, to reach Vronga. This time, we are not going to rest with the horses... I hate to see horses die, but... that is how it is." He glanced at his boots, his gaze downcast and sad.

"We are, as you can probably guess, or if you remember, Knights of the Black Dawn. Does that sound familiar?"

Zhy closed his eyes and black shapes danced in the fog. But nothing solidified. "No, not yet."

"Well, I am sure it will come back to you. In any case, you and your companions were traveling north. One was a mercenary, or warrior type, and the other a small-man. A mage." Through the fog, Zhy could see their faces, but they had no edges or features, and shimmered out of sight. "You—not you personally, but your friends—engaged two of our members in battle. One was erased by magic, and the other stabbed—but not before a sword fight. You killed him.

But you did not mean to, I believe. My companion seems to think you did. But that is no matter.

"My name is Yulchar and the gruff one is Huyen. Normally, we do not ever release our names in public, for doing so betrays the Order. But times are different. The world has changed, and everyone is in grave danger. The Order may pursue us, but we take the chance—they do not know what darkness lies in wait for the world.

"One of our members left us to hunt you down. Her note said that he was killed, too. I guess he was right about the warlock..." He trailed off, and the sad look returned. "I—I almost killed him before he left, perhaps I should have, before Ar'Zoth got him."

"Ar'Zoth..." Zhy whispered. "That name... yes, that name I remember." A man standing in a door, arms high in the air, yellow teeth and then falling. Falling. *Falling.*

"He killed you. According to this lady, Cerease, her son killed Ar'Zoth after he killed you. He waited." Yulchar shook his head sadly. "And now he has assumed that role."

"I don't..."

"He sits atop a demonic horde—something far greater than what is under the Temple of M'Hzrut. At least, that is what we think. Huyen wasn't allowed much time in the Archives. In any case, some say the Temple of M'Hzrut protects us all, but we are convinced that is not the case. Not anymore. Somehow, something was lost or went horribly wrong. No warlock should have been exiled up there. No mad, raving, lunatic warlock. But all that is behind us now—"

"Wait," Zhy replied, putting up a hand. His mind caught on the word "Archives," and he paid little heed to the rest of what Yulchar was saying. "I thought—" but then the memory faded as quickly as it came. He had a brief image of blood and sparks of light. *Archives? Had he heard of them before? Who had mentioned them?* The image of a man with a scraggly beard came to the fore, but then was replaced by Yulchar's handsome face—that was his name, right?

Yulchar thought he understood what Zhy was thinking. "You thought we were villains or thugs? Well, your friends probably did. We do not know how you ever reached

Ar'Zoth, but it was good you did, even though things ended the way they did."

"But—"

"I don't understand it either!" Yulchar cried with a wave of his hand. He looked confused and as lost as Zhy felt. No wonder he seemed to ramble. "I should not say 'good', but I cannot think of any other word... no, it was not good that you died, only that she... well, that she... rescued you, so to speak. We are unsure how Cerease's son got there to replace Ar'Zoth. How did she get you? Too many questions!" He sounded almost frantic, a stark contrast to the determined, level-headed man he had been earlier. But Zhy could fully understand his predicament. "We have to know. We have to find out. But we don't have time. Hurry!" He stood suddenly.

"Drink this tea—it should be cooler by now. There are new clothes," Yulchar said, pointing to the pile as he abruptly left the bathing room. Steam from the heated room billowed out into the bright and cold air.

Zhy grumbled, but eventually exited the warm bath, dried himself hurriedly, combed his hair with his fingers, and drained the lukewarm tea in a gulp. He thought briefly on what Yulchar had said—some of the gaps were starting to fill in, but he was utterly lost on the true reason for his involvement. *If I was dead, and if this woman brought me back, why? Why me? Why not the others who were with me?*

When he arrived outside, Huyen and Yulchar were atop their horses, scowling at the main road. As soon as he stepped into the cold air, he regretted not drying his hair fully, for the warmth of the bath was immediately frozen by the late-autumn chill. He hadn't got himself fully upon his horse before they sped off. Cursing, he kicked his own animal and followed.

What can the hurry possibly be?

φ

As day turned to dusk, the power of the new horses became readily apparent, for he was almost fully bent over the pommel of his saddle in an attempt to reduce the roar of the wind. The bath had helped his muscles, but riding at such a pace for so many miles was quickly erasing any benefits of the hot water. For the most part, he kept his head down as they rode hard through forests of leafless, lifeless trees.

The land had transformed from a lush and colorful display of colors into a dull and depressing gray. Where the forest floor had once been a multi-colored carpet of birch, maple, and aspen leaves, it was now a dead brown. Leaves no longer blew away in the wake of the horses, but crunched underfoot like dead skin. Long branches clicked together in the rough breeze, and clouds of dead leaves would swirl into the air. A smell of decay and fester was borne on the breeze, and one could detect snow in the air. Leaden clouds rolled across the sky, burdened with moisture. Zhy swatted at a fly, before he realized that no fly was white. Snow! Tiny flakes eddied in the air, but not yet enough to cause his companions any concern.

Finally, dusk turned to full dark, with only a sliver of a moon in the sky. Zhy watched in amazement as a white orb flickered into existence between Huyen's fingers. The man waved his hands slightly and the orb followed ahead of the horses, providing a bright lantern.

Zhy wanted to ask how he had done it, but the man seemed to sense his thought and looked back with a scowl. He then kicked his horse and shot forward. Zhy's horse followed of its own accord.

After what seemed hours of speeding along in the dark, Yulchar suddenly called for a stop. Zhy's legs were slick with horse sweat and stained with a thick, brown slime. The horses panted, their great chests heaving in the darkness.

Huyen found a flat area a few paces off the main road and threw his pack down violently. To Zhy's surprise, the knight unrolled his bedding and dozed off to sleep without so much as a word. His light blinked out and Yulchar and Zhy faced each other. High, thin clouds blocked out most of the moonlight, but they could see enough to locate shapes that were trees or rocks.

"No fire?" Zhy asked.

Yulchar shook his head. "No time. Find a level spot."

As Zhy fumbled with his sleeping bag, the had a brief vision of a man fighting with a traveling pack and sleeping bag, and another man stood over him, laughing. He discounted the memory as useless, and as he unrolled his own bag, he heard the faint call of a whippoorwill before dropping into a deep sleep.

Chapter 2
A Voice Out of Nowhere

We all hear voices in our heads. Who speaks? Who are we talking to if we dare reply?

Cleric Bertrand

*A*las, I can reach you. Your mind is so closed when it is awake, little one. I see you are with the Knights of the Black Dawn.
The voice sounded strained and careworn, as if the owner had struggled long under an illness or depression. Zhy thrashed in his sleeping bag, but his eyes remained closed. He floated in the indigo haze of a deep sleep, and yet the woman's voice seemed to pull at him physically and he was tugged upward into a separate part of his dream. It was a dream, wasn't it?

In dreams, he had had lengthy conversations with Kahl, with women, with people long-since dead, and even with himself. It was not unusual to hear people speaking in dreams, although given his current exertion, he would have expected a death-like embrace of the sleeping world. The voice repeated its earlier statement, but he shrugged it off, feeling his dreaming body trying to wriggle into the pure black of oblivion.

But the voice continued.

Zhy... Zhy, please answer me. I know you are there. I can see you.

He groaned.

Zhy, the woman's voice repeated. It was a sad, soft voice, and slightly grating in its tone of—what was it, anyway, he wondered? Pleading? Exasperation? Hopelessness? Yes, there was something deeper, something determined in that voice. Still, he rolled over again, trying to force himself out of the dream.

Zhy, please answer me. I know you hear me.

"I'm only dreaming," he finally muttered.

If you want to think so, the voice replied. The sad and tired woman's voice continued. Her voice trembled slightly, sounding as if, as if she had just finished crying. *My son murdered me. And now he sits in a castle, far away, working to destroy the world.*

"Destroy... How...? What are you talking about?" In a mirrored situation of his waking experiences, he had a hundred more questions to ask, but only a few came out, muttered into the roll of clothes he was using as a pillow. His companions snored nearby in their own oblivion. He could hear them snoring... Was he awake? No, he assuredly was not, he convinced himself. This was a deep and disturbing dream and he was simply adding the sounds of the waking world to it.

You died, Zhy. You died. The abruptness of this statement shook him and his legs jerked. She seemed to sigh and continued. *I snatched you away at the last possible second, but I had to let you die. I'm sorry. Things will now be very different. No one could reach you until that happened."*

"Then this is a dream," he muttered and tried to float away from the strange voice. But it pulled him back.

No, Zhy, it is not. You are not dead now, and you are not dreaming... I was the only one who could rescue you.

"What do you mean?" Why was he talking to her? Who was she? He did not remember many women—he remembered very little of his life before. Her statements were the prototypical fuzzy phrasing of dreams, and thus were his responses. But in the far reaches of his mind, these were questions he needed answers to—the bright memories of snow and rock were too sharp and too overpowering to allow any other thoughts to seep out.

What other meaning could there be? She sounded almost irritated by the question.

"I don't understand how dying and being brought back to life is a good thing," he snapped. His joints, muscles, and bones had gone through an incredible jarring on the horse, and it seemed every last fiber in his body screamed in an agony of dull and throbbing pain.

You will, perhaps, appreciate it later. I can understand your confusion and your pain—your body was almost completely crushed.

"So why even bring me back? What possible purpose could that have?"

You were the only one not yet gone by the time I got there... the others had already passed into the final resting place.

"Others?" Her mention of others brought forth a flicker of a memory.

Yes, your friends. They are gone, sadly. You are the one, the only one, who knows the area, who can help these men kill him.

"I am no use to anyone, dead or alive."

He could see her shake her head. *Enough of that kind of talk, Zhy. I saved you for a reason, and it was not out of any whim.*

"But you just said I was the only one left! I guess I wasn't smart enough to go that this 'final place' or whatever you call it. There was a long fall and my head was probably smashed—so now you've rescued an idiot." If he could convince her that he was worthless, perhaps she would leave him alone.

That ploy may have worked with others, but not with me. You will see the point to all of this, I hope sooner rather than later. The three of you have a long journey and you must deal with a very dangerous person—not the man who killed you, but he might as well have.

Zhy grimaced and sighed. If this were a dream, he could take comfort in her absence in the morning. If not, what horrors of the mind did he have to look forward to for another thousand miles? It was a thousand miles, right? He thought he remembered. "Fine, I will play your game. For now. Who are we going to kill?"

My son.

"Your son?" he barked. It only got stranger. *This is just a dream, a very bizarre one.* As long as he remembered that, the strange conversation would not seem so out of place. If only he could fall back out of it and get some sleep!

*Yes. My son... he once had a name, a nice name. He counted turnips in our field, played the sutan... I mussed his—*Zhy could hear her forcing a coldness into her voice. *Now he calls himself Ar'Zoth and he wants to rule the world.*

The name didn't register at first. In the purple void of the dream, his mind suddenly raced past the image of rocks and snow and focused on a long and familiar face. A smile floated past and then vanished. *Father.* If this were truly a dream, then what would it hurt to think of his father? And in the way of a true dream, his focus shifted rapidly. "If you're dead, is my father there?" The question leapt from his lips. Memories of his father were as cloudy as any other, but for a brief moment, he knew the face; he knew who the man had been, and that was enough.

She sounded like she was crying again. *Your father was here. He tried to reach you. But he is gone now. He was helping my son, in fact. He wanted to tell you something—*

"NO!" Zhy screamed. The dream had turned to nightmare. In some small station of his mind, a stern voice warned him not to believe those who purported to talk to the dead. *Never call their names, never call on them, and never talk to them. For they are liars and they will amaze you when they can reveal a loved one's past—but they are cheating you. They read you. You give them clues and you don't know it. Avoid them. Run.* The voice faded as abruptly as it came.

In his rage, he tried to kick the sleeping bag off of his body, but he was wrapped in it, and the fabric made a stretching sound. Frustrated, he pushed the bag down to his waist and sat upright on the hard ground. He bellowed into the dark, "No more! Out! Away!" Gone. Gone! Always gone... gone forever.

Yulchar stirred, but Huyen kept snoring. "What is the matter, Zhy?"

"Voices!" he spat. "There is a woman. But how? It is not Mother. Who is it? Is it me? Am I mad? " He was frantic. His mind had not registered the fact that he had mentioned hearing his father's voice before.

"You heard your father's voice?"

"I—" He broke off. "What? What did I just say?" *Am I still dreaming?*

"You said you used to hear your father's voice, but now there is someone else?"

"I said that?" he asked. Had he said that? Yes! He had asked the woman about him, hadn't he? So, he had had a father, and he was most likely dead. Try as he might, the memories simply stopped. Why could he not remember his own father? "No, I was talking about a woman."

"A woman?"

"Yes, a woman. Talking in my head. She was telling me... about my—" He stopped. "About my father, but she was lying."

"Why was she lying?"

"She's dead! That's why!" Zhy veritably screamed. *I am either dreaming, mad, or... or drunk... Drunk? How could... wait, had she said that she wanted us to kill her son? Her own son?* His head fell heavily into his hands and he squealed in frustration. There was too much, too much! Dead, alive, rocks, falling, blinding snow and sun, dead women, dead fathers, dead... dead sons.

"Zhy?" Yulchar was asking. "Zhy, do not worry. You are not mad." His voice was suddenly soothing. "Now, tell me. Are you sure that there was a woman—a dead woman— talking to you?"

"Yes," he whispered.

"A woman!" Yulchar blurted, his voice tinged with excitement. "That is she! It must be!"

"Her? Oh..." His thoughts raced back through the day, what the man had said as he stood on the stoop. *Some woman. She is dead.* "How?"

Yulchar shook his head. "I said, I do not—"

"Know how these things work!" Zhy snapped the sentenced closed. He sucked in the cold night air. "I wish I knew!" His fists were balled and he pounded his knees; he forced away the tears of frustration behind his burning lids.

"You must find out everything you can. Who is she? Why you? Who are you? What did she say?"

Zhy thought a moment. What had she said? Only seconds ago, it had been vivid in his mind, but now there were only blanks.

"She said... she said she was trying to find something."

"Find something?"

"No, wait, she was worried about her son. He was someone else." His face was a slate of confusion. Yulchar leaned on his elbow, his face patient. Given Huyen's disposition, Zhy expected him to be breathing fire.

"Yes, that he had killed someone. Maybe her."

"Did you get a name out of any of this?"

"No. Yes!" He paused. "Ar'Zoth," he finally whispered. As soon as the name crossed his lips, something familiar tickled his brain. Something horrible. *No. NO! It cannot be...*

"What?" Yulchar pushed himself off of his elbow and bounded to his feet. He paced in the dull moonlight.

"Ar'Zoth. She said the name Ar'Zoth!" Zhy repeated, louder. As if saying the name would somehow coalesce those horrible memories, or at least make them go away. The only change was a sudden shift in the clouds which revealed a full moon just below the tops of the trees. He hadn't slept very long.

Suddenly, Huyen leapt from his bedroll, sword in hand. "Demon-spawn!" he snarled. The glow of the full moon caught the blade of his sword and sent muted flashes into the forest. In the bright light, Zhy could make out his companions as clearly as in the day. Where had he seen a man draw steel so fast?

"Listen, listen!" Yulchar barked. "This is far bigger than us." Huyen's face was a distorted, angry mass, with glaring eyes and a raging crease across his forehead. Yulchar matched his stare with one of his own. "Do you wish to turn out like Gryn and seek revenge? Isn't it obvious?"

"It's obvious that he was one of these three that Gryn was chasing—one of those in league with the warlock. Who can say that he is not in bed with the demons?" Huyen growled.

Zhy glanced nervously at the twisted face of Huyen and his gleaming sword.

"The only thing obvious to me," Yulchar replied softly, "is that this was *one* of the three, yes. But he was the only one who never engaged the Dawn, who never started a fight."

"And how will that help us?" Huyen spat. "Surely not in a fight against Ar'Zoth!"

"No, but he might be..." Yulchar almost whispered, his voice faded, and his gaze was on something far away. As quickly as it came, the mood vanished and he looked at Huyen, speaking as if Zhy were not there. "He will help us, surely."

"How?" the other man snarled. He scowled at Zhy, and a small scar under his lip made it look almost like a bat, a sneering, bat, with dripping—

A bat! The thought struck Zhy with such force he nearly fell back on his bedroll. An expression of horror ignited upon his face, and his nostrils filled with an unholy scent. Then it was gone.

"Is something wrong?" Yulchar asked, after seeing Zhy's body jerk.

"No, I remembered something," he stammered. "But it's gone. A bat. Some kind of large bat." He tried to recall the memories, but all that remained was the fleeting smell, and that was replaced by the scent of dead and decaying leaves, wet with snow and rain.

Huyen's scowl deepened, and low growl seemed to emerge from his throat. "A gherwza. I knew it!" His sword thrust forward—

Yulchar's arm was a blur as it lashed out and gripped the sword hilt. Huyen held it firm, but did not fight. His eyes locked on his companion's. "I think his mage companion killed it. Please stop this. This man is not demon spawn. We can be sure of that."

"Oh can we?" Huyen whispered in a voice that was quiet yet fiercer than any battle cry.

"Yes, for now. Something is very wrong. We need his help. Until we find out otherwise, keep that sword in check."

"Why? Can't you see this man bounces like a stuck rabbit? Screaming at voices, and—"

"We've discussed all this already, Huyen. How would *you* act if died and suddenly woke up?"

"I'd kill myself for a demon."

Yulchar sighed. "I seriously doubt that."

The crotchety knight grumbled.

Zhy scratched his head and then thumbed his earlobe. "This has to do with Ar'Zoth. She said her son is now Ar'Zoth. I don't understand." He looked up at the full moon, wishing he were up there, rather than in a freezing, fireless campsite with two assassins. One who wanted to kill him, and the other to save him. *Either up there or dead*, he thought bitterly.

"Son," Yulchar said quietly. Huyen had sheathed his sword and set it by his bedroll. He lay back down, but Zhy assumed he lay there, listening, ready for another chance to strike. His brashness reminded him of someone, but the name and face refused to come to the fore. "Ar'Zoth killed you. Gryn, who was one of us, was chasing after you, and then he was going to deal with the warlock. There was never any word again from him, so we assume Ar'Zoth killed him, too."

"That's at least one thing that is cleared up, I guess," Zhy said with a catch in his throat. His gaze had returned to the moon and he had a brief image of his own father—how could he remember something so far back, but not how he died? "But you can't expect me to be able to help you kill him."

"No, no, we do not," he said sadly. But there was a hint of something in his voice. A knowing. "You died helpless, but you are no longer a helpless creature. We cannot expect you to battle a great warlock. But you can still help us."

I am helpless—I can't remember a thing! He took another longing glance at the moon as it sidled lower behind the spindly branches of a large birch tree. As the black tentacles waved in a small breeze, they looked like fingers, beckoning. *Beckoning? Or shooing away?* Zhy wondered. "Such a relief," Zhy said with a yawn. Yulchar's mouth formed the barest of smiles.

"Sleep. If she comes to you again, let her in. Talk to her. We need to find out more of what happened and why. We are still trying to understand. We know that we do not have much time. Sleep. A couple of hours. Then we ride. We are close to Vronga."

"And what about him?" Zhy whispered, indicating Huyen.

"What about me?" the knight replied gruffly.

"Well—"

"Huyen here would have gone with Gryn, I suppose, and been killed by Ar'Zoth. But he followed orders—better then than he does now—and remained with me. Now he seems to think you were in league with the warlock and perhaps the Dark. Is that not right?"

Huyen coughed. "I wanted more information like you did," he said flatly.

"Funny, that. You still seem to think Zhy here has something to do with demons?" He shook his head. And to himself he muttered, "Why do I always get the insubordinate ones?"

"I was never in league—"

"How do you know that, Zhyfrael? How? You remember names and parts of things, but not everything. How do you know you weren't traveling with demon spawn?"

Yulchar threw up his hands. "Listen, why are we having this conversation?" He was exasperated. "We need Zhy; that is what she said. Ar'Zoth *was* a demon. That much we know from the letter. That does not prove Zhy and his companions were, you know that, and you knew that when we started. This ends now."

"Is that an order?" Huyen replied, a dangerous edge to his voice.

"That is an order," Yulchar said.

"Good night then." He sounded far from satisfied, and his reply was too quick. But Yulchar had settled him down for now, and for once, at least from Yulchar's point of view, he had given an order and had it accepted. He looked at Zhy, his expression blank.

"I don't think he likes me," Zhy said softly.

"I don't," Huyen replied from his bedroll.

Yulchar sighed. "You had best get some rest. Perhaps if she visits you again, you can find out more information." With that, the knight lay his head down and snored.

I wish I could sleep, Zhy thought bitterly. These men were used to traveling and sleeping in the wild. He lay down, a small root in his back. No amount of shifting seemed to help, so he moved his blanket a few feet away. The moon sidled across the sky and he watched as it slowly dipped beneath a large hemlock and was gone.

He thought on the dead woman's words, on the journey thus far, his pieces of memories, and of Huyen. The man would kill him if given the chance, he knew. Zhy feared that no amount of convincing could do any good—at least as long as his own memories were so clouded. He was no demon, was he? He had not been in league with them either, had he? Why had they traveled to see Ar'Zoth? And why had Ar'Zoth killed them all? Zhy at least understood Huyen's anger and suspicion, but it was going to be distressing to watch out for his own neck during the journey.

By the time sleep reached him, Yulchar was loading the horses and barking at them to take their leave.

Only a bare hope of a sunrise was visible beyond the trees. Frost hung everywhere, even on his blanket. It clung to his chin and he wiped away the icy covering with a groan. Muscles ached, and his head throbbed from lack of sleep.

"Hurry... Zhyfrael," Huyen barked. "There is not much time."

Not much time. I'm getting sick of hearing that already.

Chapter 3
An Abandoned Farm

It is said that Death is the End. There is no more. But I have spoken to the Dead. Some walk among us. Some are truly long buried, but they remain as loafers in this world. They hang onto the plane between this world and the Void, in an attempt to finish what was undone in Life. Many will wander forever in such a vain attempt.

Prophet Zher'wen

The farmhouse was empty. Someone had removed the body and buried it near a Temple inside Vronga. All that remained was a field of dead turnips, some pumpkins, a hill with a massive stone set into it, and an empty farmhouse. The horses were gone, and the only item left in the stables was a single sutan, sitting on a bale of hay.

When Zhy's companions stopped suddenly before the front door, he was confused, but slowly realized that his must have been that woman's home... the dead woman. They had said something about a farm, hadn't they? Or had she? *A dead woman who was talking to me.* They dismounted quietly.

There was strangeness about the place, and not in the fact that it was now abandoned. As they approached the farm, Zhy never saw the farm or the fields, even though both were directly off of the Crown Road. A low mound of dead grass sat perfectly aligned between the road and the farm—the eye would catch on the low rise, and then skip past the farm to the copse of pine and poplar that bordered the edge of the farm. By then, the average traveler would have been long past and never seen the residence. Wagon ruts led around the south side of the small knoll and to the farm. Were it summer, grass would be growing in the ruts, but now only a stray blade of clover grew in the matted depression.

"Let's have a look around," Yulchar said, patting his horse. Huyen grumbled and stomped off, muttering.

Zhy's companions left him to his own devices, and he wandered the farm. Every so often, their paths would cross as they, too, sought something. Huyen would grumble and Yulchar would nod respectfully. But were they looking for? There was nothing here of interest—the place had long since been abandoned, and it was waiting for new owners, or the blanketing snows of winter. Zhy took a last look at the sutan—perhaps the only thing out of place here—and went into the kitchen. Maybe there was some food left over.

Yulchar pulled out a dusty brandy bottle and set it on the kitchen table. "Fine vintage, that. Care for some?"

Zhy looked at the bottle with wonder, as if he'd never seen brandy before. A wobbly vision came to mind, of a man stumbling and falling, but then it faded. "No, never had it. Don't care to either," he replied. He thought he heard the man gasp, but when he looked up, Yulchar's attention was directed elsewhere.

"Not much left here, apart from this, and some knickknacks. Oh, and that sutan out there," Huyen replied. He gave the brandy bottle a sneer, then turned back into the main living area, looking around at the emptiness with an air of total loss.

"I don't understand what I'm supposed to be looking for," Zhy said quietly.

"We do not either. There is really nothing here. We have already been here once and come up empty. Anything of value that was here is now in the hands of whatever guards were here before us."

Zhy nodded slowly. "I wouldn't doubt that... so, if you don't mind me asking, what drew you to this place? Why here?" *And how did you find it?* he wanted to ask.

"That is a long story and we do not have—"

"We don't have time," Zhy finished the sentence for him, a bitter edge to his voice. "If I am dead, which I think I am, or am dreaming—" He waved off the brewing protest. "—I have all the time in... well, I have a lot of time." He pulled a rickety chair across the dusty floor and sat down. The pine chair creaked in protest. He sat, looking up at Yulchar.

The knight dry-washed his hands, and with a heavy sigh, pulled the other chair to him, sitting down with obvious irritation. His glance darted around the house, no doubt seeking Huyen.

"Well?"

Yulchar folded his hands on the table and looked hard at Zhy, his gray eyes sparkling in the dust-covered sunbeam that angled through the window. "We didn't exactly know to come here. Our group had experienced some setbacks—" He looked at Zhy with sadness. "—and made our way to Vronga, trying hard to run from our troubles. Troubles we had no business getting involved in. We lost two of our own, and possibly Gryn to—" He stopped abruptly, his eyes sharp. They bored into Zhy's, who only returned a blank look.

"Yes?"

"You do not remember?"

"Why should I?" Zhy slammed his fist on the table. "Why should a dead man remember anything?" he snapped. The frustration was too much, but the anger quickly boiled away to surrender. "I—I'm sorry. I—"

"I guess I should say that I understand, but I do not. But I am sorry. I hope that your memory returns to you."

"So do I."

A tense silence filled the room. Dust from Zhy's outburst floated up and was caught in the ray of light, and for a moment, Zhy saw the shape of a man, drowning, his arms reaching to the sky. Was he that man?

"In any case," Yulchar continued, with another glance around the room. "We were going to try to meet some of our Order's members in Vronga and get reassigned, but we overheard a guard talking about this dead woman. Quite a few people seemed to have known her—rather, her husband and their boy—and were concerned. It seemed like a major event here, and with a city like Vronga, that meant something might be important related to... related to our work." He looked at Zhy again, but he only nodded slightly. "We asked the guard, and explained we were also interested, since we had just come from the North, and there were strange goings-on. He gave us directions, and we found the note... it was right there, on the table." He pointed at Zhy's hand.

Zhy moved his hand away from the table and stared at the knotty pine.

"But it is gone now... must have blown away or been taken."

"I see. Well, I—"

"And the lady has not visited you since you—since last night?" Yulchar broke in, seeming eager to change the subject.

Zhy shook his head. "No."

"Let's hope to Sacuan she does, and soon. There is not much time." He chewed on his lip while Zhy thumbed an earlobe.

At that moment, Huyen stomped in, his face set in a scowl. "Well...?"

Yulchar shook his head. "Not a whole lot," he said slowly. Huyen cursed softly. "Can't be helped... listen, Huyen, take two horses and get the supplies. We'll take one last look around and get a meal started... there are some things left over, I'm guessing they aren't poisoned. Then we must be going."

"Going... where?" Zhy asked.

"Zhyfrael, it is not yet time for you to know," Huyen snapped, then left with an irritated wave from Yulchar.

"Impetuous. He'll be straightened out soon enough."

"Why do you call me Zhyfrael? It's Zhy, please."

"That is what the lady wrote," he replied. "But we all know of Zhyfrael. It is a bitter part of Welcfer's history. And any Beldener worth his salt should know the history." He cocked an eyebrow at Zhy.

Indeed, Zhyfrael and her—her! A woman! Her great folly, letting in the savages to rend and tear and destroy everything in sight. Zhy pounded the table again, softer this time, frustrated that he could remember something like that, but not what was important. As the image faded, he saw a smaller man float by in his mind's eye, a small-man, a man from Welcfer, who had told him the story. But a glint of sunlight caught his eye and everything went dark again. "I don't need to be reminded. Apparently, I already died for that. Possibly twice."

"What do you mean?"

"I don't know," he snapped. He stood suddenly and walked out of the farmhouse.

Yulchar muttered something about the fields and wandered off into the rows of dead turnips while Zhy poked around the stables. He picked up the sutan and tried to play a chord, the ten strings were difficult to adjust to, and he couldn't get his fingers to make any discernible sound. Nonetheless, it was a very beautiful instrument.

"Why is a sutan laying in a stable?" Yulchar's questioned, startling Zhy. He turned. "And, I am sorry, Zhy. Tradition and history go very deep in our Order."

Zhy only nodded. "Strange, this. Who would leave it behind?" *A sutan! A sutan... had she said something about a—*

"We hope that the lady would have told you, well that and seven hundred other things. I hope she comes to see you again."

I don't. I don't understand any of this. It is senseless. If I was dead, why not let me stay dead? I can't seem to remember much about living.

He nearly jumped at the hand on his shoulder. "I am sorry, son." The voice was suddenly soothing, even with the rough edges. "Fighting the Dark and demons for so long, we often get lost in our mission. We forget about people. To Huyen, you are still a tool to be used to get to Ar'Zoth. I can't imagine what it must be like to be dead—and then alive. I'll try to give you that if I can—that peace, anyway. Time alone, I mean." The man struggled to get the words out and they sounded forced, but Zhy accepted them tentatively as an honest attempt to soothe him.

I'll probably wake up soon anyway. "Thank you." Zhy set down the sutan and returned to the house. He had the same look of loss and confusion as Yulchar. *What was so important? What am I missing, if anything?*

"They took away the poisoned tea," Yulchar was saying as he rooted through the cupboards. He had found some turnips that were still decent and some dried meat; there was a pan and some fat and he got to frying both items together. The fat smelled slightly rancid as it heated, but Yulchar poured out spices in heaping handfuls—after sniffing them for poison. "So you could make some I suppose, although... on second thought, never mind."

"Poisoned tea?"

"A spicy-sweet tea, apparently, they drank it a lot here. Found a cup next to her and a Healer came, took one whiff, and knew it was poison. Someone killed her."

"Her son."

"Maybe, but—wait, how did you know?"

"She said so—said her son murdered her." *She had told me, hadn't she?*

"Well, that proves that, then. Straight from the dead woman's mouth. So, the idiot child did it? Interesting. And where is the man of the house? Folks said he was a strong, loving man who just up and left."

That proves it? That proves nothing! "Left?"

"Disappeared, more like it. Had this wife and idiot child, and the farm, and left. Before he left, though, locals in Vronga said he came to the university with a young man, and they were desperate to find a mage. They dragged some old guy out of an inn where he was drowning in his cup, then that was the last."

"Why at the inn?" Zhy's foggy mind was trying to process all of the information, but only holding onto small bits. Somehow the inn stuck out as important.

"All the other mages were busy with final examinations or research. This guy was almost ready to retire, so they sent him. For what, I do not know. They were very close-lipped about it all."

"And they disappeared?"

"Yes." Yulchar stirred the sizzling food.

"Maybe the mage kidnapped him, or..."

"Yes, but everyone disappeared. Everyone. Why?" The knight shook the pan and the smell of fragrant spices filled the kitchen.

"And the son is gone?"

"Yes."

Zhy scratched his head. *It's where, not why. Probably abandoned his wife.*

"What was that?"

"I—" he started, then stopped. He had a vague memory of someone else reading his thoughts—a large man. Not fat, just muscle. With a sword. He shook his head. "Where, not why. Maybe he just wanted to leave his wife, so he killed her and left. But where? And what in the name of—of... What is the point of bringing me back from the dead for it?" He scratched his head and scowled, surprised at his own emotion. *I can't even remember how to curse!*

"That is a good point. But we know the where. At least we think we do. We need the why."

"I don't understand. You know where they went?"

"Yes, but did they go together? If we follow and get to Ar'Zoth, will we be facing the others, including the idiot son?"

"No, I... wait." His head spun and he sat down on a pine chair. "She said her son was up there. Trying to destroy the world. What does that mean?"

The pale man went a shade paler. "Sacuan help us all," he breathed. He set the pan off the heat and sat down himself. He collapsed in the chair, his vision blank and his face splattered with worry. The food sizzled on the hearth.

"I don't..."

"Is that what she said? I hope Huyen gets back. We don't have much time. If the son... it makes no sense. But yet it might. The son... the father. Not together. Where is the father?" Suddenly, he jerked, then grasped Zhy's arm. Zhy gasped in pain—the main's grip was stronger than an orca's jaws. "Zhy! You must find out more! Must. Ask on the way. She may reach you—in there. Are they together? What happened? Did the boy kill the father? What? Who was the third..." He trailed off again. "Protector..." he whispered.

Zhy merely stared. Yulchar's gaze went to the kitchen, then to Zhy, and when his eyes met his, they were hollow and wide.

Yulchar's voice trembled. "The Temple. They went to the temple! Damn Huyen, where are you?" He slammed his fist on the table.

"What... you don't mean? Oh no..." Zhy groaned. He had a memory of a temple. Far away. There was a fascination with it, by someone. And anger and sadness. When had awoken in Belden, there had been a small miniature temple at his side—was that where he had been?

"She better reach you in there. Do we go to the temple or to Ar'Zoth? Or both? Can we? Is there time? Does it matter? I—" His voice gave out in a hoarse whisper, but his mouth still moved, mouthing silent words that were curses and blessings and everything in between.

"Where?"

His mouth kept moving as if he were raving.

"Where?" Zhy repeated, a little louder.

"In the Tunnels."

"Tunnels?"

Yulchar pointed a shaking hand out the kitchen window, clearly indicating the large stone slab in the hill. "There."

"I don't see anything!" Zhy barked. "Just a stone!" But when he looked again, he could see how the slab might be a door. Set perfectly within the side of the shrub-covered hill, nothing grew in front of it, save a stray dead turnip plant, its leaves black. It could be a door, if one had the imagination of a child...

"That is the entrance, Zhy, the entrance to a very secret, very long tunnel system. Well, not a system, just one long tunnel that stretches from here to the Temple of M'Hzrut. Or near to it, anyway. But you said Ar'Zoth. Rather, she said Ar'Zoth." Why was he rambling? For such a tough man, he liked to prattle from time to time. "So that means we have to get out short of the temple."

Zhy let out a sigh of relief, but he wasn't sure what he would be relieved about. It was too fantastical to be real, and he pinched his arm just to ensure he was still awake.

Fool! Pinching your arm, like a child. Of course it's fantastical. Everything is fantastical.

"Because I'm dead?" he asked himself.

Yulchar shuddered as if struck. "Excuse me, what did you just say?"

"Oh, sorry, nothing, just thinking about something. So, you said there are tunnels—rather, a tunnel behind the stone?"

Yulchar nodded.

"A secret tunnel?"

"Of course."

"And how do you know of it, and why, if you knew, did you not...?" He trailed off. *Not what?* Why *would* anyone go blindly into a tunnel, even if they knew about it? Who just takes off on a long journey without knowing all the right information, and where they are going, who they are going with, and what might face them at the end? He thought he heard someone laughing, and looked up to see Yulchar with a smirk on his face.

"What?"

"You were muttering something..."

"And what is funny about that?"

"Nothing..."

"So, these—this tunnel, it's a secret?"

"Yes."

"And you know about it?" Yulchar nodded. "Who else?"

"I'm sure a few people."

"I'd say the people that live here may have, and maybe the guards, probably that 'Protector' you mentioned, maybe a stray hermit, or an uncle to—"

"That's enough, Zhy," Yulchar said quietly, his voice soft but deadly.

"So what do you call the tunnel?" Zhy asked. He could feel his face heat.

"The Tunnels of Woe."

Zhy burst out with a hoarse laugh. "Please wake me up or bury me or something, but stop with the silly names. First there was—" He broke off. There was what? A man with a puerile name, but what was it?

"Why do you find the name funny? Once you get down there, you will not be laughing. I can assure you." His demeanor had changed dramatically, and he glowered at Zhy.

"I don't know," Zhy replied. His smile was slow in fading from his face, but the icicles in Yulchar's eyes were enough to temper his mirth. "It just sounded funny, that's all."

"There is nothing funny about any of this, Zhy."

Chapter 4
Winter

Snow, snow, beautiful snow! How your brightness and cleanliness cover the world with a warm, welcoming blanket. Alas, such beauty does hide a sinister reality: Such a warm-looking blanket can freeze, smother, and strangle you in its relentless pressing.

Prophet Vron'Za

Winter was looking to be delicious.

I woke from an enjoyable dream and was staring out at the frozen landscape, a smile across my lips. For now the castle was silent, except for the hiss of a fire and the simmering tea. She had been silent, thank whatever demonic god there was, and I was left in peace to look out at a sliver of a world that was going to die.

Far beyond, in the cities like Belden City, Darvein Harbor, Vronga, Port Havren, a clawing madness was approaching the huddled commoners in their collective safety. Death. Demons. Blood. A great wave of ripping talons and rending teeth.

"Ah!" I breathed out loud. The expectancy was profound, my hatred of mankind bottomless.

I looked to the east, staring at the Spires that blocked my view of Welcfer. Yes, even Welcfer would fall. Whatever trivial population lived there would soon be devoured.

But, alas, I was hungry.

"Rabbit sounds good," I declared to the empty palace. My voice echoed strangely. Rooms and rooms, and only I was there. It left me somewhat sad, but also relieved... but we've been down that road. Still, I repeated: "Rabbit. A nice juicy rabbit..." *I wonder if I can snare an arctic hare...* "Ha!" I laughed. Ever the poet. Should I write something? There was paper, perhaps I should write this down so if anyone survives they can find out...

The only words that came to mind were a piece of an old children's story. I repeated them into the empty air, repeated them a dozen times: "Toil and labor, toil and labor, without sport, Bimb will be dim." I could have written it a hundred times over and over and over... but a grumbling from my stomach stilled my would-be author.

Giving up on the rabbit, I shuffled to the kitchens... there was still dried meat and some turnips.

It was going to be a delicious winter.

Chapter 5
Unleashed?

Demons walk and talk, and they are inside of us all. If we do not deal with them appropriately, they will cover our souls with depredation. And they will cover the land with their filth.

Cleric Gorand

The death of Ar'Zoth created a great deal of havoc among the demons already loose in Belden and Welcfer. Directionless, they wandered aimlessly, often into rivers or lakes. Some would become unhinged and foam at the mouth before expiring. Gherwza flew blindly into trees or hillsides.

One rational demon—if one could put that term to such a creature—made its way across the snow-covered track of the Crown Road, shuffling tiredly against the deep powder. No caravans had dared pass in either direction for days, and not even the Counsel Guard ventured past. Most likely they were holed up on some farm, snuggling serving maids or bottles of brandy. *Humans are incredibly weak*, it thought to itself.

A wild screech and a crash off to the east startled him. "Another blasted *gherwza*," he growled. "No sense of direction, no leader."

The death of Ar'Zoth, and his sudden replacement by a helpless imbecile came as a great shock when it occurred,

as if someone had jumped from a cistern of boiling water
into a snow bank. But the demons that were loose in Belden
and Welcfer should not have had any trouble with a
transition, as sudden as it was.

But then... something else had happened. As if the jump
from boiling water to snow continued with a leap into a
raging inferno. Everything somehow just—stopped. And
stopped with such a jolt that he, himself, had staggered and
run headlong into a support beam of an inn. Thankfully, the
patrons had given him wide berth. A connection had been
severed; the constant voice in his head had suddenly gone
silent. What had happened? Why had he lost his direction?

"He's gone!" the demon muttered.

He took a few aimless steps, then stopped suddenly, his
meager boots scuttling across the snow.

The Black Dawn! What were they up to? Were they
behind all of this? Perhaps if he could somehow get inside—
become one of them? It would be a grim and difficult task—

"No, too cliché," he thought to himself after churning a
few pieces of that idea over in his mind. Possessing others
was difficult and getting into this body had been quite a
chore. Infiltrating the Black Dawn from within, while
appealing, seemed somehow a waste of time, especially
since this new—event—had seemed to wreak such havoc
already. Sure, he knew there were countless demons
beneath the earth, but it would take too long for them to
reach the surface, and when that happened, what need was
there for the Black Dawn?

There has to be a better idea, he thought bitterly, his
face set in a scowl.

He walked ever northward, against all instinct to go due
south, to Belden City, where he could do the most damage.
There was no voice guiding him in either direction, but he
assumed most demons would try to make it south, where
more of the soft human flesh was. But he would go north.
North.

Great honor awaited him in the north.

φ

The people gathered as usual on a warm winter evening in far south-eastern Belden. Earlier in the day, the cold rains had stopped, leaving a lukewarm sun to dry everything and provide a little warmth to the region. No snow ever fell here, but still, winters were dreary and damp. Inside the temple, worshippers talked idly about sons and daughters, crops, and the weather, but every so often one could hear the word "demon" being whispered. Hard stares were aplenty at first for these people, but soon a small tide seemed to wash over the citizens, and the hushed whispers became open dialog that quickly turned into heated yelling.

"Children, children!" the elder exclaimed, shrugging into his blue silk robe. He sauntered to the front of the temple and stood before them, for now eschewing the podium. But the talk continued on in a dull roar, and he finally raised his hands and repeated his cry, only louder.

Slowly, the noise abated, and faces full of worry stared back at him.

He sighed and pushed up his wide sleeves. So now it was in the open, and he would have to forget his well-planned sermon and address this or there would be a riot. Rumors were rumors no longer, and missives he'd received from other cities not buried in snow had confirmed the worst. There were demons on the loose. His mood soured and he stared into the throng, not noticing that someone—a nut farmer—was talking.

"So what are you going to do?"

He tried to remember what the man had asked, but it was a blank. "Do?" he asked quietly.

"Aye," the gruff man spat. His hands were calloused and rough, and he clutched a hat in his hands. Beside him, his bulky wife stared at the floor. "Why, only yesterday I was checking the trees when some animal flew overhead and made a terrible sound. I think it crashed into a tree, over on Winslep's land." He gestured behind him and the man known as Winslep nodded gravely.

"Animals—birds—sometimes die, yes." He tried to don his best pious voice, trying to find some other explanation. But it was too late.

"No. No bird like that. That were a bat. A giant bat." His nervous hands had nearly crushed the cloth hat to pieces.

Raising his head, he looked at the elder—his gray eyes cold. "That was a gherwza!"

With that the patrons erupted—a dozen conversations happening at once. Even in the temple, he could hear curses and cries of frustration laden with foul language. All the elder could do was look on. Let them rage. In the dark of winter, fears and terrors often grew best, confinement and cold weather had a way of sprouting such horrors that festered in men's minds.

Again the roar abated, however slowly, and he gestured for them all to sit on the benches. All complied, except for one man on the middle right. He was short and stocky, his head a gleaming dome of dark skin.

"Yes, Voraam?" the elder asked quietly. Today's sermon was definitely going in the bin.

"I saw a man on the docks yesterday. Looked like Old Man Felnur, but he's been dead twenty years. He walked down to the water. Then he walked right across it—for a time—before he finally sank." Someone gasped. "Where he went under, there was a big puff of smoke." More gasps. He waved them off with irritation. "And now we hear of the g-bats. Demons walking around. So I ask you—" He jabbed a large finger at the elder. "What are you going to about it?"

"What can I do about it?" he repeated softly.

"Not just you, but all of the elders."

He sighed slightly. "Son, what can we do? We are but holy men, guiding the people of this land in their ways. Do you want me to tell you to do something to these creatures? Are you asking me to allow you to—" The word *kill* was almost impossible to utter. But Voraam saved him.

"I'm not asking for permission to kill. They seem to be doing a good job on their own with that. No, after all these years of telling us demons were rare, or kept locked away at the temple, and all of that, now we see them loose! Why? And what are you going to do?" He was a simple fisherman asking for help from his Holy Elders, and at the same time, he seemed to be asking several questions underneath questions. Questions he knew the elder did not want to answer.

And he did not. A hand seemed to grab his stomach and twist it into several different shapes. Had he never gone to Vronga, he would not be standing there, exposed like a melon-poacher in a flash of lightning. Voraam knew it. How he knew was another question, but rumors easily spread. And not all rumors were fanciful tales. Some were true. Horribly true. The man's brown eyes pinned him where he stood.

"Voraam," he started, struggling to keep his voice even.

"So, what is going on?" a young woman asked, but remained seated. "This is terrifying my children. You say we never have to worry about demons, and yet they fall from the sky and walk into the sea!"

"Madam—"

"Fa says that when the demons walk, it means the temple has fallen," came the voice of a boy of about fourteen, in the far back. *Leave it to youth to sulk in the back*, the elder thought. He opened his mouth, but other voices kept rising—not in the cacophonous roar as before, but each allowed a statement to be aired before chiming in.

"I saw a man like Voraam saw; he was in the woods out by my place. Never saw him before, but he was very old—"

"Something hit the large oak tree, but when I went to look nothing was there—"

"What other creatures are out there? So far we only hear of bats and old men. Are there other things we don't know about?"

"So has the temple fallen?"

"No, we'd all be dead!"

"I saw a bat. I knew it was, very big, but it kept flying!"

"Children, children! Please, be assured the temple is safe!" he bellowed. "I'm not sure—"

Voraam interrupted again. He spoke quietly, but his voice was stern. "What I want to know," he began, setting his meaty hands on the pew in front of him, "is what you are going to do." A finger again pointed at the elder, who grimaced slightly. "The temple may be safe, aye, but something has happened. And I want to know." He stopped.

"Do you mean the Protectors?" the Elder asked, hesitation and hope in his voice. Hope that the question truly centered around the Protectors that almost everyone knew about. Hesitation that he meant something else. His heart sank as Voraam slowly shook his head.

"No."

"What then?" he asked, knowing with sickening finality where this conversation was leading. *Out with it, son,* the Elder thought. *The lid is off the coffin and the dead will not go back in.*

"I mean, what about the Knights of the Black Dawn? What are they up to?"

A few voices rose in murmur over that, mostly confusion, thankfully. But that would not last. Those few who knew of the Knights often kept the secret, as hard as it was to keep a secret for hundreds of years. But now... The lid was most assuredly removed and flung to the far winds.

"The Knights?" he asked.

"Don't pretend that you don't know what I'm talking about." Brown eyes that were well-honed swords were leveled at the elder.

A young, well-dressed man stood. His voice was refined and silky. The town's only teacher was smart, too smart for his own good, and tended to dig into places he was not allowed. Perhaps he and Voraam had shared an ale or two. "You cannot for one minute pretend that an order like that could be kept secret forever," he purred. If he had joined the Holy Orders, he would be near the top with that voice. "What about the Knights?" he asked.

The Elder sighed heavily and finally sat down on the dais. His stomach was still a knot of terror.

"Who are the Knights?" someone finally dared to ask.

The elder started to speak, but the teacher explained in his silky voice. Explained what the Knights of the Black Dawn were, and how they fought a constant battle against demons. Oh, sure, he had seen men all clad in black, fighting creatures on his travels, and dug into as much research as he could find, always running into brick walls laid forth by the Holy Elders. He finally put it together, but kept silent, for he did not want any vengeance exacted upon them. But now, all had changed. What had happened to the vaunted Knights?

"Something has happened," the elder breathed, staring down at the scuffed wood floor of the temple. "The Knights... well, yes, you are right, Teacher Rhys. They do exist." Another wave of gasps. He thought he heard someone faint, but dared not look up; instead, he addressed the floor. "And I am sure they are busy working on this new—development. Nothing has happened to the Knights, I mean." He was rambling. Never since his indoctrination had he felt like such a novice, struggling to spit words out to this elders. "It is a—disturbance. We cannot quite explain it. I have missives from other temples who say the same thing. It is very odd."

"A demonic invasion is odd?" Voraam shouted. "Odd? No, Elder, blue weevils in grain is odd. This is downright evil! Even if all we see are the ones who cannot survive, who knows what others are out there. It could be an invasion for all we know!"

"What have we done wrong to deserve this?" came a timid voice near the front.

A thousand things you have done wrong, the Elder wanted to say. *You and everyone in here. Some of you shorting the weights of your goods, others selling rotten nuts buried in the barrels of good ones, a man slinking around with another man's wife (or even husband), a wife proclaiming love for a man she hates, only to get his money. You are all vile and deserve the evil that befalls you.* These thoughts floated through his head, but he suppressed putting voice to them, if only because of a lone timid voice: *This is terrifying my children.* Unlike other elders, he believed children to be innocent. What sin was ever so great it punished the children and the innocent? For years he had dealt with indiscretion and sin on a purely individual level—a summer cold could be attributed to your lies about the number of ales you had drunk, or a pimple the result of a filched turnip from a field. These were easy ailments to throw back in the face of the individual, as a means to somehow force them to adapt a moral and righteous way of living. And he always took it upon himself to remind them that sin weaves complex knots, and we need to make sure to keep knots that are simple and straightforward (as straightforward as a knot could be). But this—this was something on a much larger scale. Perhaps it was punishment for sin, perhaps the demons were out to claim their due, to swallow the evil and subsume the hedonists. But children? Babes? Who could look a child in the face and tell them they will starve because his daddy slept with the innkeeper's daughter?

In front of the open-mouthed worshippers, he put his head in his hands, the large folds of his robe swallowing his face. When it emerged again, tears streamed from his cheeks. The lid was off and not going back—let them see his emotion. There was nothing left to hide. "You have done nothing wrong," he choked, against all the drilling thoughts that bore into his mind, all the teachers and elders who would tear off his left ear could they hear him now. "Nothing."

A hushed silence fell over the temple. Even Voraam was subdued in his response. "What kind of a disturbance?" he finally asked in a near whisper.

"I wish I knew," the elder replied after he regained control of himself. "It seems as if somehow the demons lost direction, or lost a leader. No, the temple stands, as far as I know, else that would have definitely been known." Thankfully no one asked how. He had no answer as to how messages could travel from the Temple of M'Hzrut to his small village, even when half of Belden was covered in snow, and with Welcfer being even more inaccessible.

"So how do you know the temple is safe?"

Can there be no secrets? He thought with bitterness. Did they have to ask every question? "I know; that's why!" he snapped, then shook himself and nodded slowly. "I apologize. I do get missives from there. Even in the winter. I am not sure how they come—perhaps by bird to Vronga and then to me. But worry not, the temple is safe."

The voices rose again in a clamor, but soon died down. Folks began to take their seats again; their eyes fixed on the Elder. Voraam remained standing, his gaze still accusing. The elder motioned him to sit with an impatient hand.

"You must trust me on this, children. It does you no good to worry over that which you cannot control. And be assured that the Knights... well, the Knights are working tirelessly, I am sure, to protect us from such creatures." He had said the word demon so many times that he feared saying the name again would bring one walking through the temple doors at any moment.

Voraam nodded his large head slightly, and the elder released the breath he'd been holding.

"I had a sermon prepared today," he said. He rose with a creak of joints and smoothed out his robe. "But given the circumstances, I am inclined to let everyone go and reassure you that others are looking out for us. As should you, too, look out for one another in this time of uncertainty."

The back rows started filing out first, with mumbles and even a few laughs here and there. Slowly the temple started to clear out, but Voraam remained—after letting his pew exit, he stood at the edge of the aisle and glowered. "Yes... Voraam?"

"I would ask your permission, elder," he began, casting a glance around to be sure he was the last one left. Only the teacher, Rhys, remained, but Voraam's eyes passed over the man as if he were an extra song book. *So they* have *been sharing an ale or two, no doubt.* "I would ask your permission to destroy such demons as I may encounter."

Rhys stood suddenly, but was silent.

Given the dark cloud that seemed to be growing over the land, the Elder was inclined to give said permission, but a tiny voice in the back of his head raised doubts. "I am sorry. I cannot grant such absolution, my son. You must let the Knights deal with this. Or let them—"

"Voraam," Rhys said softly, "we are a peaceful nation. We must remain so, even if it means we have to allow such creatures to wander—sooner or later they will be dealt with. They will."

The large man spun suddenly, his voice thick with frustration. "But you said—"

"I know what I said, and that probably in the heat of things. Now that I've had time to think, I—"

"But there is no more time to think!" Voraam bleated. "Such time is long past, with the demons loose, who knows what they will do? How long before they stop killing themselves and start killing us? And our children?"

The elder put a hand over his stomach, as the image of dead children flittered across his vision. *It is scaring the children*, the voice echoed. No, it was not fair! It was inherently unfair that the innocent should ever suffer! But if he let one man take matters into his own hands, there—

"Voraam, if you are allowed to kill demons at will, where would it stop? There would be a bloodbath," Rhys said sternly, as if reading the Elder's thoughts. "And not only demons would die, possibly. No, not possibly. Definitely. Innocents would die, too."

"I would only kill demons," the man protested, but weakly. His face had gone blank, as if he were picturing an out-of-control battle.

"You say that now, my good man, but I don't know if it would stop. What if you 'saw' a demon and it turned out to be a goat, or a horse, or, what I fear the most, a child? When the hunt is on, and the blood is spilling, everything looks like prey. This you should know—that the Knights are there for a reason. They are disciplined, and will not go killing everything they think is a demon." Rhys made his way slowly over to Voraam and put a hand on the man's shoulder. "You are a good man, Voraam, but we are living through a very dark time, and I fear if given a weapon, things could get out of control very quickly."

The teacher had put words to the small voice in his own head. A senior elder could not have said it better, and he mentioned as much. "That is why we cannot allow killing. In fact, I want to draft a proclamation. If anybody kills anything intentionally—even a demon—they will be tried as if they killed a human being." He waved off the protesting Voraam. "We cannot allow any type of war to start."

"What kind of war?"

Rhys responded softly. "It would not be war, Your Grace, it would be a slaughter. Annihilation. And very few would survive."

The Elder nodded gravely. "That is how the proclamation will stand, for now. Killing is forbidden. Now go. I have to get writing."

He walked the two to the entrance, and as soon as the large doors slammed shut, he fell against them. The "change of direction" would mean an organized militia of some sort, which really meant that he would have to allow killing. And, if Rhys was right, and the elder knew deep down that he was, even an organized militia could turn into a pack of bloodthirsty wolves.

"The Knights better have an answer and soon," he muttered.

Chapter 6
Buzzing

Oh, buzz, buzz, buzz, buzz, buzz! I'm a fly! Buzz, buzz!
To the far winds! To the sea, to the sand and the shore.
I buzz!

Mad Hereald

Flies were buzzing. Even in this bitter cold, I could hear them. When she wasn't talking to me, blocking my every waking thought, there were flies.

FLIES!

Flies and giant beetles! Crawling under my skin, scratching at my bones, and eating through my flesh. The scratching and scrabbling were relentless and unforgiving, both within and without. I could hear the clawing deep down below, echoing through hundreds of miles of rock, up through the courtyard, through the snow, past my windows, and into my head.

I screamed and threw the pewter cup against the hearth with such violence that it was crushed against the stone in a spray of hot black liquid. "Sacuan be damned!" I screamed. "And the flies—take them all away. I want them out!"

Snow lashed the window panes, only adding to the horrible cacophony of sounds that were assailing me, driving into my skin. Flies and snowflakes seemed to be in my head, next to her voice, and they hurt. They HURT.

"Sacuan be damned!" I screamed again.

OUT, came a hiss from below. *Out, we want OUT*. I could hear them scratching and clawing each other, copulating in the festering heat of perversion, and inching ever closer to the top. They could work their way out through the rock. I knew they could, and they knew it too. But how many would die in the attempt? As fast as they could reproduce, they would die out, eat themselves, or slaughter one another trying to scramble to the top. They need me more than anything, both to keep them at bay, and to finally release them. But I couldn't! I couldn't!

She screamed again and I was flung to the floor with a creak of joints. A black pain swallowed everything.

φ

A low hiss in the back of my mind woke me. I was splayed across the sofa, legs pinned in odd directions and my hands bent under my torso. Each limb had fallen asleep, countless needles digging deep into my skin; when I tried to stand, my bloodless feet gave out, and I tumbled to the floor.

The hiss continued in my mind, as if something large was emitting its last breath—its last few trapped gasses before expiring.

I could not control them; it hurt too much—The demons were rudderless!

It would not be long before the horde broke through the surface, but they were still trapped. What froze my heart was the fact that almost every demon awake in Belden and Welcfer was now wandering aimlessly, killing itself or even others. I could no longer control them, either! Something had severed my connection to them, and now, they were as useless as the pewter cup that lay smashed on the floor.

Buzz!

"No!" I screamed, grabbing my skull.

She had done this. I knew it. The vile woman and her scheming! I should have known. Sacuan curse me, but I should have known. All those years I had talked to Lyn, why did I not guess that killing *her* would have sent her searching for me? Perhaps he talked to her before he left?

No, he had never mentioned her, but it was possible he had planned something in case my—no, he would have surely taken action earlier. But...

It was too much.

I stood to fetch another cup, but my legs were weak. With a groan, I collapsed back on the sofa. There was much I had to do—many things I needed to figure out—the most important being *her*, but I couldn't move. Against a million protesting thoughts, I leaned back on the soft cushions and fell asleep.

ϕ

You cannot continue this, Bimb.

The voice came through the dark. Mother! Was I still sleeping, or was I awake? My eyes opened and I looked at the cold heart. No, I was awake. Painfully awake. My lips could hardly move, so dry and cracked were they. I forced them open. "Mother, leave me alone! You cannot stop what has been started."

I am going to stop you.

"Then who will control the demons?"

They will work that out—right now they are coming. Coming for you, and there is nothing you will be able to do about it.

How was that possible? She was obviously lying. She was stalling, for what I couldn't guess. She was dead and in her place and could do nothing to stop me. But she was succeeding only by keeping me occupied with her pointless and meaningless voice. I needed her to go away! This was starting to border on the ridiculous. The dead never hung on like this before, but, of course, a mother would.

"Why don't you leave me alone?"

I can't and you know it. Something inside of you died. No, you died, Bimb, and you must come back.

"I'm not dead!" Why was she crying again? "I'm not dead! Do you hear? I am alive in more ways than you can imagine. He saved me."

He has doomed you. Lyn led you here in an attempt to save his son, but all the while, Ar'Zoth was destroying you!

I wiped away something from my eyes. The buzzing continued, but if I tried very hard, I could make it go away. "You don't know what it was like! Everyone my age was able to do every fun thing they ever wanted to, and I was stuck counting turnips. When Ar'Zoth came to me, it was like being released from the restraining house!"

She was silent for several seconds. *You don't know what it was like to have to raise you, do you? No idea of the pain I had to endure, knowing that I... that I...* She trailed off, sobbing.

I felt a flicker of empathy. I tried to crush it, but I still heard myself apologize to her.

It was not your fault, Bimb. It was mine. I am so sorry that—

"Silent!" I screamed, finally able to destroy any feelings. She had made me what I was, and if she felt the need to carry that guilt past the grave, that was not my problem. No, I needed her to get out of my head! She was interfering with very important work. I told her as much.

You are a sick little boy, she said quietly. *And they will find you, and I think they will have to kill you. Perhaps your own death will make you think.*

"I will never die!" I hissed. Ar'Zoth had promised me nearly eternal life here, especially should I be able to release the demonic horde upon Belden and destroy every last living thing. Living forever was impossible, but he promised that I would live longer than anyone. He promised! And now she was interfering.

Bimb, you—

"Silence!" I screamed. "You—" The hand grabbed my stomach again, but I willed away the pain. If only I could get this vile woman to leave me alone—there was too much to do and already the horde was starting to slip away from me. Who knew what was happening in greater Belden or Welcfer? For all I knew the demons were already marching and eating everyone... and I was missing it! My delicious winter! How could she take it away from me? I was stuck here with a band attached to my stomach and a mad woman crying in my skull.

No, you must listen to me...

She prattled on, but I stopped listening. There had to be something that I could grab onto, some string, rope, fiber, or particle that could be used to get her to leave me alone.

Buzz!

No, stop, I need to hold on, I need to find it! When I reached for the spaces between, she seemed to sense it, and the knot tightened. Something about tea... why was she talking about tea, of all things?

... Like a cup of soothing black tea, he is. They are. They will cut you down and free the world from your vileness.

Who was mad? Certainly not I. Tea? She was blathering on about tea when I was slowly losing my grip on everything? I wished I had listened... what in the name of all demonic rites would tea have to do with anything?

"You are mad, not me, Mother." The word felt like a thick tar in my mouth.

No, Bimb. They are coming. They are coming. It will not be long before they smother, drown you and stop you.

"What does that have to do with tea?"

Tea? She sounded confused. Of course she was confused; she was utterly mad! Crazy and beyond help! *I was talking about what a relief they will be for you, like a hot mug of tea, soothing away your problems...*

"Trying to kill me is not very soothing."

It will be for the world, Bimb. For the world...

I think she prattled on some more, but I thought again of tea. Tea! Of all thing that she could—

Tea! My mind suddenly snapped to attention upon further thought. That could be the answer!

Ar'Zoth told me about tea, much about tea... I missed him. Well, no, I didn't.

There were many ways to serve tea, from large leaves steeped in water, to crumbled up particles, and even tea in little cloth bags. Most tea was a brownish black, but others were green, and even some very expensive blends were white. White! They called it that, only because the water never got darker than amber when you boiled it. But that wasn't the point. When you made tea, you took two separate things—leaves and water—and you boiled them together, or boiled one, and added the other. What started as clear water ended as a green or brown liquid.

And there was no way to put the tea back into the leaf! That is what she was doing to me, wasn't it? She was the insipid liquid that oozed from the pure tea leaf of death and had spoiled my clear, pure water. I was steeped within her vileness, rather, her vileness steeped within the work that I had to accomplish. But how could I possibly get her out? If I could find that... I could expel her.

"Yes, Mother," I said to something she was asking. "As long as you leave me alone."

I will never leave you alone. Besides, you weren't listening, were you? I didn't ask you a question. I told you— they are coming!

"Will you stop saying that?" I spat. "I get it. They're coming. Your invisible friends, they're on their way here. Thank you, but you need to leave me alone. I have too much work to do." Who were they? More of her dead friends? Or was she just rambling on, the lifetime of drink not fully washed away with death? Most likely she was still drunk. The dead can't talk to the—

With that thought my heart sank slightly, but I quickly recovered. I was stronger than Ar'Zoth! It didn't matter if she brought an army, I would kill them all! They would be stuck at the base of those non-existent stairs, or I could slaughter them at will as they tried to cross over the mountains... I was safe and had nothing to worry about.

Buzz!

I'll go now, but I will be back.

Good, she was going to go. Thankfully. Once she left, I could get to focus on what needed to be done.

But before I do, I will leave you this—

The band around my stomach tightened and I collapsed in a heap. Whatever was strangling midsection was no longer confined to my stomach. It edged up into my heart; it nearly sucked the air from my chest. As it crept higher, it finally attached itself to my head. It was supposed to have been a delicious winter—There was a quick burst of searing fire before everything went black.

Chapter 7
Into the Tunnels

I oft wonder what we have created. Such a waste for the Tunnels to have only one purpose. We must add a new exit, and that near what is called Gray Gorge. This will allow us to move our "special" cargo to its location.

Adel Forshen, from a letter to High Cleric Bertrand

Huyen arrived with two horses fully loaded—huge packs hung from the sides, and small saddle bags were filled to the bursting. Long pieces of slightly curved wood were attached precariously to the gear. The knight rode atop one horse and skillfully guided the other with a leader harness.

Yulchar ducked inside and brought out the pan of now-cold turnips and meat. The men ate hurriedly and the pan was tossed unceremoniously back in the house—rodents and other wandering animals would at least have a snack.

With a mouth full of food, Huyen walked to the horses and pulled down a massive pack. "Zhyfrael," he muttered as he heaved it at Zhy. It had straps for the back and another strap to secure it around his midsection. Zhy struggled to don it, and it nearly tipped him over backward. Huyen laughed mirthlessly as he slung his easily onto his back, complete with the long slats of wood sticking up. "Sleeping bags are in those, with other gear," he growled.

"Where to now?" Zhy asked, knowing the answer and cursing himself for asking.

Yulchar pointed to the large stone slap tucked against the snow-covered hill. "In there."

Huyen grunted in agreement.

Following numbly and somewhat clumsily with his heavy pack, he let the two men lead him to the stone wall they claimed was an entrance. And as Yulchar recited a string of complex numbers, the stone slab slid out and sideways, revealing a black chasm. *Now where have I seen that before?* Zhy wondered. As if in a vivid episode of déjà vu, he watched Yulchar and Huyen walk into the dark and simply vanish.

Something seemed to push his pack and he stumbled into the darkness, hoping—and knowing? Did he know?—that he would emerge in light. Or at least a world lighter than the purest black. There was a thick smell of must, dirt, and moisture.

And after a few paces, he heard the slab ease shut, took a deep breath, and pushed his foot forward just one more step. Indeed, there was light, if a muted and disconcerting blue. The glowing runes were spaced out a few hundred feet apart ahead of him, but when he looked behind, there was only black. He dared not imagine what horror lurked in that darkness, what vile demonic creature, or... his mind wandered and then snapped back to focus.

The lights were like rectangular sconces set in the wall. A metallic plate was attached to the stone with what looked to be round spikes or nails—though Zhy wondered how one would bore the hole for them. Magic, more than likely. The light fixture itself was a translucent, glass-like material with four small ridges that encircled the see-through material. Behind the glass one could make out the actual light source—a clear, oval-shaped rune that, beneath the blue glow, looked as if it were covered in smoke.

His companions were bathed in the strange light, their pale faces almost glowing indigo. Dull-brown packs looked nearly orange in the light, and the bindings on the wooden slats reflected the light in odd, miniscule flashes.

He looked to his right and wondered aloud where the Tunnels led in that direction.

"Just a blank wall," Yulchar replied calmly and started walking. "Are we going north?" he finally asked after mindlessly following them for quite a while. And how far to go? *This pack already feels as if I'm carrying a small village on my shoulders.* The strap along his midsection eased the burden, and he found that by tightening the strap considerable weight was shifted, but it was still very uncomfortable to carry. His entire body ached and they had only gone a dozen paces.

As if reading his thoughts, Yulchar chirped: "I have powders for the aches, and even some to keep us awake. Do not worry. And there is plenty of water here. Listen," he said, cocking an ear.

In the black voids between the lights, water could be heard dripping in an odd cadence. *Drip drip-drip drip drip drip-drip-drip drip drip-drip.* It was comforting to hear water, for he knew they could survive for a while on their rations with water aplenty.

They seemed to be slowly descending into the earth, though there was no reference by which to judge, but he felt as if the pack pushed at him at each step, as it would walking down a gentle hill.

"We are on an incline... rather, decline," he said.

"Aye," replied Huyen with a grunt.

"We will level out shortly... and yes we are descending slowly and will eventually be hundreds of feet below the surface when the tunnel levels out."

As they walked, Zhy fell into a rhythm and idly counted the lights as they went by, but soon got distracted by the dripping of water and gave up. He tried to think of himself hiking on a long journey, but it was very unsettling to be so deep underground with the knowledge that above their heads were uncounted tons of solid rock. Zhy looked up into the darkness, but the blue light faded before it could reflect any ceiling.

"And why would something like this be built for just a small number of people? Imagine what could be done in the winter! Food. Food! People starve in the north, don't they?"

His voice sounded too loud in the space, and it echoed briefly on the rough stone walls.

Didn't they starve up there? he thought. *With all the snow... they must.*

Zhy could see Yulchar nod his head slowly.

"Sacuan's—" He broke off. It was not worth it. If the world could be threatened by a single man, it only stood to reason that enormous amounts of effort would be spent on an underground highway to a temple that absolutely no benefit to anyone. *What an absolute waste.* Their footsteps echoed dully in the sodden atmosphere and were quickly swallowed by the rock and the damp.

"So these tunnels go under the mountains?" Zhy asked in a valiant attempt to force down his anger at the situation.

Yulchar nodded in the blue light. "Straight under the Spires of Solitude. Well, the little range that blocks Welcfer from Belden... they call that part of the Spires, but it is really split by Gray Gorge, so it really is not part of it. You have been up there, and we come out a few miles or so north of Gray Gorge."

Zhy couldn't help but whistle. "Great grinding goats," he muttered, his hand drifting to his ear. *Where had that phrase come from?*

Looking up, he realized it was more than tons of solid rock—entire mountains stretched up into the heavens. It was an unsettling thought to know that if any part of the tunnel were to fail, they would be crushed like gnats. *How could anyone dig a tunnel through mountains?* he wondered.

Huyen stalked a few more paces ahead with what Zhy thought was a curse, and no matter the pace Yulchar or Zhy set, he always set himself apart. *Grumpy old dog,* Zhy thought, and his breath caught as the gruff man turned his head slightly.

Patiently, Yulchar explained the Tunnels and how and why they were built. "It took several Ages to complete Tunnels, but when the High Cleric orders something, it gets done. The Orders did not want to have to go overland during winter or chance the dangerous route to Foltrag, so they came up with the idea of the Tunnels—odd name, since it is just one long tunnel."

"Were there plans for more?"

"Possibly... they probably thought they could build a crisscrossing network, but with the roads all converging in Vronga, they must have decided to just go from there. I am sure finances played a part, too. But the name stuck... it sure has a ring to it."

Zhy grumbled. *A fancy name for a superior method of delivering necessities—used only by a useless bunch of Sacuan-worshipping fools.* His foot caught an edge of stone and he stumbled. He had asked the same question it seemed a hundred times (and would ask it again), but it was only appropriate: *Where had that thought come from?*

"So through tithes and such they paid for it. It took a great deal of magic to bore through solid rock, burrow under villages, and keep the water at bay."

"Keeping it secret took the most effort," Huyen said suddenly. He kept his distance, but he had his head bent in thought.

"I would say."

"You sound skeptical."

"Well, you know about it, who else does?" Zhy asked snidely.

"Listen, Zhyfrael, I did get a brief look in the Archives, although the Keeper would have wrung my neck had I not divulged the Order."

Yulchar grimaced. "Yes, while I asked around for your residence, Huyen was able to get some information."

"I see, and what did you find?"

"What we have just told you, Zhyfrael."

Zhy chuckled. "I also meant, what did you find out about me?"

"Plenty. Some crusty innkeeper said you lived in that run-down house. Said you had left on a journey with a stranger and would not be back for a long time, if at all. He knew of you."

"Did he say anything else about me?"

"No."

"I see." He understood little, although he had vague images of an inn and an innkeeper. Why had Kahl said nothing about Zhy? The additional knowledge could have provided at least a candle in the darkness of his memory.

"In any case, I had to retrieve Huyen and make haste for your house, and then we were off. So the Tunnels *are* quite secret, but that does not mean they are entirely unknown, either."

"I see," he repeated. He suddenly felt as if he were moving much faster than he had. "We *are* going downhill, aren't we?"

"Other magic is at work, yes. If you feel as if you are stumbling down a hill, well, that feeling might not go away."

"Why?"

"Even though we will be traveling on level ground, it will feel much faster than above ground. Some say that is magic working—we move faster through the Tunnels. But others claim that is simply the fact that the ground *is* level, dry, and that there are no curves. Whichever-" He shrugged. "—the journey will be much faster. Long, yes, but faster."

He nodded in agreement and they walked in silence.

"How do we know when it's day and when it's night?" Zhy wondered, his voice echoing dully in the Tunnels. To his right, a large droplet of water splashed into an unseen pool.

"We will not, but these magical lights will, apparently," Yulchar replied.

"How is that?"

He scratched his head. "They will dim slightly when it is night above."

What a strange place, Zhy thought. *This cannot be real.*

They walked quietly for several hours, the crunch of their boots on stone the only sound, and the blue lights became somewhat mesmerizing. And while the tunnels were warm, there was still a dank coolness and every so often their breath would steam out into the tunnel and be caught in the blue light, casting an eerie fog. Their footsteps would echo for a mile or two, then stop, as if something far away were swallowing all sound.

Zhy could not help but cast a backward glance along the tunnels. It was maddening not to be able to see visually how far they had come, for even the blue lights would vanish into the distance, and become swallowed by the oppressiveness of the place.

"Tunnels of Woe indeed," he mused quietly.

No one answered, but he could see them nod in the dimness. Of a sudden, the blue lights flickered, then dimmed.

"Let us try to find a dry spot to bed down, although I am afraid this will not be the most comfortable place."

"It sure doesn't feel like night."

"Yes, that is part of the danger here. One could travel for days, not knowing day from night. But soon you would collapse and even die. No, trust the lights, as much as you distrust your own intuition."

They continued on for at least a mile before they noticed a slight widening of the tunnel. The ground, while still hard and cold, was dry here, and the sounds of dripping were quite far off. Resigning himself to the fact that this would be his home for the foreseeable future, he unrolled his donated bedding and attempted sleep in the eerie blue glow.

ф

Zhy started to drift off to sleep, but the far away dripping seemed to be growing louder and louder. What was once a slight plop soon became a massive splash, like someone had hurled a house-sized boulder into a pond. He bolted awake, panting, hoping it was a dream. But Huyen and Yulchar were wide-awake, swords drawn. He drew his own small knife, not knowing what he could possibly do with it.

Dim blue light cast odd shadows on the wet rock. Beasts and men alike danced before his eyes, and ha squinted violently, trying to parse out real from imagined foes.

"What is that?" Zhy barked.

"I do not know," Yulchar replied. Another huge splash echoed through the tunnels. The lights flickered, dimmed, then went completely dark.

Zhy gasped in terror.

"Quiet!" Huyen snapped.

In the utter darkness, visions of all sorts of horrible things danced in his mind's eye. He could hear the Knights' knuckles crack as they tightened their grips on their sword hilts. Perhaps they even prepared to cast spells, but he faced only black. Apart from the shallow breathing, there was absolute silence. No dripping. Nothing. Only quiet breathing.

Then they heard it. It was very muted at first, and far, far back in the tunnels where they had started. The sound of wings flapping. Large wings. The leathery sound of something giant whooshing slowly into flight. Whatever it was, it was slowly gaining speed—faster, faster, faster.

"Wh—"

A massive screech filled the air, and Zhy ducked instinctively. At the same moment, a bolt of light flashed from one of his companion's hands and bolted into the darkness. Zhy waited for some sort of impact or explosion, but the blue tendril simply faded into the vast tunnel. Just as quick as the first noise came another screech. Closer. Less than a hundred feet. Then another deafening roar. And again a bolt of light shot out, and again it missed the creature and faded into the void.

Suddenly, the magical blue lights blinked on, but only for a brief second before going dark. In that brief light, however, they had seen enough. They sat frozen in horror, for they had seen the shape of an oversized gherwza. It was black and dripping wet. Its razor-sharp teeth dripped something green. As it passed them, it flapped its mighty wings and launched itself faster through the tunnel. The stench from the flapping wings was unbearably thick and cloying, and it hung in the windless tunnel. There was another, softer screech, as it continued through the tunnel and disappeared.

Soon water started dripping again, as if the demon had somehow terrified the very water into cowering in fear.

"I—" Yulchar began. The lights flickered on again, but in their previous dull glow. He stopped and looked at his companions.

"Why didn't it kill us?" Zhy wondered in a whisper.

"I—Perhaps it was trying to escape. I do not think it was hunting. It looked almost—almost frightened."

"Frightened? Frightened! How could a demon be frightened?"

"I—I don't know."

"How...how did it get into the Tunnels? The door shut behind us and there is no other entrance." Huyen coughed. "I think we should pack up and keep walking—I have lost any motivation for sleep."

"I think—"

"It could have been hiding where we came in," Zhy offered.

"That could be," Yulchar said. "But unlikely. Too big to sneak in, we would have heard it."

"But—?"

Yulchar interrupted him. "We always assumed the Tunnels ended there, but maybe they do go farther toward Belden City... we just do not know of any other entrance... so yes, it is possible."

"I think we should hurry up and get out of here," Huyen rasped.

"We cannot walk ourselves to death because we saw a gherwza in here. We have a very long way to go and can't afford to kill ourselves walking. Our pace will be careful."

"Is that an—"

"Yes, it is an order, Huyen! Stop with this. It sounds like the bird has gone farther down; perhaps we will run into it, or maybe it's gone away, somehow. Maybe there are openings big enough for such creatures, but such openings, well, I have never heard of them!" He looked up into the black void. "Stay alert. Stay alert."

"I wonder if Zhyfrael—"

"No, he did not! Go back to your bedroll and sleep."

Huyen coughed, but grudgingly returned to his sleeping bag. Zhy returned to his as well, but sleep was nigh impossible to find. He kept hearing the screech of the enormous bat and the constant dripping of water. Everything felt damp and slick with moisture.

Thankfully, he slept soundly and did not receive any visitors.

ϕ

"I found something of interest in Vronga," Huyen said of a sudden. His voice was either a snarly rasp or a growl, and there was little variation.

They had broken their fast in silence and continued on their slow march northward. Zhy worried his bedding and sleeping bag would mold from the moisture—especially without the ability start a fire for warmth. The others paid no heed to his concern.

"What was that?" Yulchar asked.

Zhy smartly kept himself out of the conversation. Huyen was trying hard to ignore Zhy, and Zhy feared if he spoke a single word, the Knight would draw his sword and strike at him.

"The store where I got the skis—" *So that is what those long thin boards are called,* Zhy thought. He knew he had heard of them. Was it Father who had talked of them? It had to have been. "—was next to not only an inn but a tea-house where some of the mages from the university would hang out."

"Yes?"

"I stopped in and casually asked about a mage, a small-man."

An image flashed in Zhy's mind, but he flung it aside, wanting to concentrate on what Huyen was saying. The constant *drip drip-drip-drip drip drip drip-drip-drip* was enough of a distraction that he had a hard enough time as it was concentrating.

"And...?"

"Well..." The man cleared his throat. "They had heard of a few small-men who had stopped in, but one in particular stuck in their memories. It took a few cups of tea and some coin to get them to open their mouths and their minds—ale would have been quicker, but alas..."

"That explains your delay in getting back to the farm."

The man continued without acknowledging. "He was a rough little man, all fire and fury—full of very rude words, they had said. Lost his horse. How can you lose your horse?"

I see you don't have a horse, someone said.
I lost it, the small-man replied.

The image flickered so fast that Zhy nearly missed it, but it was there and for a moment two names floated to the tip of his tongue and then danced away.

"That sounds very strange," Yulchar agreed.

Huyen nodded. When his head dipped back, his hair got caught in a reflection of the blue lights and a thin trickle of water against the western rock wall. The lights created an illusion of lightning striking, Zhy thought, and again a hazy picture dashed in front of his eyes: a small-man flinging around lightning bolts.

"A small-man," Zhy said quietly, he thought under his breath.

"Yes, a small-man, are you deaf?" Huyen snapped. Zhy's mouth opened, but he snapped it shut.

"Now—" Yulchar began.

"It's quite all right," Zhy said. *Drip drip drip-drip-drip.* "I just remember something about a small-man—that is all. I think he lost his horse, but I can't quite remember."

Huyen continued talking, seemingly ignoring everything Zhy had said. "After some chatting, he had left, and said he was headed down to Belden City."

"Any mention of a farm or a boy?" Yulchar asked.

"I asked, but each said they remembered no such discussion. Only something about having to 'find those bastards before they find me,' whatever that meant." The grumpy man scratched his head. "Or was it 'find those bastards to make it three?' Nobody was quite sure what he said, but the only word that came across was 'bastards' for whatever reason."

"He sure wasn't going to get very far on foot!"

"No, but maybe he was hoping to meet up with someone."

"But if he was running, if he said he had to get away before he was found..."

"I know. It makes no sense," Yulchar snapped. "Maybe he was going to that farm for whatever reason."

Zhy padded along silently, watching the blue lights approach, then pass by slowly. He had the strange sensation that the ground was moving under his feet, as if he were merely stepping along a sliding slab of rock that raced northward. "How fast are we traveling?" he asked suddenly, ignoring Huyen's glare.

"Faster than you think," Yulchar replied. He then turned to his companion. "Very strange business, that. A small-man without a horse, headed south to Belden City. And something about 'bastards.' Did you get any other useful information?"

"No, except that a few weeks—maybe a month—after the man was seen going south, one of the mages was convinced he saw him again, this time riding through town. On a horse. This time he was going north. And he was with two others."

"Maybe he found what he was looking for."

"Perhaps, but it only makes it that much more confusing. Unless he found who he was looking for, and..."

Yulchar shrugged.

The image of a small-man riding a horse seemed familiar, somehow, but as hard as he tried imagining how that would look, nothing coalesced. He had a brief vision of a beggar in the street, and an argument, but nothing further.

"I think you were chasing something that did not need to be chased," Yulchar said sadly after they passed a few lights.

"What do you mean by that?"

"I vaguely remember a man like that," Zhy answered for him. "And something about a horse, too, but everything is still cloudy."

Huyen grunted.

"Well, I guess..." Yulchar started. "It still does not answer anything about the farmhouse and the woman!"

"No, it does not," Huyen snapped.

"Then why are we talking about it?" Zhy added.

"You are not; we are," the gruff knight retorted.

Huyen sniffed loudly, triggering a flash of a memory in Zhy. Who else had sniffed like that? But the surly knight was talking to Yulchar: "But it is a start anyway. I think that small-man was one of his companions." He waved at Zhy with irritation. "A dangerous little bastard himself."

"Now, Huyen, I think you may have forgotten what we are doing here. If nothing was found regarding the farmhouse or the boy, I am not sure we've really learned anything."

"It was not a complete waste of time, if that is what you are insinuating."

"Of course not, but—"

"Ach! Just forget it then. As much as I hate to admit it, if we do not fill the gaps in Zhyfrael's memories, we may not survive the confrontation with Ar'Zoth, or whatever his name is."

At least he admits it, Zhy thought with a half-smile.

"I am not sure we can do that for him, though. He has to do it on his own. Perhaps this woman can tell him—"

"I wish I could believe that!" Huyen said. He sounded exasperated. "There are too many questions surrounding her, and him, and everything else that I do not think I can trust things as they appear."

I don't either.

Yulchar shrugged. "I am not long on trust either, but think about it. *Something* is pulling us along. Something led us to that farmhouse. Why had the guard not found that note? For Sacuan's sake, Huyen, we almost rode right by that farm without seeing it. Do you remember?"

"Aye, I do. The blue jay caught my eye—strange bird flew almost straight down to the field, and then was up again with a worm the size of Darvein Harbor in its mouth." There was a mirth in his voice that Zhy had never heard; it was reassuring, but unsettling to hear the bristly knight speak so easy. "I never would have seen that farm..."

"And the guard let us look around without question."

Zhy strained to hear the last few words and then realized he had slowed his pace. He took a few steps forward, as quiet as he could. Still, he remained a pace or two behind the men as they talked. The brief levity in Huyen would only last so long.

"Maybe Sacuan is at work here," Yulchar added.

Huyen spat. "No."

"Why not? We have a dead woman talking to Zhy here—"

"So he says."

"Listen, the note—"

"I know what the note said! And yes, I do think the dead can guide the living, but not Sacuan... he has been gone far too long. I do not think they stay around long."

Suddenly Yulchar spun and addressed Zhy. "Did she say anything about death? About how..."

He started at the sudden address. For so long they had been talking as if he weren't there. *Your father was here, but he is gone now.* "Nothing specific. Only that some people were 'there,' wherever that is, but many were 'gone.' I still don't—"

"So that is why it is not Sacuan," Huyen continued. "But something *is* going on, I give you that."

"The note, Huyen, the note!"

"I *know!*" he exploded. "We have had this conversation already. Why are we having it again?" *So I can hear it,* Zhy thought. Yulchar was deliberately repeating a conversation so Zhy could understand more. His respect for the knight was increasing.

"That note was written after death—it had to have been. She—I do not know how, but she did it. Or someone did it for her."

"Who? Who else can talk to the dead? And if they can, why go get Zhyfrael and drag him all the way back here?"

"That is an excellent point. So she must have written it, but how?"

"Ack, I do not know!"

"I... I am glad you found more information in Vronga, and I hope it will be useful. I think we do need to rely on this woman—that is, let Zhy relay the information to us."

"I think we can handle Ar'Zoth just fine on our own."

"Would we even know to go after Ar'Zoth, if not for that note?"

Huyen spat. "Sacuan blast it, you are right. Sacuan be—" He spat again. "So we do need him." The sidelong glance he afforded Zhy was a dangerous mix of loathing and acceptance. As if he would slice Zhy into small pieces once Ar'Zoth was dealt with.

"Let us see what this woman has to say, Zhy," Yulchar said, turning to address him. "Keep your ears... or mind... or whatever it is... open."

Zhy nodded.

"And let us hope we don't run into that gherwza," Yulchar said softly, which elicited a grunt from Huyen. Zhy groaned inwardly—he did appreciate being reminded of that incident.

Huyen's hand drifted back to his sword, and he gripped the hilt briefly before letting go.

Chapter 8
Foltrag

How do you grieve when you think they are still alive?
How do you know that you should mourn their passing?
Where will you find it in you to shed tears for a person
whose knot you assume is whole?

Prophet Broundoun III

Freezing rain pelted the Welcferian capital of Foltrag, coating every surface with an other-worldly sheen. It enveloped the masts of ships in the harbor, leaving a double-image of beams and ropes as it froze. The cobblestone streets were a smooth sheet of glass, and anyone who dared to venture out found themselves sliding rather than walking. Inns and taverns were packed to the rafters with those stranded by the storm. A flash of lightning and a clap of thunder harkened to the bygone summer, but the eerie sound of rain freezing against window panes, metal, and roofs was unsettling. Nobody knew how much weight the structures could hold before collapsing under the weight of the ice, and the storm offered little hope of lessening.

The common room of Zhyfrael's Folly was packed beyond capacity, and the sutan player had long abandoned his chair for a seat at the bar—he had tired of constantly bumping the neck of his instrument against the patrons. No one seemed interested in music—they preferred to keep the noise level in the room high, in an attempt to drown out the constant roar of the rain and the tinkle as it froze solid. Lodgers in the upper floor had also moved down for the beams creaked, and icy rain found its way into small corners. A fire roared in the hearth, but the chill of the rain and the uncertainty of the storm seemed to affect the warmth generated by the flames. Everyone seemed to be talking at once. But the conversations had no direction, and the patrons would repeat themselves—always an ear cocked to the windows or the ceiling.

Nearly every person in Zhyfrael's Folly was a small-person, save the odd traveling merchant from Belden. No doubt their ships were now blocked in from the ice, and here they were stuck. But, apart from the low bar, the small beds, and the slightly lower ceilings, the Beldeners saw no reason to dislike Foltrag. The women were loose and the food was sublime.

Another crack of thunder brought with it a man falling into the common room. His feet had slid out from under him while he gripped the long brass handle, and his momentum carried him face-first into the fat legs of a patron. With profuse apologies to everyone, the newcomer pushed the door shut. Ice pellets showered those closest to the door, and hands furiously wiped away the cold liquid.

"Drunplug!" a voice boomed over the commotion. Suddenly the noise in the room vanished. The only sounds were the crackle of the fire and the constant clinking of ice against the glass. All eyes moved from the innkeeper, who had addressed the man named Drunplug, to Drunplug himself. Where at first the focus had been on getting the man upright from the storm, now everyone noticed he was still in full armor, sans his helmet. The metal plating had been covered in a smooth membrane of ice; water slowly began slicking his gear and trickling on the wood floor.

Drunplug raised a gauntleted hand and waved to the innkeeper. His voice was deep and booming, which seemed to unsettle the customers more than the storm. "Greetings, old friend!" he boomed. He eschewed addressing men by their first names—in fighting the savages for so many years, he'd learned that a friend today could be a rotting corpse tomorrow.

"What brings you in here in this blasted weather?" the innkeeper asked. He weaved his way through the crowd and stood in front of Drunplug. The men clasped hands fiercely, and Drunplug patted the innkeeper gently on the shoulder. Once the sound of the freezing rain filled the common room again, conversations renewed in earnest. Even with the great warrior in their midst, they were intent on covering up the sound of the deluge.

"Well, I—" The large man stood, gesturing to his spot at the table, but Drunplug waved him off. "No, but thank you. Come, we can talk in the kitchens." That raised a few eyebrows, but otherwise the room had resumed its normal roar.

The innkeeper leaned against an empty cask. His wife made a face as he waved her out to the common room and gave him a scathing look, as if to say "I don't care if Sacuan himself is here, you get out there and tend to the place!"

Drunplug laughed. "Ah, the work, it never ends."

"And the same for you, I suppose."

The warrior sniffed. "Such savagery, such absolute savagery, my good man. If it weren't for the rain, I'd be soaked head to toe in blood. As it was, I was washed clean by the time I reached the gates. But then..."

"The ice?"

"I could have crawled here faster! I know some men know how to use those skis, but I just slid sideways for six miles before I covered even one!" He laughed again, but it was forced.

The innkeeper raised an eyebrow. "What's wrong?" he asked, his voice full of concern. "If you are fresh from battle, why did you come here?" *Instead of your headquarters,* he thought.

Drunplug tried to smile, then sighed. He sagged slightly and seemed to deflate. The fierce warrior evaporated into a man who carried a tremendous burden. His smile fell, lines of worry crisscrossed his leathery face, and his once-bright eyes were a dull and tired gray, underlined with thick dark circles. "I—I came here to find my son, actually. I expected to see him, or his lowlife companions in the common room."

"Darrell's not here."

"I'll be damned!" the man spat. "He left home two years ago. Two years, man! I—"

"I am sure he is still padding around Belden, avoiding the inevitable."

Drunplug shook his head sadly. "Savagery. No, he would not take that long, no matter the task. I fear something has happened to him. He was always a bit hot-headed and ill-tempered, and... well, they—I mean, Belden, has plenty of influences I'm not sure he could turn away from."

"He's a grown man. He can handle himself. And quite powerful in the magical arts, additionally." The innkeeper's son had studied with Darrell and had nothing but glowing accolades for the mage. Whatever spell they were learning, it seemed Darrell could master it quickly and more efficiently than even the instructors.

"Maybe he went mad already," Drunplug said to the floor, ignoring the innkeeper. "Or got into it with someone more powerful."

A shake of the head. "I don't think many men are more powerful than Darrell. Your son was by far the most talented. Elders had told me that, time and again, over several brandies of course!" He sucked in air. "And mad? Why would you say that?"

"Oh I don't know... he always said that he had strange visions and heard voices from time to time. I always let it go, but worried he might do something rash."

"Don't worry, Drunplug, he's as sane as any of us. He's smart, that's all... too smart sometimes. But I'm sure he's alive."

At that the small-man chuckled. "I would like to believe that he was—is, but I still feel as if something is sticking in my heart and twisting it."

"I think you just miss him. That's understandable. Wait a little longer, before you—"

A gauntlet waved him off. "No, I would not. We still have another excursion in a few weeks. If this blasted ice ever stops," he added with a glance to the ceiling. "I just fear the worst."

"As any parent would, Drunplug. So..." he began, hoping to get the man's mind off his son. But the warrior had a point. Two years was a long time to be gone from home. And, while the mage was very powerful, the innkeeper had heard stories of warlocks and demons and creatures called Wights. Belden was a dangerous place, and while he gladly traded with Beldeners, he knew the merchants did not represent the rest of the people. Beldeners were untrustworthy and shifty people. They were soft, to boot. When faced with a superior mage like Darrell, who knows what trickery they would employ to defeat him, even if there was little cause to do so. "How was the battle this time?"

"Oh, good, I guess. We may actually be gaining ground. I wish we had not returned here, though."

"Why is that?"

"Well, this blasted freezing rain for one. If we'd stayed in the field, and if the rain reached that far west, it would be a distinct advantage for us."

"Hmmm, well, that could be. When you say 'gaining ground', do you mean we might be..."

He shook his head and sighed. "Well, this is the seventh tribe this year that we have almost completely wiped out. But every winter we find ourselves in this position—" Another gesture to the ceiling. "Usually it's snow, but the ice makes it doubly hard to go out and continue the battle. And by then tribes have moved and cycled members—they breed like demonic rabbits. It was always that way, though. But we must remain strong." He tapped the door frame to the common room. "We can't afford another Zhyfrael's folly. Ever again."

"Aye, that," the innkeeper replied. "Aye, that." He stared at the floor and there was silence in the kitchens, save for the sound of the ice falling outside. It seemed to be lessening, but maybe he was just getting used to it.

"Do you have any rooms—no I suppose not."

"Well, some of the patrons in the upper floor came down here and are taking cots in the common room. Said the sound of creaking beams and the small leaks were too much for them. So, yes, if you don't mind..."

"I'd sleep outside, I'm so tired, so yes. Thank you."

He would skip dinner tonight, though he was starving. Tomorrow, he could eat as much as he could fit in his belly, but for now, exhaustion from the journey and his great disappointment at not seeing Darrell were enough to still any more desire for human contact.

φ

The room was uncomfortably small, and the beams indeed creaked. A small drip of icy water could be heard in the corner, but Drunplug tuned it out. As he dozed off to sleep, the small knife in his heart seemed to twist again.

"I hope you are safe, Darrell. We need you home," he muttered with half-open lips. "You are the only hope against the savages."

He had told the innkeeper nearly a bold-faced lie. True, they had succeeded this time, but the weather was worse on the Plains than it was here, if that could be imagined. Further, he had not succeeded in killing their leader, for as his troops returned for Foltrag, he had turned in his saddle to take a last look at the battle. And standing, his face covered in blood, was the savage clan leader. He stared hard at Drunplug's men as they retreated, raised his spear into the air and then turned to the wounded.

Drunplug had to fight every instinct to stay atop his horse. He should have roused his men to return and fight. After all, they could have easily destroyed the wounded man. But who knew if it was another trap? The savages had been expectantly very experienced this time. There was organization and a cleverness they had heretofore lacked. And so, against every screaming nerve in his body, Drunplug had turned around.

If they were going to go back and face the hordes, he needed help. He needed Darrell. For his son, he'd move any obstacle. While the innkeepers wanted him for his "personal" services, Welcfer needed his magic. His unbelievably powerful magic.

Drunplug whispered to the dark, "Son, with your power we can destroy them utterly."

Chapter 9
At the Temple

When dealing with the Dark, action is necessary. Contemplation, prayer, and meditation are worthy endeavors to determine a course of action. But such sedentary pondering must come to an end, and action must be taken.

Cleric Hrozon, Order of the Knot

Fanlas set down his fork. The turnips were incredibly sweet and filling, and the piece of dried caribou only complemented the starchy vegetable. He watched as the old mage and both Protectors ate in silence, eventually setting their own utensils on their plates.

"I think it is time we dispensed of some of the rules," the old mage said, wiping grease from his shock-white beard.

The young Protector sat up straight as if poked with a spear. "I really don't think—"

"It doesn't matter anymore," the old mage replied with a wave of his hand. The older Protector only stared. Fanlas wondered why the man still kept up his illusion as an elderly person. Perhaps that was part of where the mage was going—maybe he had tired of the charade and wanted make a change. Or leave this place. "I finally realized what I was seeing when I saw Bimb following us."

Fanlas dipped his head slightly. The others around the table regarded him with sympathy. By now it was common knowledge, and a topic of much discussion, as to what Bimb was up to when he left the Tunnels. When Fanlas had shared the map that indicated Ar'Zoth's location, there was much heated discussion about what that meant. Apparently the old mage had figured it out—or thought he did.

"And why is that?" The "old" Protector asked. "What did you see?"

"I saw a demonic host, larger than we could have ever imagined. Sitting below ground." He took a sip of water. "And it was not beneath this Temple."

A murmur spread through the small group.

"Further, I think we must prepare to do something about it. Other Protectors will be here in a few months. That could be too late for everyone, but it might just have to be that way."

"Prepare to do what?" Fanlas asked.

The mage waved a hand. "First things first, young man. It is time we shed these appearances and this constant charade."

The older man grumbled, muttering something about tradition.

"It's quite true—" the old mage heaved a deep breath. "Tradition is important, but not if it gets in the way of the more important work. That is, if we are to survive, Heayar."

The old man quivered, as if struck. "You have broken the seals, Wrenflang. You have broken them forever. We are now doomed."

Fanlas hung his head in his hands. *Wrenflang?* Fanlas thought. *Bimb had called you "Ugly Nose."* That memory stuck like a barb in his heart and he hurriedly took another gulp of water to drown the lump that was forming. "What does—what does he mean?" Fanlas asked softly, setting his cup down.

"He means," the young Protector—Sorchal—replied, "that for countless centuries we have protected this Holy place under anonymity. So that no one would be named, who bore the weight of the world on his shoulders." He tipped his mug to his mouth and grimaced. "And my name is

Sorchal." He made a sour face at that, as if hearing even his own name was a bitter reality he dreaded facing.

Heayar raised his ancient head slowly and stared at Wrenflang—how much Fanlas wanted to call him Ugly Nose now, for his bulbous nose seemed to be much larger, and his look a mixture of exasperation and despair. "Fanlas, it saddens me that you have been brought into this."

Fanlas pulled his mug of water closer to himself, but did not lift it. "No, it should not sadden you. I agreed to follow along. Perhaps I had some deep down knowledge that Bimb was following me, and so I took comfort in that. But when the knife turned in my heart and Wrenflang—" He gestured to the white-bearded mage his son had called Ugly Nose. "—put words to the darkest fears a man could have, I realized my presence here was not accidental. I now think Bimb had something to do with all of this."

Wrenflang nodded sadly and stroked his white beard. Heayar hung his head in his wrinkled hands and Sorchal merely scowled at his empty plate.

"So there are no demons underneath the Temple?" Fanlas asked.

Wrenflang touched his beard as he shook his head slowly. "I did not say there weren't, but this is not the only place."

How many are there? Fanlas thought. He opened his mouth to ask as much, but "old" Heayar coughed. "I have felt them here, and I still feel them. We cannot leave, if that is what you are suggesting."

"We cannot leave yet, but we must plan to," Wrenflang agreed, bowing his head slightly toward Fanlas, then Heayar.

"The Tunnels do not lead to this place on the map," Sorchal pointed out.

"No, they do not." Wrenflang scratched his cheek and reached for his water.

The room fell silent. In the background, they could faintly hear the hiss and pop of the fire.

"What would we need to bring if we went cross country to this... to this place?" Fanlas asked slowly.

Heayar sighed heavily, but Wrenflang answered, "Apart from warm clothing..." He smiled briefly. "Perhaps a few items from the altar, and ourselves."

"This place must remain as whole as possible," Heayar said sternly. "But you could take a number of things."

"You would not be coming?" Sorchal asked.

"I—this place... it is my home; it is what I protect." He suddenly sounded like the older man he had portrayed. "And we cannot leave it abandoned; there *is* a disturbance here, and there is something to guard."

Wrenflang nodded. "I believe that would be—"

"But he—he is far more powerful than any mage!" Sorchal protested.

"Not exactly," Heayar said softly. He gave Wrenflang a long look, and the mage returned it with a slight nod.

"What...?"

"I do not wish to draw undue attention to myself, but I have sat in the stead of warlocks from time to time." He looked uncomfortable and fidgeted with his fork. "I will be able to join you on your journey."

"Let's take a look at that map again, Fanlas," Sorchal said absently. His gaze was locked on Wrenflang, and when the older mage returned his stare, he jerked and looked at the table.

"Do you now understand why that lock came apart so easily?" Wrenflang asked of Sorchal.

The young man kept his head lowered, but muttered an affirmative.

"And how I knew that Bimb was back there, and how I could even see the demons? There is much I have learned that I regret learning, but I believe I can help. I wish there was another way."

"And I wish I had known that earlier," Sorchal said, "when we went to find you. You may have saved a lot more trouble if you had told us everything."

At that Wrenflang snorted. "Told you? A Protector? One who guards the Temple against the demonic underworld?" His head was a flash of snow-white as he shook his head. "No, I could not have told you any of that."

"Why not?" Fanlas asked.

"I worried that the reaction would have been the same as if I had told a Knight of the Black Dawn."

"I'm not sure I follow."

The mage sighed. "Some—no, many of those who have sworn their life to protect the world against demons are not so fond of warlocks. In fact, they even go so far as to call them demons. I've heard their ramblings before."

"But you're not—"

"Son," Wrenflang said, turning to face Fanlas. "You are under great strain, I know, but I have been trying to explain that many of the skills I have, the powerful spells I can use—those I learned from warlocks."

Fanlas's head spun to face Sorchal as the man gasped audibly. All color had drained from the man's face.

"It is true, and it was a large factor in my agreeing to join with you. I knew you the moment you came into that inn back in Vronga. From the look on your face, I knew something was wrong, and if it had anything to do with demons and demonic magic, that you needed a warlock."

"Are you...?" Fanlas wondered. Sorchal went from pale white to green.

"No. Very close, but no. I have studied with them, learned from them, even helped to strip the powers from one on a south-sea island. But I do not have all of their abilities. Enough, but not all."

"But you knew Bimb was behind us. You saw past his simple-minded state, didn't you?"

He nodded sadly. "Yes, I saw that, but I could not read it fully. There was a mix of dark and light, and when he left the Tunnels, it went purely dark."

"But you could have—"

"We have been through this before, son," he said, putting a bony hand on Fanlas's massive shoulder. The man did not flinch, but dropped his eyes to his empty plate. "The world is in grave danger, and I truly thought it was here... I could not have known Bimb would go... to that place, or what true evil was there. Looking in the past, one always finds the answer, but that answer was not there when one was living it. Do you understand?"

Fanlas wanted to smash his fist down and crush everything in sight. Instead, he simply cracked his knuckles.

"Yes." How often had he planted a field of turnips only to realize later that the soil that year was better suited for potatoes or other root vegetables? Not until a few rains and he could see the sprouts start, brown and spotted. The past could not be undone.

"Perhaps he is in charge now, have you thought of that?"

Fanlas shivered at that. He looked at Wrenflang with horror in his eyes. *No... no, Bimb, no, you did not...* "What if whoever is there has control and power over him? Or..." He let the thought go unspoken. There was a cunning in Bimb, behind the veil of idiocy, behind the mind of a demonic being. Far in the back, there was an unscrupulous cad who would seize any opportunity no matter the opening.

"Yes, and that is why you should have done something!"

"What would I have done?" Wrenflang barked, bony fist slamming on the table. Glasses and utensils rattled. "Killed Bimb outright?" All color drained from Fanlas' face, and Wrenflang put a bony hand on the man's huge forearm. "No, no, of course not. But we... we are now in this precarious situation and we need to get out of it. Somehow. Do you have any idea of what I should have done?"

Sorchal colored. "I—I don't rightly know, but I wish we—"

"You can't put the river back into the spring, young man," Heayar replied softly. His voice sounded out of place as he spoke up for the first time. "And you can only know the past, not the future. It is not worth fighting about something we knew nothing of... we can only move forward."

Wrenflang nodded slowly, then set the plates right on the table. Sorchal eventually apologized and stood slowly. "Let's look at those maps."

Fanlas stood in unison with the others. The entire situation was confusing, but whatever squabbles the men need to work out seemed resolved for now. He assumed that Wrenflang was a powerful mage, but the way he responded to Sorchal indicated that he was perhaps far more formidable than he had first assumed. To stand in for a warlock meant he matched the power of one—was he powerful enough to hold the demons at bay?

And the most horrible of all questions started to float to the fore. If Bimb had been guided by this demonic warlock, and if he were now—the thought made him shiver—in control, would it have been better if Wrenflang had killed him?

How could one ever think of killing one's own son?

Chapter 10
Splintered Dawn

CƷ

We must keep ourselves whole. Dissension or subversion of the Order will destroy us and endanger the entire world.

Adel Forshen

The only indication of a building was the low snow-covered roof of a hovel. It was full winter this close to Gray Gorge and the tiny, nameless village just off of Crown Road was in full hibernation. Citizens were huddled in their low in-ground huts, snuggling under blankets, reading by firelight, or more likely sleeping. Firewood had been gathered, cut, and stacked; food had been canned, dried, or stored; and only children would venture out to play in the deep snows. No one paid the odd house at the edge of the village any mind—the villagers were ever timid and shy and ignored the fact that black-clad men would come and go from the structure.

One such man entered the hut and shook the snow off his coat and hat. A dark set of stairs, hidden behind a bear hide, led down into a massive corridor, as big as several inns' common rooms. Doors that led to sleeping quarters and offices lined either side, while the room itself was arrayed with long oak tables. Some held swords and other weapons, others were piled with musty books, and the rest held food. The room looked like a hive for black flies, for it swarmed with men clad in black, like himself. Here, no one wore the black veil, but each carried one easy to hand. The newcomer scowled and made straight for a table piled with books.

An obese man was hunched over a volume and muttered to himself. He didn't look up until the newcomer coughed. "Ah, Orfel, glad to see you," the large man breathed. "Do the demons dance in the winter?"

The man named Orfel grimaced. He was unused to speaking names. But here, where it was supposedly safe, men were free to be open about whom they were underneath the coverings of the Dawn. Although no one did. So used to covering their names in public, they extended that gesture here, and rarely mentioned names to each other. Except for the obese man at the desk, that is...

"Greetings, Master Dran'Za. Yes, the demons dance. And they dance with the Knights."

"That is good to—" He cut off abruptly, his normally purple face now a sheet of white. The book fell closed. "What?"

"Indeed," Orfel replied, moving a large volume off of a chair to sit down. He stood stock-straight in the chair.

"Explain yourself."

"Two of our members seem to have broken off," he said flatly.

"Broken. Off? What does that mean?"

"Tell me," Orfel said, avoiding the question, "what have you heard of Huyen, Yulchar, Gryn, Lorfel, and Roterran?"

"Not a thing, why?" The obese man shifted his bulk and his eyes widened. "Not a thing in several months. Which is not unexpected, but Gryn... Gryn..."

"Was traveling with Yulchar and Huyen," Orfel finished. "They were expected six weeks ago."

A heavily-padded fist pounded the table, knocking a small pamphlet to the floor. "Sacuan help us all," Dran'Za whispered. "And you say they dance? Do they dance or have they been hurt in some way?"

"I have reason to believe they dance." He set his hands on his knees, gripping them tightly. *Dran'Za couldn't dance a step if he had a sword to his throat—the fat lout and his nonsensical catch-phrases!* "Late in summer I traveled the road between Belden City and Vronga. Something drew me to a spot—a perfect site for camping without being seen. Our—colleagues—had been there, it was obvious. Long gone from the site, they left only one thing. A burned section of earth that surely had been a man." He paused and looked into Dran'Za's puffy eyes.

"So who died?"

"I have no way of knowing, but does it matter? We all wear the trinkets." He fingered his nervously. "Only one spell can get through that. And either it is a superior mage or a demon."

"Warlocks have that ability as well," the fat man reminded him.

"What is the difference between a warlock and a demon?" Orfel spat. "In any case..."

The fat man had opened his mouth to say something, but closed it. "Go on," Dran'Za said flatly.

"In a small village I noticed people milling around an inn. I went inside and asked what was going on. The innkeeper took me aside—he took me for some of the Counsel's men! A body lay on the floor." He paused for effect. "It was Roterran."

The obese man let out a cloud of fetid air and closed his eyes. "How did he die?" Dran'Za finally asked.

"He was stabbed in the back with a small knife."

Dran'Za whistled. "Dancing indeed."

"It turns out three young men had the room that night. A warrior type, a small-man, and another man who the innkeeper could not describe. I believe the small-man was the one who killed one of the others."

"Or all of them."

Orfel shook his head. "I doubt that. I heard other mutterings in inns that people saw two men dressed in black, sneaking through the woods. This was only recently. Two men. Not three. And where they were, I can assure you, no other members are. That leaves one more unaccounted for. And it raises the question as to where these others were going. And why? They should report back here, but they have not. Especially Gryn. Where has he gone?"

Dran'Za stared into his meaty hands.

"I think Gryn is dead. And I think the other two are up to something. A dance. A deadly dance. I'd like your leave to find them and deal with them."

The obese man sighed heavily. "You have very little proof, Orfel. What you say sounds reasonable, but you honestly have nothing to base it on." He held up a hand at the protesting knight. "And how can you assume the other two are up to something evil? What if something is hunting them? If so, they would not lead whatever it was straight back here."

Orfel sighed. The man had a point. "You may be right, but something is very wrong. Very wrong."

"It is the middle of winter here!"

Not in here, it's not. "It warms me to know you would sit here, reading and eating, warming yourself by the fire, while your fellow Knights are dying in the snow." He offered a thin, mirthless smile.

Again the fleshy fist slammed on the table. "That is not what I meant," he snapped.

Irritated, Orfel waved a hand. "All I ask is a waiver for my next mission, and leave to track these men down, or track down whoever killed them."

"And where will you start?" The look on his face asked the question, *and why?*

"Reldan, of course. That is where it starts—where I know I can start." He didn't mention anything about the burned inn south of Reldan. That would be covered in snow and not worth searching. Had knights died there? The villagers would be in no state to help him now, and they had pointedly avoided him before. Not worth stirring anything up, unless he had to.

The obese man sighed heavily, his chins wobbling. "I guess there is not much that will stop you, is there?" He picked up a book and absently thumbed through it, not looking at the pages. "Why did you even bother to come here? Reldan is a long way back south."

He knew he was wasting his time and effort. But to go without permission would have doomed him. As much as they both knew he would go on his own path regardless, he had to ask. "You know the answer to that question," he said softly.

Dran'Za nodded. "When are you leaving?"

"Now."

"Now? You won't stay for the meal? It is fine today, a roast—"

"I could care less what you eat, while the villagers above hope they can survive to the next day on what they have stored."

"I—" The man threw down the book, his hackles rising.

"And I'm skiing," Orfel continued bitterly. He could care less for whatever excuse was offered. "The snow has been slow, but I think it will be faster today."

"You are going to ski—*ski* back to Reldan?" Dran'Za shivered in disgust, his massive frame wobbling like a stuck orca.

"How do you think I got here?"

The big man breathed heavily and snatched up a dusty volume with a fleshy hand. "Then you best be going."

Orfel stood and caught a whiff of something cooking. He was hungry. Very hungry. But there was no time for that now. He nodded to Dran'Za and left without a word. He expected a cold reception, but not that cold.

Slowly he ascended the stairs, shrugged into his coat, and went out into the snow.

Orfel nodded to a new arrival and snatched his skis that lay propped against the hut's wall. He strapped them on, grabbed the birch poles with a curse, not caring who heard, and pushed off across the blanket of snow.

φ

Dran'Za snored. He had his feet propped on the desk, his body thrown back into the chair, and his massive head lolled on his fleshy neck. A book lay open in his massive lap, but soon slipped from fat fingers and fell to the floor. Days had passed since Orfel had been here, but reports of demons had not ceased—there had been a slight lull today, however, and the obese leader had dined heavily before dozing in his chair.

"Dran'Za!" the newcomer snapped, and the fat man shook so violently he nearly went falling to the hard floor. In a dull roar of coughing, snorting, and sneezing, the man put himself together and faced the man.

"Where have you been?" he barked.

"Have you been outside in the last three months?" the man spat. "It takes a long time to ski here from the west coast."

"What is it with skis?" Dran'Za wondered.

"Pretty good transportation, if you ask me, next to those funny long shoes people are using." He scratched the side of his head in irritation. "Look, where's Orfel?"

The obese man shook his head, trying to clear cobwebs. This conversation was directionless, and he hoped he was still dozing, for nothing was making sense to him. "I'm sorry, what is it you want, Tralen?"

"I need to find Orfel."

"Why?"

Tralen sighed. "Do I need to explain?"

"I think that would be appropriate, since you are supposed to be a thousand miles away from here, on the Opal Sea near Sorang. So first I must ask what you are doing here."

"I don't see why you would need to know that. You just need to know that I am doing the most good to rid the world of demons. Anything else is mine to—"

"Your arrogance is going to get you in more trouble than you can imagine," Dran'Za snapped. Of all the Knights, and indeed, of all the people he had ever met, Tralen was the last person he wanted to deal with today. Or any day. "Now tell me what you are doing here and why!"

The man colored slightly, then raised his head in defiance. His nose edged toward the oak-beamed ceiling. "Why, you—" he began, but was cut off as a page raced up to Orfel and tossed a sheaf of papers on his desk. Tralen snorted, but the boy paid no heed.

"What is this?" Dran'Za asked, picking up the papers. His huge frame shifted uneasily as he scanned the documents. With a curse, he crushed the papers in his huge hand.

"S-sir, it's like that all over. Notes from everywhere," the boy responded.

"Thank you, you may go." The boy bounded away nervously and still refused to address Tralen. The arrogant knight sniffed loudly.

"So tell me again, why do you need to find Orfel? When this is happening!" He brandished the crushed wad of paper.

"When is what happening?" Tralen asked impatiently.

"As if you did not know! Demons, everywhere."

"Everywhere?" he asked as if questioning a child on the veracity of a tall tale.

"Indeed. Flying into trees, walking into lakes, starting themselves on fire. And yet here you stand, asking to find Orfel. I might have told you had this information not arrived. But, no, now I must question your actions, young man. That letter was from Sorang; it seems an entire village decided they wanted to form a militia and hunt demons. Don't worry, they were talked out of it, but someone mentioned *us*. Not sure who, but we were mentioned. And no wonder, since you weren't there!" The man was purple by now; a vein in his corpulent neck pulsated angrily.

Tralen stammered, but Dran'Za didn't let him finish. "Why? Why, why, why?" He pounded his fist against the table, knocking more books to the floor. "Why are you here?"

"I'm here to find Orfel," he snapped. "I had no idea that demons were loose; I haven't seen a single one."

"You're lying."

"Lying about wanting to see Orfel?"

"No!" He slammed his fist down again. Only a few books remained on the once-full table. "I've had enough of you. Out. *Out!*" he shouted, pointing violently at the stairway. "Leave and do not come back until you have completed your mission. You have left the innocents near Sorang exposed to demons."

"Finding Orfel is far more important than killing a few wild bats in a back-woods village."

"Why?" Dran'Za snapped.

Tralen clenched his fists. "I do not believe I have to tell you that."

"Yes, you do. You've pushed the limit on several things, and you've gotten lucky, but this is too much. What do you need from Orfel?"

Tralen's hackles rose. He was surrounded by Orfel's own men, and if he refused this plump excuse of a man, he would be cut down without a thought. Dran'Za had no right to know his intentions, and it angered him that he had to come here to find Orfel. He could either admit his suspicion or he could find himself dead.

"Orfel is in league with the demons."

Dran'Za was purple, and more discolored veins popped out of his forehead. "Out! Out of my sight!"

"I will come back, Dran'Za," he snarled. "I will come back with *proof*." *And I will kill you, you fat lazy bastard*, he thought.

Silence. The huge man studied the arrogant knight for a moment before sitting back down. He said nothing as he grabbed one of the remaining books and cracked it open. Tralen stood for a few moments, then turned away toward the exit, but a cough from Dran'Za stopped him.

"You will please leave your weapons behind."

"What?"

"Do you honestly think I would let you walk out of here with your weapons?" he replied, not once lifting his eyes from the book. "You are not removed from the Order, because that would mean I would have to kill you. No... think of this as a leave... you are being suspended until you can prove your claims are true. But you will not do so with your sword."

The look on the man's face was priceless—a child who has had his favorite toy taken away. Only Tralen was going to lose more than a precious trinket. Dran'Za waved to a heavily-armed knight passing into the kitchens. The warrior stopped and put a gentle hand on Tralen's shoulder.

"Remove this man of his belongings—save his clothes and skis. See that he never returns here. And then get yourself to Sorang as fast as you can." He paused. "He can keep his trinket," the fat man said with a chuckle. "Let's see how much good it does him."

"Don't you want me to..." the man asked. It sounded as if he were chewing on rocks.

"No," Dran'Za said with a smile. "No, he said he was going to come back with proof. I fear that he will come with violence instead—a sword is not a hard item to find. When he comes, I rather look forward to that encounter. He underestimates my ability to defend myself, apparently." A twisted grin worked its way across his fleshy face, and then quickly vanished. "Go!"

Tralen started to protest, but the burly man forced him outside into the snow. How had the fat man known he would try to come back and kill him?

"You are lucky," the warrior said. "Were these normal times, he would have had me kill you. You'd leave thinking you were just being sent out for a time, and then stare as the sword slid into your soft belly. I'd like to do that, you know. It would be fun." Before Tralen could reply, however, he found himself face down in the thick snow. He waited for the inevitable boot or sword to the back, but all he heard were faint footsteps as the man returned inside the building. Slowly, he pushed himself up and wiped the cold white powder from his face and hand. With a curse, he strapped on his skis and pushed off toward the north.

When he retrieved a hidden sword from behind a birch tree, Tralen smiled.

Dran'Za's reaction was all that he had hoped for. There was the very real risk that he would be killed outright, but knowing the fat man, he gambled on being able to push him over the edge without losing his head. And in that, the odds were stacked strongly against him—no knight had ever left the Order with his life, at least not in the manner by which Tralen was departing. A suspension? That is what Dran'Za had called it?

Tralen had long thought that Orfel was the one responsible for the deaths of Huyen, Yulchar, Gryn, Lorfel, and Roterran. There had been whispers Huyen in Vronga, only recently, but he discounted that. A few old mages sitting around sipping tea were not reliable witnesses. Huyen and Yulchar were nearly brothers—why would they not be together? And, at one point at least, all five were together. Why would that no longer be the case? He had to think Orfel had done something. Members of the Black Dawn disappeared wholly from the view of normal citizens, but not from Dran'Za. And not from Tralen. He made it is business to know where everyone else was. It meant no sleep and little food, but when one distrusted everyone apart from himself, such work had to be done. Who else could protect the world? Surely not fat Dran'Za.

Dran'Za may very well make good on his threat to kill Tralen, but Tralen knew that if his plan succeeded, he'd be immediately brought back into the Order, and hopefully attain a spot at the very top. And Dran'Za would have to resort to begging for food. He laughed at the thought of the obese man begging in the streets of Vronga or Belden City.

With a glance at the sky, he grimaced.

Blizzard!

He dared ski only a few more miles and then stopped to construct a snow house on the ley side of a massive white pine. Only an hour or so after he had settled into the hut, the wind howled outside. This storm would set him back, but hopefully by only a day at most. And if it was setting him back, it would be setting Orfel back as well. The fool had made the mistake of telling that innkeeper that he was heading north. Knowing Orfel he'd stick to the main road and would keep a slower pace. Tralen could easily catch up to him.

And Tralen was going to kill him.

Chapter 11
Dreams of Sleep

Whoever talks to the dead is either a charlatan or a prophet. The dead have gone and are no more—should they spend moments in the places between death and final peace, beware, for their business is unfinished.

Cleric Hyun, Order of the Knot

Zhy?
The voice drifted along the dark void of sleep, and he could somehow see it floating there in his dream, as if the waves and particles of this telepathic speech floated as a physical entity. For a moment, he felt as if he were dreaming of his mother and her soothing voice. But the voice in the dark was timid and sad—as if the woman had seen every horror imaginable in her lifetime and had gone blank. Never had he spoken to anyone in his dreams, for they had been... *What had they been like?* he wondered. Had he ever dreamed before?

Zhy? she repeated. The voice was soft and didn't jar him out of his sleep, but he still felt roused from a slumber. The pads Yulchar and Huyen had brought were helpful on the cold and damp stone, but it was not the same as a bed, and so he floated between the waking and the sleeping worlds, unsure of where he was when her voice flowed through.

"Who are you?" he asked. In his dream, his own voice sounded different to him. It was more hoarse and full of a coarseness that he did not recognize. Did he sound like this when he was awake?

I must thank you for going along. My son's life is at stake.

"Who are you?" he repeated.

You should know. I'm Bimb's mother.

"Who in Sacuan's name is Bimb?"

My son. And my name is Cerease.

"Wait. Are you... the woman these men keep talking about? Did you live at the farm? The farm near Vronga?" Of course she was, he chastised himself, but his questions seemed at times to float off of his lips without thought or direction.

Yes, I am. And yes, that was my home.

So it was a dream. His mind had simply put together the events and scenes from the past days and created a dead woman. He could play along for a while before he fell into a deeper slumber. When he opened his eyes, he was surprised to see dull blue lights glowing in the distance. *So, a dream within a dream*, he thought. *Clever, very clever.*

"How did you write that note?"

The note?

"The note at your house—the one the knights found. They said it described my death and where to find me."

There was no note.

"What?"

They saw one. They think they did. I can't talk to the living, Zhy, well, not many living people. She let out a soft laugh. *But sometimes I can impress minds. They both thought they saw a note. But what they picked up was only a blank scrap of parchment.*

He had no response. What other illusions was she up to?

Don't tell them, please. I don't—

"I won't."

You can close your eyes again... you only think you are awake.

"I—so you are doing it to me too?"

Indeed. You are still sleeping.

"Why are you talking to me?"

You were the only one left... the only one who had not gone to his final peace before I got there. It took me long enough to find Bimb, I—

"The only one left? Where?"

You know the answer to that question.

He knew it, barely, but enough floated through the void that he remembered. It was enough.

> *Snow covered nearly everything, except for the craggy rocks and the odd patch of barren earth. A beam of light extended out from a gnarled hand and held him above it all. A word was shouted into the frozen air. Suddenly the colors whirled and spun—images of childhood passed quickly by, and soon it ended with a sickening crack.*

"There are parts that I remember," Zhy said hastily, trying to cover the memory of falling with something more pleasant. But the vision returned time and again, and he could not shake the tumult of pale rock and shock-white snow.

You should be thankful that I saved you. You should be doubly thankful that your body did not explode! But there is much work to be done, yet. You will have many difficulties in the near future... but I have saved you. And I thank you for agreeing to go along.

He hadn't exactly agreed to this adventure, much like another one he had been on. Or had he objected then? "So why me? And was I dead? Who are you? And who is Bimb?" The questions poured out, though there were many more waiting for answers.

I will answer all of your questions in time, but for now I wanted to thank you. As you get closer to the North, your companions are going to rely more on you—and me—to deal with him.

"Who?"

In good time. Dawn is breaking. But thank you.

The voice faded and was replaced by a loud grunt from Yulchar. So dawn indeed was breaking, Zhy noticed with a groan of his own—the blue lights were slowly flickering into their full intensity. Standing to pack up is bed roll, he realized with a start that his eyes were open. Had they been open the entire time?

Was I dreaming?

Hoping that everything was indeed a dream, he breakfasted silently and followed his companions, choosing not to say anything more about the strange voice. They walked in silence most of the day, and it seemed as if the racing motion he had felt earlier was abating; even Huyen and Yulchar noticed that their walking was taking considerable effort.

When at last the lights dimmed at the end of the day, each man collapsed on the hard ground and fell to sleep. They were too tired eat.

ф

Bimb's Father is not with us, here. He is not with Bimb— Ar'Zoth he calls himself now. The voice nearly jolted Zhy upright on his mat. He felt like opening his eyes to see if he were still asleep, but dared not to. As long as his lids were closed, this could remain a dream. If he could will it so, it could be so, but a slow, cold feeling draped its way across his mind and he knew that this could not be any dream— that he was talking to a dead woman.

"Leave me alone," he groaned. His sleep had been so deep and so complete that the sudden jolt from oblivion was as irritating as it was sudden. What was she talking about anyway? Had she been talking the entire time? Or had he somehow wandered into her space, into her thoughts?

I wish I could. I can't keep this up forever.

"Why were you talking about Bimb's father? Is he dead too?"

No, he is not dead. He is very much alive and at the Temple of M'Hzrut of all places.

"The Temple of—that sounds familiar somehow." Of course, the trinket! The wooden trinket that somehow lay next to him. The trinket he had smashed against the wall. So she had somehow brought that back, too.

Yes, I'd hoped it meant more, so I left you with your companion's small model. But now I'm not sure it means anything... but Fanlas is there, guarding it. Acting every inch the Protector that he is. I miss him...

"So he is not going to help, or is he? I'm confused."

No, no, I don't think so...

"Then why—oh never mind." He wanted to drift back to a dreamless state of oblivion, wanted at least one night of peace without her interruptions.

I'm sorry, Zhy, to bother you again... I'm so very glad you decided to help.

"Help? Is that what you call it? I was dragged out here—by these—these whatever they are. And by you. I didn't really decide anything."

Yes.

"Why?"

I had—I have—very little time left in this place before I am taken away. My son is dead. He died the moment he killed me. And now...

Zhy thought he heard sobbing. What the woman was saying made little sense. And if she had little time, why didn't she get to the point, and stop worrying about her husband and a temple that had no bearing on anything? "Isn't your son still alive?"

Not the son I raised. No. Just as you are no longer Zhy. Yes, you are alive. But Zhy is dead. Long live Zhy.

He absently scratched his arm.

You think you are going to awake from this, and maybe you will, but not in any way you can imagine. Right now, you need to follow and listen. Listen to me. My son is a very dangerous man now, and as much as I hate to wish the destruction of my flesh, he must be destroyed. Zhy heard a sniffle in the back of his mind.

He could not begin to comprehend what it would take for someone to want to kill their own son. How bad could a man be? The thought trailed off and again an image of snow and rocks flashed before him: a whirling, spinning blur of white and gray ending in a red cloud.

"Great Sacuan..." he muttered, although the name sounded hollow.

Sacuan's a man, not a god, Cerease said, almost absently. *Don't waste your time praying. I prayed for a healthy son. I prayed that my drink—I prayed. I prayed! And look what I got!* This time the women descended into heaving sobs.

"Cerease?" Zhy whispered to the dark.

I'm sorry, Zhy. I need to stop crying. I thought death would take away my emotions, but somehow they seem stronger. I hope they aren't this bad on the other side.

"The other... side? I thought you were already—"

No, I am gone, but I'm not quite over the threshold. Don't worry about it now, young man. With any hope, your time is far off. I had a wonderful boy who never grew up. Knew the number of the stars, the blades of grass in our field, and could play the sutan better than any trained musician. But he... he couldn't read, write, and could barely take care of himself. And now... all that is gone, but what is left is an evil sorcerer!

She seemed poised to descend into another fit of sobbing, and Zhy wasn't sure if he should let her or try to calm her down. For Sacuan's sake! Here he was considering conversing with a dead woman as if she were a distraught woman at the inn, carrying on over her husband's misdeeds.

Zhy, your father—

"No!" he barked, coming awake suddenly, wrenched from the dream. There was a brief flash of vertigo and he felt as if he spun uncontrollably for a few seconds before landing in the waking world. "No, no, no, do not play that game—" He broke off as his eyes fluttered open to view the dull blue surrounding him.

Neither companion stirred. Only Yulchar muttered a "are you all right?" before returning to sleep. The surly knight didn't bother to wait for a reply.

"No, I'm not," Zhy replied, but each man was too exhausted to rise. He lay back, hoping to stare at the lights until dawn. Dawn? Or when the lights got brighter? But as soon as he closed his eyes during a yawn, he nodded off.

This time he did not dream.

Chapter 12
Investigation

❧

While our secrets may seem to sustain us, they only drive us farther down a path of degradation.

High Cleric Bertrand

T he day before had been bright and sunny, but now cold, dense cloud cover dimmed the land, providing a taciturn, disheartening gloom over everything. Orfel smiled, despite the murky scene—with the slight melting of the snow yesterday and the quick change to cold, the surface of the snow was almost a sheet of ice. To prevent his skis from slipping, he produced a tin of specially made wax—a mixture of beeswax and pine tar pitch. The concoction was a sticky, cloying mess, and he was careful not to get any on his gloves. Carefully, he spread the thick mixture over the bottoms of the skis and rubbed it in with a cork. He wrapped the cork in paper and put the tin and cork back in his pack. Once he strapped on his skis, he veritably lurched over the glazed surface and raced towards Reldan.

The crunch of the steel-tipped poles in the crusty snow, coupled with the gentle swoosh as the skis slid out in long strides, provided a muted harmony to the cold forest. Orfel let his thoughts wander as he skied, trying not to dwell too heavily on what he was undertaking.

Dran'Za's bloated face hovered briefly in his mind's eye and he spat on the frozen ground. What a worthless excuse for a man. Sworn to the Holy Order and yet a gluttonous, flatulent old fraud. And to put the apostrophe in is name! What further shame it gave to the order. No doubt his name was simply Dran or Dren, or something otherwise meaningless. And to hoist upon himself the vaunted apostrophe was an insult.

Perhaps he could deal with him later. Right now, his focus was on Reldan.

φ

Reldan was just as deeply buried in snow, but the well-worn footpath to the inn was a clear sign that the villagers had not completely hibernated inside their homes. Just outside of the village, he had doffed his black coat and shrugged into a thicker wool garment.

"Aye, so you are back, sir?"

Orfel was surprised the wrinkled innkeeper recognized him, but alas a good innkeeper would make a note of every face. That he greeted him while seeming to serve several patrons at once, however, was impressive. The common room was packed full of locals—perhaps the town's entire male population. One stumbling man was just vacating his stool, and the ragged innkeeper motioned Orfel over.

"Greetings, and yes, I have returned."

"You picked a strange time to return. How did you get here?"

"Skis."

"I see. Nice crust out there today, I imagine." The innkeeper smiled, and Orfel returned it with one of his own. "More questions about those boys, is it?" he finally asked, shifting nervously.

"Yes, but I need a drink and a meal."

"Aye, but it may take some time. Kitchen is right well busy tonight. There's talk of a blizzard and everyone wants to fill up in some way."

"Blizzard? How do you know there's a blizzard coming?" Orfel asked, nodding with a smile as the innkeeper set a hot mug of tea in front of him. *He's good, very good, to remember even that detail. Perhaps he'll remember more of the "boys" who were here.*

But he would have to sit and sip tea for quite some time as the innkeeper flew from patron to patron, delivering ale, brandy, wine, and steaming plates to the guests. When at last he came up for air, he addressed another grizzled customer. "So, a blizzard's a coming, eh?"

A ragged throat cleared itself of phlegm. The old man sat at a table dead center in the room, and as soon as he opened his mouth, a silence fell over the inn. All that accompanied his proclamation was an occasional pop and hiss from the fire or the odd creaking chair. "Aye, as I so said before. Can feel it in my knees. Plus," he continued, his eye strangely on Orfel, "look here at this." A bony hand reached for a saltcellar and he shook some grains out. Or tried to. Only a few fell onto the table and he swept them away with a well-veined hand. "See?"

Orfel only stared, but he heard a few voices mutter in understanding. *What black magic is this...?* Orfel wondered, then reproached himself—old wives' tales and superstition did not necessarily indicate magic. He needed to step away from some of the blind assumptions his Order held. "I'm sorry. I don't follow," he said respectfully. He took a careful sip of the tea, though it had cooled by now.

"No?" The man cocked an eyebrow. "And the chairs, they creak. Do ye hear that?"

Orfel nodded.

"Ah. So in summer and in winter, if salt don't pour and chairs creak, even in the heat of the fire, a storm is coming." He said this with finality and returned to his meal. Slowly, the noise in the room resumed its hum.

"Blizzard's coming," the innkeeper said, setting down a plate of roast mutton in front of Orfel. The potatoes were mashed into a kind of paste and fried turnips were served alongside. He tucked in with abandon and it was not long before his plate was clear.

"Thank you," he said finally. He sat and sipped tea, staring at the wooden bar; after a few cups, the inn started to grow quiet again, and the innkeeper at last approached him, wiping the bar with a towel.

"Aye. So, these boys..."

"Ah yes. I wonder if you remember anything else about them?"

The man scratched his chin. "I believe I told as much as I remember. Sat there where old man Krych sits and took a large room. Never heard much out of them. Stayed two nights—bought a great deal of equipment from the traveling vendors the first day. Left early the next."

"Please, if there is anything else..."

He thought hard on that, but shook his head. "It was busy, as busy as it was today—well, not quite that, but during the harvest and all..."

Orfel drained his tea and took a shallow breath. He had only hoped for the barest slivers of information, but the haggard innkeeper had provided him with even less than that. It had taken a great effort to get here; perhaps he would stay a night himself if it wasn't full—

"Come to think of it..."

"Yes?"

The innkeeper refilled Orfel's cup, his lips a thin line. Steam curled lazily into the air. It seemed thicker somehow, as if the atmosphere had gotten heavier. *Perhaps a storm* is *coming.* "There was something—probably nothing."

"It could be something."

"Well, they sat there, they did, and an older man talked to them for quite some time. I didn't catch all of the conversation, but—"

"Did you know him?"

"Sure, it was old Rersha—he died, they said. Poor man. Died just a few weeks ago."

"And they were talking to him?" *And for quite some time?* That was most definitely not a small oversight! It occurred to Orfel at that moment that the old man had never asked *why* he was interested in the three travelers. As a Knight, he often assumed he carried a deal of authority over people, though they never quite knew what kind of authority he had. But why should that always be the case? Would the innkeeper have assumed Orfel was looking for the boys for other reasons? He shuddered.

It was all too possible. Since one of them had been a small-man, it was more than possible—it was the truth, he realized. A gruff man, standing on authority, had come to the small town looking for a group of men, one a small-man.

What else would he be after? He was not a Counsel Guard, he was not a Protector, and he was not a Holy Elder. Too often he forgot that people did not know his station and would never believe if he told them. To others, he was most likely an old creep who wanted some skin time with young men. "Aye. I think he gave them quite a scare too. Was probably prattling on about demons and the like. Their eyes were all whites at one point. One of them, the burly one, assured him they wouldn't go there... wherever "there" was."

"Did you ever figure out where?" His interest was suddenly piqued, and he sat bolt upright on the stool. If the man had assumed Orfel's intentions were less than noble, it would stand to reason that the innkeeper would have said nothing. But now, during the depths of winter, there was no harm in sharing the information. He could have cursed.

"No, but they said they wouldn't go there. Thought I heard the word 'zithy', but that's not a word, is it?" he said absently, scratching a large tuft of facial hair he had missed while shaving.

"No, no it isn't," Orfel said, suddenly much paler. *Zithy? No, he means seith. A seith!* They were headed to see a seith. Did that mean they worked for him? Is that what they were discussing? He shivered. He needed to get to the north and follow the trail... somehow, some way. These "boys" were far more dangerous than he had given them credit for. In league with a warlock! Or were they chasing him? Was he chasing them? In any case, he had gathered further evidence that the three travelers had been either looking for, or working with, a demon. Warlock, seith, demon—to Orfel they were all the same vile creature.

I must find them. They had killed Roterran, Lorfel, and quite possibly Gryn, Yulchar, and Huyen. Killing a single Knight of the Black Dawn could be attributed to luck. Killing two or more indicated a far more dangerous foe. He would have to be very careful.

I will kill them.

Orfel set down his empty cup and waved off a refill. "I thank you, and I hope to see you in the spring." He stood and paced to the door.

"You are not staying the night?" The innkeeper's face was a mask of concern.

"I cannot stay. No. I believe they are dangerous."

"Dangerous? How so? Rersha was more dangerous than they; he once tore a man's arm off right there in the bar. Nasty old man."

Orfel scratched his ear. "But why?"

"Man had stolen his best chickens and sold them to some wandering merchant. Rersha was evil. Downright evil. Even as old as he was, he could kill you with a look. No, these boys were right scared by him, and they left. I'm positive they went back south, though some said they saw them ride north. Maybe it was..." The innkeeper blinked several times in rapid succession. "I don't know. Maybe they did go north. But what of it?"

"I've become more and more convinced that they were up to something."

"And why is that?"

"Wish I could say."

The innkeeper wiped a nonexistent crumb off the pine bar. "And just who are you, if you don't mind me asking?"

"I wish I could say," he repeated, noting how hollow it sounded. "I can only tell you that I work for the Light."

"That so? Then, you are wasting your time with them. Long gone, they are. Gone and hopefully someplace warm. Rersha, now I would send you after him, but—"

"He is dead, I know," Orfel replied with irritation in his voice. "Still, I have to find out for sure. I think they killed some friends of mine."

The innkeeper snorted. "Is that so?" he repeated.

"I—"

"I think you've been into the Zor'Tarak, is what I think. But, it's your funeral."

Orfel wanted to slap the man, but he could also see his point of view. To reveal himself as a Knight would be foolish and earn him a slap of his own, possibly. No, it was best to strap on skis and leave this place, no matter what the locals thought of him. "It just may be."

The innkeeper eyed him warily and then a look of understanding crossed his face. "I've been convinced of things myself, things I had to find out. I don't regret that. But I'd ask you to stay... at least wait out this storm."

"I have skis."

"They will do you no good in a blizzard."

"I will find a way," he said flatly, doubting every word as it left his mouth.

"I hope you do. If you find the need, I have rooms here or can make them." His voice was suddenly sad and tired.

Orfel slapped a few extra coins on the bar. "Thank you."

"Good bye, sir," the innkeeper replied wearily.

Chapter 13
White Blanket of Death

ぱ

Who is the hunter and who is the prey? When it comes to matters of Dark and Light, beware of unseen foes watching you. When you conquer an enemy of the Dark, another may lurk in the shadows and strike when you are unprepared.

Cleric Archean, Order of the Knot

The village of Reldan lay ahead. His eyes lit up at the opportunity to tuck into some warm flesh. Raw or cooked, human or beast, it did not matter. Hopefully, he could have a great deal of both. Given the deep snow and the threat of more snow, the entire village would be inside, all trussed up for the plucking. But as he ambled toward the door of the inn, the familiar shape and gait of a man caught his eye.

"Demon hunter," the man spat, watching as Orfel strapped on his skis. He watched from behind a large tree, and suddenly the thoughts of wanton hedonism vanished, replaced by a murderous rage. Once Orfel had traveled for several minutes, the man followed on foot, oblivious to the snow slowly freezing his feet. He only saw red. Red and two even tracks in the snow that would lead him to the demon hunter.

His host body was frail, but he pushed it forward. Pieces of exposed flesh began to freeze and turn from red to brown, and finally, black, but still he walked. Snow began to fall slowly from the thick sky; it fell into the space between his coat and his exposed neck, rolling down his back, melting on the skin briefly before freezing again. The host body screamed in protest, but he shrugged off the resistance and took one step at a time.

The tracks were not as easy to follow as he had hoped. Cold air had frozen the snow, giving it a thick sheen, atop which the demon hunter was flying. Still, there were the odd-shaped holes every few paces, which indicated the ski poles. He could follow those for a very long time, even if the snow increased in intensity.

Which it did.

He started to panic when he noticed the holes filling with snow and quickened his pace. The small toe on the host body's left foot finally turned to a black char and fell off the foot with a sickening *pop*. Stuck in the boot, there was nowhere for the loose digit to go, so it rolled under the foot proper and was crushed into a black, sinuous, pus-filled pile that squished when he walked.

Kill. I must kill the demon hunter.

ϕ

There *was* a blizzard. A great, howling wail of wind— wind that ripped at shutters and tore at roof tiles. Snowflakes were driven hard enough to shatter glass, and in vortices where the wind whirled, it left behind drifts seven feet high, curled in bizarre shapes. His father would call the storm a "ring-tailed ripper," whatever that was. He had only traveled perhaps four or five miles before the great, white wall howled down upon him, slashing his skin with swords of snow; nothing but white surrounded him and he completely lost his bearings. No way to make a shelter. If he even so much as thought about opening his pack, it would fill with snow in seconds.

So he stood there, hands gripped tightly on his poles, and tried to remain upright. *I'm going to die if I don't find shelter*, he thought to himself, trying to force down a growing panic. *But I can't see! I'll just spin around in circles.*

He screamed into the storm in frustration, but all he could hear was the roar of the wind and the tinkle of snow as it drove against his face. Cursing, he pushed his skis forward, and although the fierce gusts tried to push him backward, he took solace in them. *North, I have to go north.* Winds seemed to be coming from the north-west. *If I just make sure the gusts are hitting from my left, I should make it.* If he hit a tree, he could try to feel it out for its species—the frozen lake he had traversed was filled with spruce. Was it a lake? It must have been. Up ahead, the forest began again, thick with birch, hemlock, and balsam. The trail was only a sliver, as he remembered it, and as long as he could keep the wind at a certain spot, he had a chance, a very small chance, of continuing northward. Until the Sacuan-blasted winds shifted.

The way forward was excruciatingly slow and painful. His solid boots were no match for the deep snow and the howling winds. His breeches and think coat soon quit holding out the moisture, and he constantly had to reach up and pull his hat down, lest it be torn away. But each time the hat would ride up on his head, more moisture would find its way in, chilling him. It didn't help that he was working hard enough against the wind and snow that he worked up a furious sweat—that only added moisture to a body already losing its valuable heat needed to survive.

Thunk. He swore furiously as his body slammed into a tree. Yet he was thankful he did not smash a ski into the solid trunk. His skis were his only hope to get to the boys. Pulling off a glove, he felt the trunk. Birch. Good, at least he was still going in a somewhat northerly direction.

Head down, he kept on, only running into one more small birch sapling as he slid forward through the blizzard. Wet and shivering, he had little time for curses or frustration—it took everything to keep his body moving in the hopes of finding some sort of shelter.

Skiing cross country presented other challenges: His poles would often land in uneven ground or strike the tops of rocks buried beneath the snow. Each time his body would lurch as the pole skipped off the obstruction, and he would have to force his body back the other way to correct his fall. This happened too often for his comfort, and each time it did, more energy drained from his body.

After several hours, his body numb and his mind nearly closed off from his surroundings, he lurched to a sudden stop and fell forward. He nearly shouted as the sound of the blizzard snapped off, as if someone had suddenly shut off a waterfall. His eyes burned and refused to open, and a strange warmth skittered across his frozen clothing—the mix of heat and icy cold triggered massive shivers and he lay on the ground convulsing.

"Why can't I open my eyes?" he whispered. After the deafening roar of the blizzard, his quiet words rang like Temple bells in his head.

When he finally was able to crack an eyelid, he realized he lay bathed in bright sunlight. Ripping off a glove, he felt around him and was surprised to find grass beneath his hand. With a sudden skilled motion, he stuck his feet out— skis still attached—and hopped lithely to his feet. He loosened the straps on the long wooden implements, stomped forward a few feet and then dared open his eyes fully.

"Am I dead?" he wondered aloud, staring at the large green field, with mouth wide open and eyes even wider. Just behind him, he could see only a wall of white. All around him, in a square a few hundred yards in area, he was surrounded by white walls, with the occasional birch or balsam peeking through as an unseen—and unheard—wind tore through the forest beyond. At the far end of the field stood a collapsing temple, long abandoned, its windows black holes. He took a few steps and then stopped.

"No, I'm not dead," he whispered again. "A reversal! A Sacuan-blasted reversal!"

Chapter 14
Reversal

᠊

There's a sunset to the east,
Sunrise coming up in the west—
North is south is west is east,
Lost is found, back is front.

Seer Zher'Wen

Orfel spun at a sudden rustle behind him. An old man was staring down at the skis, his head covered in rapidly melting snow. The creature looked to be nearly ninety-summers old, his face nearly all wrinkles. The snow melting from his head revealed a pale, liver-spotted scalp, dotted with spikes of coarse silver hair. His eyes were black, infinite pools, wide in a feigned wonder. A gnarled, frostbitten hand reached up to stroke a shriveled chin, and he leaned a little to one side, as if something was affecting his leg or foot.

The knight's hand shot up to his medallion. He fingered it quickly, then let his arm fall to his hip; his sword whispered from its sheath, but it nearly slipped from the moisture of the rapidly melting snow. He gripped it until the tendons in his hands screamed from the pressure. "Who...?"

But he knew the answer to that, with one look into those eyes, and at the sight of the nearly blackened hands—no human man in the last years of life could survive the snow, wind, and blasting cold without protection. And here this creature wore neither cloak nor coverings for hands or ears. This was not human.

"Ahhh," the old man nearly groaned, but his ancient voice sounded more like leather being dragged across a stone path. "So, that is how you got here ahead of me." His bony finger pointed at the skis.

"Ahead—wait, no... Who are you? I have only just arrived."

The man laughed. "So then I am still faster!" With a blur, the demon was suddenly yards away, his back to the old temple. Orfel spun, keeping a hand each on the medallion and the sword. "And do you practice the magical arts?" he hissed.

Orfel dared not answer. Instead, he was a blur of motion; the sword spun clockwise in a downward motion—an attempt to lure the opponent in one direction—and then it was suddenly slicing from left to right, from bottom to top. Such a quick motion would have cleaved anyone with inexperience, and surely an elderly old man who had puss oozing from his boots, and a black ear slowly falling from his head.

But this was no ordinary old man.

A brief second before Orfel's blade would have decapitated the man, he again moved in a blur and was four feet away. A purple tendril of light suddenly arced forward from his bony right hand, and Orfel rolled away. Behind him, an explosion shook the small clearing, quickly followed by the crash of a large hemlock as it thudded to the ground. Orfel didn't bother to look, but sprang to his feet—as much as the heavy boots would allow—and charged.

Something hot struck him in the face, sending him sprawling backward. His sword flew from his hands and he growled in frustration.

"I can't touch you with that—piece of jewelry," the old man hissed. His eyes widened, the dark pools a swirling blend of terror and vexation. Thin eyebrows raised, and bottomless creases slid across his leathery forehead, while his ears seemed to pull back like those of a frightened hound. "Not yet. Not yet. I will, however. The choice is yours. Follow and try to stop me, or I will erase this entire forest searching for you."

With that, the man spun and ran to the crumbling temple. He moved with a blinding speed that defied his older body. He must be using some sort of an illusion spell, Orfel thought as he dove for his sword. Even a possessed person was subject to the abilities of the host body. Unless... Orfel wondered if some other force was at work; what if the rumors were true? The wild mutterings of the villagers were something he tended to ignore. They had been prattling on about demons and how *gherwza* were seen flying through forests, and the dead were seen to be walking, only to kill themselves in some strange fashion. Apparently, there was some basis in these rumors. *No*, he thought, *no, this is isolated. I am a Knight of the Black Dawn. I am a target!*

Still... What if everything *was* changing amongst the demons? There was no more time—that cliché was getting old, but it was the reality. He needed to get to the boys as soon as he could, needed to save them, or kill them. Should he run? Take his chances in the snow? No, the demon was a priority—leaving it to its devices would only keep his backside exposed. These thoughts flashed across his mind for a bare fraction of a second, and soon he was sprinting to the temple, his sword in hand.

But what if he sent them? What if they *sent* him? That would be the most likely situation. And they probably were all huddled in that temple waiting for him. *Preposterous.*

The entrance was a gaping black hole, out of which the stench of the underworld seemed to emerge. A foul, damp odor assailed his nostrils, and he was still paces away from the crumbling stone entrance. The moment he set one booted foot atop the lowest stair, a green tendril of lightning screeched from the void. He ducked instinctively, and as his weight shifted atop the stone, a chunk of stairway crumbled like sand, sending him toppling. Orfel grunted in pain as a small slab of granite smashed into his kidney, and a pointed shard dug a hole in his right leg. He cursed and rolled to his feet. The bottom stair was almost completely destroyed, but he leaped onto the top stair and quickly cradled his sword in front of his stomach, curled himself into a ball, and rolled blindly into the opening. Another bolt of lightning shot out, grazing his skull and leaving a brief stench of burning hair.

He dove to avoid another flash of light, but in the split second of illumination, he could make out the form of the old man standing at the far end of the temple. Shapes of rotting pews sat hulking in the utter darkness. *No one else is here*, he thought. As he tumbled away from the bolt, he again winced as his left side cracked against one of the old pews. The wood gave way immediately under his weight. *This is senseless*, he thought, *I can't see anything. He's lured me in here to kill me!*

The alternative—running from here like a frightened schoolboy—was not any better. No doubt the demon possessed the ability to destroy much more than a crumbling temple and a wandering Knight of the Black Dawn. Orfel had to figure out how to survive, or broken ribs and bruised kidneys would be of little consequence. As he lay panting atop the shattered wood, he suddenly wished he hadn't been so hot-headed in his pursuit of the demon.

But there's no—Sacuan blast it!

Again, he flung himself across the dust-filled floor as a green bolt obliterated the pile of rubble he had been lying on. He had no time to look in the brief moment of light. *Maybe he'll say something. They always say something, don't they?* he wondered to himself. But the demon remained silent.

He felt like a trapped animal, running from one end of the cage to another. It was only a matter of minutes before the demon would hit him full in the face with one of those lightning bolts. And he had no way of seeing where the obstacles were before he struck them—either the magical spells would kill him, or he'd crack his head open on the stone or the pews—

That's it! he thought. With a hurried prayer to every single prophet that had ever been born, he leapt up from behind a pew, then dove sideways. Not wishing to remain stationary for any time, he rolled underneath another pew. In that moment, the demon played into his wishes and unleashed another green tendril. This time it struck the center of the wooden bench, and as Orfel had hoped, the dried wood burst into flame.

Now I see you.

In the dull flame of the fire, Orfel saw a brief but disturbing view of the temple; it nearly sucked the air from his lungs. The temple resembled any other temple he had visited in Belden, except for a few minor and glaring differences. Age and decay had rotted pews, frayed wall hangings, shattered stained-glass windows, and crumbled stone. This could be accepted. However, it was obvious that this temple was also a complete reversal of any temple. Instead of oak, cherry, or pine pews, the visible wood here was a deep black. It looked more the color of dried blood. *Is that—?*

Another crack of lightning struck nearby and he dove back into the relative safety of the rotting pews. The first fire had burned intensely and it was now nothing more than cinders; the fresh blast of magic, however, ignited another, sending up the stench of sulfur and rotten meat.

The stonework on the inside glowed red in the firelight—it too most resembled the color of blood. In the place of a square altar sat a stone slab in the shape of a seven-pointed star. Threads from red-stained coverings clung to the decaying stone—or was it bone? If he could—

"For Sacuan's sake!" he blurted, diving again, then cursed himself the fool.

"I will burn this entire temple, worm!" the demon hissed.

Orfel dove back to his previous spot, avoiding a magical bolt and burning pew. His glance darted quickly around the temple, desperately trying to piece together the structure in the scattered pictures he was allowed.

A long trough ran from the altar to the front door. It was made of stone, chipped and fragmented like the rest of the place; its bottom stained a reddish-brown. Flecks of—something—were scattered along the bottom of the slowly sloping runnel.

If he had looked up to the ceiling, he would have emptied his stomach—had there been anything to empty. Attached to the thick oak beams were long and rusty iron hooks, and small pieces of bone, fabric, and jewelry clung to the curved rods. The beams were so thick that the rot had not yet compromised their structure.

A subsequent blast and bolt of fire allowed another glimpse of light, and Orfel took his chance. How many times had he been lucky, darting to and fro? This last gamble seemed futile, but better than being systematically murdered by an aged demon—rather, being left to burn alive. The fires burned quickly, but if enough pews were ignited, or Sacuan forbid, the upper supports, the whole place would come crashing down upon him in a roar of timber and a raging pyre.

The knight sprung to his feet and bounded forward—in a single leap, he hurdled the trough, his sword up and swinging. A thunderous roar filled his ears and he instinctively closed his eyes as another brilliant flash of green energy exploded in front of him. It worked. His medallion had functioned, although it left his ears ringing and his lungs burning. The old man grunted and Orfel heard him shuffle sideways, but the knight had already guessed which way he would duck; his sword arched in that direction. The curved blade was at neck level.

Orfel's arm felt as if he had struck a solid metal bar. The sword reverberated with an audible clang. It vibrated with such violence, he nearly dropped it. Instead, he pulled it violently back and struck lower at the creature's legs.

His sword only cut the air.

Some plan that was. Now, how did he—

There was a loud crash, but it was not magic. It sounded like another pew being shattered. Orfel thought he heard a faint grunt and a wheeze. He leapt toward the sound, swinging the sword again, and once more felt as if he had struck a tree.

If the trinket didn't allow the demon to cast spells against Orfel, it surely allowed the man to cast a protection against himself. There had to be a way. Orfel had only killed *gherwza* and the possessed frames of ancient, shambling men. Never anyone like this. There had definitely been some sort of paradigm shift for this to be happening—either this was a particularly strong demon, or the Pillars had been compromised (or worse, broken), or—Sacuan forbid—there was a true demonic invasion underway.

A shuffle of feet alerted him to the man's movements. *I just have to stay as close as I can—and think of something.*

Orfel found himself chasing the demon around the temple, making sure he struck him now and again. His arm was nearly numb from the exertion, and the darkness was nearly absolute. The fires were only a few lumps of glowing specks in the dark—the dead, dry wood had burned hot, but quick, dying against the stone. His eyes had not yet adjusted and only added frustration to the series of events.

A clank of something metal—no doubt a hat hook on a pew falling down or an ancient window latch finally giving way—caught his ear, and he nearly laughed. He took another hop toward the demon, struck with the sword for good measure, then made his final gamble. Either this would work or he would die here.

And many more would die as a result of his failure.

He followed the footsteps again, the sword now in his left hand. And with his right, he removed the medallion as quietly as he could. He would have to be as accurate as he had ever been, even better than striking an arrow with another arrow in mid-flight. This would have to be even more perfect than that.

With another prayer, he tossed the medallion toward the sound—toward a target he could not see. The rattle of the silver was the only indication it had landed on anything, but the muted cry of frustration was a beacon. Tossing the sword into his right hand, he thrust it forward.

The sword sank easily into flesh, opening the demon's stomach. Entrails and blood flowed freely into the trough. Orfel removed his sword with a curse, then swung again, slicing the demon's head off—the knight's arm recoiled again, for he had sliced from shoulder to shoulder, his thrust so violent he took bone and muscle in his attack. The severed part thudded to the crumbling stone.

Orfel stooped down, fumbled against the stone, stomach lurching at every slimy, slithering horror upon which his finger brushed. His fingers found purchase on his precious medallion; he snapped it up, turned and ran.

He wanted out of this evil temple. The magic that clothed this place felt like a foul blanket that he struggled to free himself from. Even though the windows were open holes and the door was long since gone, absolutely no light shone in. And that after he had dispatched of the demon.

That meant some essence of it still remained.

Orfel knew the general direction, but soon slammed his knee into the side of a pew. The old wood creaked, but his knee seemed to creak even louder and he cursed. Turning back to his right, he stumbled and fell to the dilapidated stone floor. His hand went out to catch himself and slipped in a warm liquid.

The trough. *I have to get out of here*, he thought, panic starting to purr noisily in his mind. The darkness was putting him on edge. *Come on, you are trained for this. Run. Run, follow the Sacuan-blasted through!*

With a grimace, he did just that. He kept one foot in the trench, and the other above, and ran lopsided, his heart pounding. *How can the door be so far away...? This is such a small building.*

The sound of bees buzzing gave him pause, and his foot twisted slightly in the confined stone drain. A small whirr slowly grew into a cacophonous drone, as if an entire hive was active inside his ear. Ignoring the pain of his wrenched ankle, he pushed forward, running awkwardly toward the door. Louder, louder, louder the sound of bees nearly consumed him. He wanted nothing more than to collapse to the ground and cover his head with his hands, but he knew that the noise would consume him entirely.

The white-hot light of outside did more to send him sprawling into the grass than the pebble he tripped over. Blind, he rolled a few feet, then forced himself to stand. His ankle turned slightly, and an intense pain seared through the torn tendons. He swore again, planted his foot with a scream and ran all the harder. When at last a cool wind touched his face, he forced his eyes open, and fell to the grass, exhausted.

Just a few feet away, the blizzard still howled. He needed to get out there, to safety. To think this protected space was unsafe was a horrendous reality that he didn't want to face.

In a reversal, up was down was back was front. And nearly dead men could cover twenty feet per jump and cast back-to-back devastating spells in a space darker than black. *There was more safety in the blinding blizzard than a warm copse of trees*, Orfel reminded himself with a grimace as his ankle gave a twinge at the mere thought.

The bees still buzzed in the distance.

His skis were fifty paces away, on the other side of the clearing, and walking to them was an exercise in walking over still-burning splinters. Could he even ski more than a hundred feet? The bindings in the skis allowed for a great deal of motion in the ankle, and he felt as if one wrong movement would separate his foot from his leg. If only he could just lie here for a while and recover—

Buzz.

Question answered. With a curse, he hobbled to his equipment. It took longer than he wanted to strap on the skis, and he had to lean on one of his poles for support with such force that it nearly snapped in two. Orfel was thankful for the incredible flexibility of birch.

He felt odd "walking" with the skis across the grass, but it would be easier than trying to put them on in a howling blizzard. With every lift of a ski, his ankle screamed in protest, but it was the only way; he could not try to strap into his skis in the snow, it had to be here. And so he would lift a ski straight up in the air, move it a pace forward and set it down on the grass, repeating with the other foot. It was exhausting work, draining him of whatever reserves of energy he had. When he reached the edge of the clearing, he took a brief look back at the temple.

The demonic structure seemed to shimmer in the sunlight. A purplish glow surrounded the decaying stone, and a thin tendril of red light seemed to shimmer out the front door. From the windows, he could see the same reddish glow, although it was nearly pink. Orfel swore he saw smoke rise from the pile of rubble that was a chimney, but then again it could be a swarm of insects, or—he didn't want to think.

The bees grew louder.

In the reversal, the sun shone brightly, but where did it hang? Was it day or night? He looked to his right, but was it west or east, or north or south? Cursing, he marked the direction he hoped was north.

With a grimace, he pushed out into the snow.

Chapter 15
A Trinket

ೞ

Trinkets, medallions, amulets, talismans, and madstones: All items the superstitious use to ward off the Dark. But the Dark can still prevail, regardless of whatever piece of metal you wear. Your actions and your thoughts must counter the dark. Not your jewelry.

Prophet Altyu-M'Zhkara

"That trinket around your neck looks familiar," Zhy said during a lunch break. He had just finished a small tin of pickled fish, and the strong aroma seemed to fill the entire tunnel. The flavor brought forth a brief image of the sea and the sun and of a strong, lean man building a large castle in the sand. *Father?*

Each man stood, their joints creaking, and readied themselves for another endless march through the blue-veined tunnels. Yulchar had bent down to tighten the laces on his boots when the silver trinket worked its way out from under his shirt, catching the blue light as it and dangled.

"Ah, this," he said, fingering it. He quickly put it back under his shirt. "Yes, it is to ward off magic. Both of us wear them."

Zhy had a brief memory of a man with a trinket like that. A dead man. "I think I've seen them before, but the man wearing it was dead."

Huyen coughed.

"It does not protect us against swords, my friend. Just magic."

"But... How did you—" He pointed at Huyen, who scowled into his jar of dried meat. "How were you able to use that magic light then? I thought those trinkets went both ways: You couldn't cast any spells either." He started at his own words. Where had he heard that before?

"How did you know that, Zhyfrael?"

"I didn't know it, I think. It just... It just came out."

Huyen grunted. Yulchar gave his companion a placid look and then replied, "If we pocket the trinket—put it far enough away from our body, like in a saddle bag or a thick pocket, we—he—can cast spells. The light he created was not very powerful and probably could have been managed even with the medallion. Isn't that right?"

"Aye." Huyen glowered, but Zhy caught a glimpse of him fingering his own trinket.

It is so strange to think that a small piece of metal could prevent people from using magic. What could they possibly be made of to block it? Fearing an outburst from Huyen, he stifled the thought and took a deep breath, and against his better judgment, asked Yulchar.

"They make them at the Universities," Yulchar replied. "They are used for training, and as a means of testing magical ability. If you can cast strong spells against weak trinkets, you pass to the next level. But the medallions we use—Knights of the Black Dawn, that is—are the strongest they forge." Zhy vaguely remembered hearing a similar answer before.

"But what are they made of?"

The knight shook his head. "I wish I knew. It feels like a sort of thin steel. I ran into one white-haired teacher at the University in Vronga once, and he was quite excited about these things, having just forged several of them. Apparently, he liked to make ones of varying size and tried to make something that could cover an entire village. But they threatened to exile him for such nonsense."

"An entire village! What good would that do?"

"He thought it could protect people from harmful magic. You see, he had this notion that magic was not really magic, but something that was everywhere. All in spaces and holes we can't see. And so, he thought if he put up a giant medallion up around a city, he'd protect people from such holes and spaces."

"But why?"

"He thought that inside the spaces were things that made people sick, drove them to insanity, and spoiled meat. He was quite eccentric."

"I don't think that's the word," Zhy chuckled. To his surprise, Huyen added a miniscule laugh of his own. "So how would you put a piece of metal over an entire city? How would people see—wouldn't it block the sun?"

"As I said, he backed away from his project quickly, once he realized he might be exiled. Who knows what he was planning."

"So these medallions, you don't know what they are made of?"

"No, but apparently they are able to reflect magical spells. Or perhaps they absorb the spell into them. I'm not sure."

"Do they have a name?" Zhy wondered.

"Everyone has their own name for them. There is no official name, and we just walk around with them on, never really thinking. I've heard *spell-shatterers, form-breakers, light-benders*, the list goes on. Each name sounds so..."

"Cliché?" Zhy offered.

"Aye."

"Time to go," Huyen said crisply. He grumbled as he shouldered his pack. The skis clacked together loudly as he flung them unceremoniously atop the bag. Wordlessly, Yulchar stood and helped his companion tighten the straps for the long wooden skis.

Well that was a nice break, Zhy thought with a grimace as he hunched into his own pack and shook his torso until it settled evenly on his back. This had been standard form for Huyen in the past couple of days—they would start a decent conversation, and the surly knight would invariably cut them off and start trudging through the dim tunnel. *Blasted fool*, he thought to himself.

"What was that?" Yulchar asked, already several paces ahead in the dim blue light.

"N-Nothing," Zhy muttered. His hand went instinctively to his earlobe, and he folded it up into his ear. *I need a bath.*

They walked for nearly an hour and Zhy took to counting the blue lights, but lost track after a hundred and seventy. The drip drip-drip-drip drip drip-drip was at times annoying and at other times, comforting. The sound of the water brought his thoughts back to a bathtub. He thought he could smell himself—the dampness of the Tunnels clung to his skin, and week-old sweat itched as it staled beneath his garments. True, they had changed their clothes a couple of times, but there was no time to wash and dry their clothes in the water. Or wash themselves.

"Is it wise to bathe in these waters or wash clothes?" he asked. In the distance he thought he hard water dripping into a pool of water.

"You must have read our minds," Yulchar said. He had tried to sound mirthful, but his voice came across as strained. They were just passing two blue lights that were not quite square with each other. Zhy had noticed this from time to time—normally the lights were set so one was directly across from another, but every other day or so, he would notice two that were not evenly spaced. Perhaps there were thicker sections of rock, such as a knot in a board. "Yes, I think that would be a good idea. It sounds like there is a little pool up ahead."

"Cold water," was all Huyen said. But he didn't protest when they washed their outfits and took turns dipping into the water. It was ice cold, but it was clean water, fed by an overhead spring. Zhy let it run through his greasy hair. The small bar of soap that Yulchar carried was the size of a corn kernel by the time it got to Zhy. He didn't mind, as long as he could wash out the grease and the stink. A piece of soap as large as a grain of sand would have been enough.

"Let's go, then," Yulchar said as Zhy stepped out of the pool. He shivered violently and used a spare shirt to dry off. He and the others donned the last clean outfits they had, although they still smelled rank after being stuffed with all of the other gear. They threw wet clothes across the tops of packs and across the skis, and the men walked slowly to avoid jarring them loose.

Ten paces down they heard a colossal splash that echoed across the walls of the Tunnels. It sounded like an enormous animal had jumped into the water from a great height. Zhy started, and his wet clothes went flying off his pack, landing on the stone with a wet slap. Yulchar and Huyen quickly threw their own packs off. The skis clattered loudly to the ground, masking the sound of steel clearing leather. Instinctively, Zhy crouched down and took a step backward as the two knights turned toward the pool, swords drawn. His attention was drawn to the water, as it rippled slowly. The blue lights provided a strange illumination to the water, as the undulations rapidly alternated whorls of blue, black, violet, and white. Quickly the ripples were severed as a large black shape emerged from the depths, the strangely hued water sloughing off its misshapen form. There was a loud screech as the thing broke the surface tension and leapt out onto the stone floor, skittering awkwardly before finding its footing.

Before it dodged into the shadows, Zhy had only a brief second to notice it was a rat—a huge rat. The rodent was as large as a small goat; its long tail curled at least three feet behind it, with thick, matted, greasy hair clumped along its body. Its teeth were razors, which glowed in the dull blue light. When it laid its ruby eyes upon the travelers, it opened its jaws even wider and screeched.

Chapter 16
An Unacceptable Situation

Are you one to admit your mistakes and claim responsibility for your actions? Or do you mutter and stammer, all the while looking for someone who can shoulder your blame? The pain may ease when you attach blame, but it will return a thousand fold.

Prophet Vron'Za

Rhys quietly packed his belongings by a single candle light, pushed the coals to the back of the hearth, and quickly dashed out his front door. He left only a short note indicating that he intended to strike out for Belden City and try to find some answers, considering the inaction on behalf of the elders. Riding through the night, changing horses, and running on adrenaline alone, Rhys made it to the capital city in record time.

The Counsel headquarters was a massive structure that took up at least a quarter of a square mile of space. Endless windows, balconies, and porches rose five stories up and hundreds of yards in either direction. A slightly pitched slate roof boasted sun-bleached tiles that peeked over the porches, and small curved tubes designed to carry away rainwater back into underground cisterns.

Sullen guards patrolled the grounds, long swords at their sides. The guards were merely a protection against vandals and the curious neighborhood child. Nobody expected a siege against the building, but it still carried the requisite ramparts and arrow slits. Double-oak doors as tall as a village inn provided a grand entrance to the keep. A narrow path branched out from the door and ended at a small gate, occupied by a yawning guard.

Taking a deep breath, Rhys approached the main fore gate of the structure. The placid look from the guard was not a good sign. Rhys thought with a sinking feeling, *He's probably shooed away hundreds today.*

"Sir?"

Rhys straightened his back and gave a brief smile. He had to make this good; it was his only chance to get in and make his case. *Smart but not arrogant, smart but not arrogant,* he repeated to himself. "My name is Rhys and I come from a small village near Sorang." The guard's hand dropped to his sword hilt and his index finger tickled the rounded end. *I'm losing ground and I haven't even started.* "There have been several disturbances in our area, and not just in our village. Reports have reached our elder that these disturbances have been occurring across Belden." The hand came away from the sword, and the bored look faded.

"And?"

And given the situation, you have no right to be blocking my entrance! He wanted to say as much out loud, but bit his cheek to stem the flow of words. *Be smart, strong, but not arrogant,* he chastised himself. "I believe the senior Counsel Guard should be made aware of the situation." *That's all you need to say. Don't tell him you're going to give them* all *a piece of your mind.*

The guard straightened to his full height. He towered over Rhys. *So that's his trick*, Rhys thought, *act the bored buffoon and then intimate the stranger. Stay strong, stay smart—*

"Do you carry any weapons?" The question seemed out of place.

"No," Rhys responded evenly.

Without warning the guard moved away from his station and stalked closer to Rhys. *Stay strong, stay smart.* The huge guard roughly patted his stomach, his hips, and his ankles. Satisfied that he had no hidden weapons, the guard straightened and took a step back. "Tell me again why you need to see the Elite Guard." The word "elite" came off his enlarged tongue in a tone of reverence and blind devotion— no doubt he had intended to give emphasis to the word, but he only reduced the perception of his intelligence.

Ah, he should have expected this. Ask the question again—try to discover any lies or contradictions. Clever. "I need to see the senior guard, officer. I need to make them aware of disturbances that have been happening in our village and across Belden."

"What type of disturbances?"

The question was anticipated, but as soon as the word left his mouth, he regretted it. Surely such a claim would get him tossed into the street. But the truth was oft better than an elaborate lie, and it was easier to remember. "Demons, officer."

"I see, well—" The look of incredulity that crossed the man's face was quickly replaced by one of concern. He scratched the back of his neck and looked around. "I see. Well," he repeated. "Only the other day, I—" He stopped suddenly, forcing a stern look back on his face.

So it's here, too, Rhys thought with alarm. Why was nothing being done? At least nothing that he could see—no increased guard presence—and surely no Knights of the Black Dawn were skulking around. Well, that was why he was here. If only this brute would let him through!

The guard scratched his nose and grumbled, but then shrugged his massive shoulders. Most likely he, too, wanted to know what was going on, and it wasn't worth a wall of pride to stop Rhys. His voice was suddenly resigned. "You may enter," he said flatly. "Go through the main door and tell the man there you need to see Counselor Gheren. And take this." The man handed him a small wooden placard, painted blue. Rhys reached for it, trying to keep his hand from shaking.

"Thank you."

As he approached the large entrance, he had to hold himself back from running headlong across the path. He willed his feet to move at a respectable pace, though his heart hammered as if he had been sprinting.

The inside of the Counsel Guard headquarters was an even more confusing myriad of corridors, doorways, and hardwood floors. Hallways, which the man at the entrance had called "wings," stretched in countless directions. Different colored rugs at the entrance of each hallway indicated which department or function was housed in that area. Rhys shook his head. He would surely need help finding his way out of here again!

He was ushered into a small room paneled with cedar. A large table sat in the middle of the room, covered in papers. Maps, Rhys noted with satisfaction. *At least they aren't completely blind.* A small stone hearth was set in the right-hand corner of the room, but it was cold. Today had been warm. Above the cedar panels, iron racks were set into the wall, and upon them lay more rolls of paper. More maps. Rhys found himself gaping at the room when a cough from behind shook him from his reverie.

"So you have some urgent news?" The voice was deep and refined, and it cascaded like rocks rolling down a hillside.

Rhys turned and was taken aback by the man who spoke. He was short, half the size of himself. His head and hands were the size of a normal man, but his torso and legs were merely miniatures. *What is a Welcferian doing in Belden's Counsel Guard?*

The man seemed to read his thoughts—or perhaps it was his open mouth that betrayed him. "No, son, I am not from Welcfer. Born and raised here in the City." It was obvious that he disdained explaining his stature, and the words were clipped. He coughed. "I am Counselor Gheren, and you are?"

"Rhys, from a little village called Jourzan, near Sorang," he said, forcing his tongue to move around the cotton in his mouth. *A real Counselor!*

"And what is it that we need to be made aware of, young man?" His resonating voice was still disconcerting to Rhys; to have such a small man use such a powerful voice seemed strangely out of place.

Rhys cleared his throat and looked the man in the eye. "There have been disturbances of late near my village. Our elder has received reports from across Belden as well, that—"

Gheren waved him off. "I know."

"You... know?" *Then why have you done nothing!* He wanted to scream, but kept himself under control.

"Come here," the small-man said, gesturing to the map table. A large map of Belden was set in the center, with four paperweights holding the edges down. Across the map were small red pieces of paper placed near cities and villages. *Demons?* "Aye, demons," came the deep reply. He scratched his chin and stared at the map.

"So..." Rhys began. "So the Counsel Guard is aware of this?"

Gheren merely pointed.

"And what, may I ask, Your Honor, is being done about it?"

The Counselor gave him a sharp look and he regretted his statement immediately. But the look faded and fatigue washed over the small-man's face. "I wish I knew. I can't seem to convince anyone else apart from a few of my closest colleagues. And the Guard? Nothing but lazy layabouts! With winter here, they hardly go to Vronga, let alone any villages farther north. And they avoid the Golden Road as much as the north."

"Why is that?"

"Something about the rains and all the marshes near the coasts. No, Rhys, I can't convince anyone. I'm sure my information comes from similar sources, as those your elder has access to. People have told me that they've seen strange things here in the City, but this is Belden City, after all. I can go down to any inn or tavern and see the dead." He sighed. "Especially that one Kahl runs," he muttered under his breath.

"I beg your pardon?"

"Oh, nothing, nothing," Gheren replied. His focus returned to the map. "So now we have some more confirmation. You say you rode from near Sorang?"

"I rode all night," Rhys replied. After putting words to his recent actions, he suddenly felt very tired. And disappointed. He had come so far, and even Counselor Gheren agreed! But...

"It is sad, my friend," Gheren said. "When religion mixes with those who really run the place—Belden I mean—nothing is ever easy. When things change, no one wants to admit the change. But, as you have seen, things have changed!"

Rhys nodded. "If I may suggest something, Your Honor?"

"You may, and just call me Gheren."

"Your—Gheren, I believe the Guard should do something. So far, the Knights have been suspiciously absent."

At that, his head shot up from gazing at the map. "And how do you know about the Knights?"

Rhys had to stop himself from sighing. "It's been something I've known about for years."

"You have not shared this with anyone, I trust." It was not a question.

"Given the current situation, I don't think it matters."

Gheren gave Rhys a stern look, but it passed quickly. "I see." He looked at the map again. "Well, that is a question I would have, but their leadership is snowbound by now. At least, as much as I know of them leads me to believe. And what I also know is that they probably aren't going to be much help."

"Why?"

"They like to remain in the shadows and hunt demons. But now, with the demons on the loose, they would have to expose themselves more than they want. So they are stuck."

"Unacceptable," Rhys said quietly.

Gheren nodded. He looked as frustrated as Rhys felt, but fatigue and overwork had worn down the emotion. He just looked defeated.

Rhys was incensed. "An Order sworn to defeat demons, but they won't defeat them if there are too many!" He threw up his hands.

"Nobody said politics would be easy," Gheren said, half to himself. "But this is out of control. I can't get any support to deal with any of this." He gestured at the small red circles. "But maybe with you here, I can muster some more support."

It was more than he could have hoped for. Not only had he gained an audience with a Counsel member, but he had confirmed that his fears were real. The hard part was going to be convincing the Guard to help. "I don't know anyone here," Rhys said softly, trying not to sound like he was complaining. He was just relaying the truth. "I'm not sure anyone would listen to me."

Gheren nodded. "Right, but things are different. Now. Look, you're smart, and you've come a long way to sound the alarm. Maybe someone will listen to that."

"Do you honestly think so?"

Gheren nodded slowly. "Wait here. Let me fetch Jafren, if he's around."

"Who's Jafren?"

"The Grand Counselor."

Rhys would have whistled were he not in such company. The Grand Counselor was the leader of the entire Counsel Guard and held sway over every Guard from Belden City to the smallest village. An elected body selected him, and he (or she, since there had been one or two during the course of history), ruled for a single term of five years. Although the Grand Counselor had final control over Belden's military, the Guard, the title was fairly symbolic. Apart from this sudden increase in demonic activity, there was little threat to the nation, nothing like the Welcferians faced on their bloody Icedown Plains. Though the nation was run by others on their daily chores, the Grand Counselor was still the Grand Counselor, a symbol of leadership for Belden as a whole.

And the fact that Rhys did not know him by name was not uncommon either: Word of the transition of the Grand Counselor came as a footnote in correspondence, if at all.

The teacher from a small village breathed out a nervous sigh—*I'm going to meet the Grand Counselor!*

Stay strong, stay smart.

φ

Jafren looked the part of the Grand Counselor. He was tall and lean with a chiseled face and a well-trimmed beard that had gray touches in its black fuzz. His hair was cut very short, and on his long, egg-shaped head, it looked like a small patch of dark grass. He seemed to have a quick smile, but he was also stern and crisp; he walked with the stiff back and measured stride of a man used to being in control. The leader's eyes were a bright blue, with pinprick sparkles studded along the edges of his pupils—they seemed to glow with their own piercing light. Thin eyebrows and a wide bridge across a thin nose only accentuated the phenomenon. Jafren's very presence in a room bore with it the proclamation that he was in charge.

"Gheren says you are asking for help with some problems?"

Rhys nodded and explained the situation. After he finished, Gheren acknowledged the facts and quietly bowed out of the room.

"Why would I send my guards out there, especially in the heart of winter?"

"Pardon me, but is that not the duty of the Guard, to protect the citizens?" Rhys was past caring if his tone was snide or arrogant. Looking at the red dots, he could hardly fathom why the Guard would not do something. Did they not see their entire population tearing itself apart? If the demons did not do the work, the common man would rise up with pitchforks and start killing whatever he thought was a demon.

"That's the problem with you teacher types." The man sniffed, fixing those eyes on Rhys. The teacher had to force himself to keep from stumbling backward. "You see only what can be written in a book or shown on a map. You have no concept of what it would take to muster that many guards to address each of these threats." He waved at the map with an air of dismissal.

Rhys ground his teeth. "I understand the logistics will be difficult, but something must be done. These people—"

"These people will have to fend for themselves until we can get there!" he snapped.

"Sir... I don't think you—I mean, I think that perhaps that may be worse than we think." He was careful not to sound accusatory. "What I saw in my own small village has led me to think that, if nothing is done about the demons, things will get worse around here. Blood will run in the streets."

He grimaced at the hyperbole. But he could see the grim future in his mind's eye—if only he could convince these men of the situation.

"What do you mean by that?"

He steeled himself for his response. "The men in my village wanted to create squads of men to hunt demons. That may sound like a good idea to have your citizenry defending itself, I can only see one logical and devastating outcome from such actions."

"And that would be?"

"I'll answer that with another question. How do you know if you are facing a demon? *Gherwzas* I can understand, but some of the possessed are simply old men. And if the younger ones are possessed, Sacuan save us, surely they can keep it secret until it is too late. Who is to say the demon-hunters won't see red and start killing everyone who they think is a demon? It won't stop there, either. Soon they will start accusing people of being in league with demons. Worse, people will be killed for *thinking* about being in league with demons... and the only outcome from that is a complete and utter slaughter."

"I see." The Grand Counselor rubbed his beard. The light scratching sound filled the room as Rhys held his breath. Jafren replied after a few moments. "What if we can get you some support?"

Rhys's face lit up at that.

A stern hand tempered the excitement. "I'm not sure how much, or from where, but I can send some missives out to our posts in the cities and villages. We'll have more luck down here, because the snow is going to cause problems."

"Anything that you can do will put my mind—and the minds of countless others—at ease," Rhys replied as he exhaled quietly. *I have succeeded! I was strong—*

"You best get back to your village and let them know that we will act, however we can. But we can't solve everything."

Rhys nodded and left with a polite and sincere thank you. He indeed needed help navigating the hallways, and when the bright sunlight hit his face, he looked out at the sprawling city with its endless chimneys, tall storehouses, and the temples scattered across the horizon.

Home? Why would I go home?

He walked down a large thoroughfare, cautious of carts and horses and foot traffic. Not sure what to do, or where to go, he eventually settled on an inn. If he returned home now, they would be over suspicious... perhaps he could send a letter back to explain his success. Voraam would probably call it further work of demons, that Rhys' words were forged, but that could not be avoided. Still, a letter should be sent, no matter the wild ideas his fellow citizens had. That would be the proper thing to do. And, after a few months, he could check back in with the Grand Counselor.

"I better find a job," he muttered under his breath. A few months' rent at an inn would be very expensive. And though he had brought with him a fair amount of coin, it was nowhere near enough in such a large and expensive city. For a moment, he thought of returning home, but images of torches and swords were too lurid in his mind and he buried the thought—no, he'd decided to come here to learn. And he'd learned more than he wanted to... his village seemed far away now. He whispered the lines of an old poem, "Gone and gone, and never back."

φ

After Rhys left, Jafren stared at the maps vacantly. His gaze shifted to the fireplace. "Would you like me to call for a fire?" Gheren asked, reappearing suddenly. Jafren almost jumped at the sound, but shoved away the reaction. He couldn't go jumping at that—not with... not with demons loose.

"No, no, thanks, I was just thinking."

"About what?"

"These demons. There is something dark covering the land, Gheren, something dark and sinister. If it were worse—one would think the Temple had somehow fallen."

"You don't think it has?"

"No." He shook his head. "We would be completely overrun by demons were that the case." He thought on that. Weren't they getting to that point already? He looked out the window at the long and level lawn. Just beyond, a city hummed with life. No, were the Temple to fall, the scene would be of unimaginable horror. *But can't a man inflict as much damage upon himself as a few demons?* he thought glumly to himself.

"Then how can all of this be happening?"

Jafren turned to face the Counsel man. "I'm not sure. Maybe there is something in the Archives."

"What would that be?"

"I wish that I knew." Another Temple, perhaps? Some hidden portal that had been suddenly exposed or forgotten? Or was some made mage or warlock on a rampage somewhere, calling forth demons and letting them loose? If he was going to start anywhere, it would be in the Archives, though he was utterly in the dark as to what he sought.

"Would you like me to send men to do some research? I could call on—"

"No, Gheren, this is a job I think I must do."

"But—"

"I know, I know," he said, waving a hand. "Work is done by the working men, and you and I get to direct everything. It's time for that to change a little."

Chapter 17
Information Please

We have heretofore done well to preserve our legacy after we have passed. Printers, copiers, and scribes have kept meticulous notes. Do not ever let such knowledge be lost—the fate of many may depend upon it.

Renalsh Horazen, First Archiver, III Age

The Archives were several floors below ground level and a thick smell of must hung in the close quarters. The paint on the stone walls peeled away in great sheets, with visible water stains in several locations. Jafren hoped to Sacuan that those in charge would figure out a way to keep all documents safe from moisture—already many were lost from flooding and damp weather. Thankfully, the more important and sensitive documents were located in a separate room that had a separate double wall for protection. Still, dampness and silverfish could wreak havoc on any room this far below the surface.

A small desk sat before the door to the inner room, and the wrinkled form of the Keeper sat hunched over a document. The ancient man appeared to be sleeping, but his gray eyes moved slowly over the tiny print on the wrinkled parchment. He straightened as Jafren approached.

"Ah, Grand Counselor Jafren, I rarely see your face down here. What brings you to the inner circle?" His voice was like the whisper of cold ash over charred logs.

He laughed slightly at the Keeper's name for the secured room. "Everything and nothing," Jafren said with a smile, which was returned.

"I'm not sure I can offer you that, but you are free to enter. Here is the key." A bony hand handed him a long skeleton key attached to a thick iron ring. "Take the time you need. Should you stay past closing, please lock up and return the key to my chambers. Do you still know where my quarters are?"

Jafren nodded. "Yes, thank you."

The "inner circle" was a little drier, but the smell of mildew still hung in the closed space. Scrolls, books, and random documents filled the room. Shelves lined the walls from floor to ceiling, and small tables scattered around the small space were piled high with items. The ceiling, at least twelve feet high held small ladders built into each wall that could be rolled along to access the upper shelves. Jafren knew there was an organization to the chaos, but the Keeper's system made it look only like a pile of junk. Which, he noted with a smile, was the intent. No one in their right mind kept the most prized documents of the land scattered in a heap.

He stood and stared at the massive collection of yellowed documents. A search for "demons" would be a good start, but he'd never finish. That subject most likely comprised of hundreds of thousands of pages of material. No, he would get nowhere going down that path. At least not at first. He hoped eventually to land on something propitious. The Temple of M'Hzrut was an equally common name to search, although it might be a start. *Which elder had started the Temple?* He thought for a few moments, starting at the wall absently.

Some relative of the Prophet Broundoun, I think. During his time at University, remembering the name was not important. But now, it was suddenly imperative to remember. Broundoun... Broundoun... he scratched his chin. "No, Brasharenden," he muttered. *Well, I was close...*

Now, where would the document be? "Where, where?" He deliberated quietly, scratching his chin. He finally threw up his hands and opened the door. The Keeper looked up, a wan smile on his face. He still held the document in his gnarled hands. "Lost?"

"Yes. I can't remember how…"

The Keeper set his bony hands on the table and gingerly set the yellowed parchment down; veined hands rested on either side. He sighed ever so slightly. "Ah, yes, how quickly we forget. There are all together thirty-two shelves in the room, plus the tables. Everything is ordered by a specific numbering system. There is a key, but I can't seem to find it—if you find it, please let me know. In any case, there are small numbers on each document. Numbers 100-200 are religious texts, 201-300 are…" And on and on it went. However, the room was not ordered by number. Each shelf had its own number, starting with the bottom shelf in the right-hand corner. The first shelf indicated number 900 to 1,000. And from there it got more complicated, because the second shelf was 200 to 300. The tables spread throughout the room contained various religious missives. One table, however, piled only with junk, was intended to be a reviewing table. Jafren committed the important subjects and locations to memory: Elders, Holy Orders (including Knights of the Black Dawn), warlocks, mages, and even the broader category of the Temple of M'Hzrut. That was only as a last resort.

When he returned to the room, he cleared off the table piled with meaningless documents and began retrieving scrolls and books based on his subjects. He still was not sure what he was searching for, but he hoped to at least find a start.

Hours passed with little progress, until he finally hit upon a glaring clue.

ф

The warlock, Ar'Zoth, exiled to penance in the North, for given his fear of the climate and region near the plass [sic], he is thus to be punished. Crimes committed: On the down-west coast, killed entire schools of orca, accidentally destroying a fishing trawler. When asked, he stated that the accidents were caused by swarms of bees and an overpowering buzzing noise in the air. Unable to control voices in his head. All powers stripped by senior mages and one other warlock. Sent to exile. Warded. Items of note: Upon final placement, suddenly showed no emotion.

"Well, it's a start, anyway. Where was he exiled?" Jafren wondered aloud. To his knowledge, very few warlocks—well, none, he thought—were exiled to the north. Perhaps if he read through the whole book, he'd find a few placed near Welcfer. But what caught his attention was the misspelling of "pass" in the document—his eyes glanced over it, but it was spelled *plass* instead of pass, or had he read that right?

region near the Plass

No wonder it had missed being catalogued! He knew the Keeper to be meticulous to the extreme, but then again, why had he not corrected the error? Or had he thought *plass* was location? Or had he simply ignored the connection between "Pass" and "Gorge?" To Jafren it was obvious, but to one who catalogued thousands of documents, it was an easy oversight.

To think, an error in paperwork could have—

Jafren cut the thought off as he lurched to his feet and began another search, but this one was fruitless.

So, there was a Keep, possibly near Gray Gorge, and a dangerous warlock had been exiled there. Why? If the—

His glance went back to the document with a snap. The word North did not look right, either. Again, his eyes had filled in spaces where there weren't any! That wasn't North—it was an N and an F jumbled together:

The warlock, Ar'Zoth, exiled to penance in the Forth

Someone had written over one or the other. Forth? Did that mean the Isle of Forth? Just a few hundred miles south of Belden City? Was there a mix-up? Which was written first, and by whom?

If they had meant to exile him to the Isle of Forth, but instead sent him to this Keep far past Gray Gorge...

"Oh for Sacuan's sake..." Jafren muttered. He quickly opened all of the pertinent documents in front of him and paled. It all made sense now. His heart sank into his stomach and he nearly vomited. Another structure, like the Temple of M'Hzrut, stood in the far north and guarded the underworld. A warlock had been there. But, something horrible had happened—a dangerous warlock had been sent to exile there instead. Jafren groaned. The evidence was as clear as it could be. It may not be enough for the elected officials, but he would have to present his case.

He gathered the documents and extinguished the lamps, save the one by the door. As he entered the musty hallway, he finally doused even this one and locked the door.

The Keeper was in his room, albeit in his small-clothes, and greeted Jafren with a smile. "Did you find what you were looking for?"

"I found more than I hoped to. I found everything I had feared to." The old man's face fell, but Jafren turned away and walked toward his own quarters. The Keeper watched him go, his face crestfallen as it peeked around the rough frame.

A moon was out—a thick sliver of white shining above the leafless trees. For several minutes, he stared out of his window at the night and watched as the black branches of the giant ash and oak swayed in a slight wind. An owl hooted.

He was about to light a lamp to prepare his case for the officials when he paused. Jafren had the evidence, but he didn't have the skill to present it. Further, they would likely dismiss his notion and send him on some other frivolous task, or worse, order him to recall the Guards he had sent out into the field. They would bicker and argue, and delay and defer for days. That would pose a danger to Belden he was not willing to face. Instead, he looked back out at the bright moonlit night, and then picked up his papers and stepped into the hallway.

φ

"Yes?" The Keeper's face was still lined with sadness, and he frowned deeply.

"Can tell me something?" he whispered quietly, leaning into the opening. "Do you know where the Knights of the Black Dawn are stationed?"

"Come in," the man said nervously, looking up and down the dimly lit hallway. Only two stand lamps still burned.

The Keeper ushered Jafren in and the door clicked shut behind him. "This is a matter of utmost importance."

"I can see that. You have not been the first to ask for such information."

"Not... not the first?" he asked, his voice shaky. Who had been here before him?

The Keeper seemed to read his thoughts and shook his head. "No, no not recently. I have never answered their query, mind you." A gray eyebrow raised slightly.

"I have reason to know—"

"And many in your very position have asked as well," the man went on, as if Jafren had not spoken. This was not going well.

He opened his mouth, but closed it quickly.

"I see," the man said sagely. "I can see it in your eyes. What has happened?"

"Something very grave and very dangerous... We will not last long if we do not enlist the help of the Dawn."

The Keeper nodded slightly. "You will have to tell me what that is."

"I—I—why?" Why, indeed? He was the Grand Counselor! In everything that had been passed to him, nothing had ever been said about the Keeper, or any special role the man played in the Counsel headquarters. None. No information on what knowledge the man possessed, or needed to possess. It was Jafren's turn to cock an eyebrow.

The Keeper returned his look with one of sympathy, as if there was something Jafren had missed. And he replied simply, "I must know." But the old voice was suddenly clean and cold, sharpened to a keen edge. The voice of ashes was swept away and replaced by one limned with hardened coal.

Knowledge is power, Jafren knew. Power over your fellow man, and power over entire nations. Knowing what others did not was important at every level, and it set one apart from the huddling, ignorant masses. So, while the Grand Counselor ran the nation, it was the Keeper who kept knowledge the Grand Counselor would not know. In essence, it made him the true ruler of Belden.

Sacuan blast him!

Jafren balled his fists and sighed. "I fear—I fear that we have a situation with a warlock who has been exiled many years ago."

"Yes?"

"Yes, exiled to the far north, north of Gray Gorge."

The Keeper paled as soon as the words left Jafren's mouth. "I see. Is there something wrong with him?"

"Much," Jafren said softly.

"And you have found this in the Archives?"

The Keeper turned a whiter shade of white as Jafren nodded. He seemed to stumble where he stood and waddled over to a plush chair where he sank with a heavy sigh. "I see." After a moment, he hung his bony head in gnarled hands.

He feels he has failed, Jafren thought with a twinge of sadness. "I don't think you should blame yourself for not knowing... I had to dig for a long time before I found out."

Silence.

"I'm—"

"It is such, as much as it saddens me," the Keeper said, raising his head. His eyes were red with worry and fatigue.

"What do you mean...?" Jafren wondered. "'It is such?'"

The Keeper sighed again. "You aren't the only one who has come here and made such a statement about that warlock."

A brief flash of rage passed across his face. "I'm not? Who else—"

"Please, it is not time for that. That time has passed. I accept the blame that our papers may not be in order, or knowledge clouded by time and uncertainty. I am so sorry... it has come to this, has it not?" He shook his head slowly, muttered a few words to himself, then looked at Jafren.

"It has come to this." He was still confused, still angry that someone else had been here and made the discovery. But the old man was correct, such worry was needless. He'd seen bad things happen when papers were shuffled in the wrong order, sent men to the north when they were true southerners. But nothing like this. Nothing like exiling a mad warlock to a site as important as M'Hzrut! Or perhaps even more important!

"Jafren?"

"I—I, I'm fine. I just... I just need to know where the Dawn is for now. That is where I will start."

The Keeper's lips parted slightly to reveal yellowed teeth, then curled back into a frown. "I will tell you where the Dawn is... I hope you succeed in your journey... Sacuan help us all." He sighed again. "But... you won't get there now, not with the snow. Unless you can ski, or use those fancy, long wooden shoes."

"I can ski."

"Then you had best hurry. Sacuan... Sacuan help us all."

Chapter 18
Wet

Cleanliness is imperative for a full and pious life. Clean clothes, clean house, clean self, and clean conscience: These are the foundations for a life in the Light

High Cleric Bertrand

Huyen slashed and the enormous rat squealed as the sword sliced a gash across the top of its spine. The sound was that of a bull being castrated—Zhy nearly covered his ears, but he kept his hands out in front in self-defense. In his shock, it never occurred to him to draw his small knife. The rat ignored Zhy and spun back to strike at the knight. Huyen danced backward and swung as the creature leapt for his throat. The tip of the blade caught the underside of the animal's stomach and sliced cleanly through the brown-mottled skin. Entrails slid out of the bloody opening with a sickening gurgle and fell to the stone with small plops. The rat, however, was able to maintain its altitude, and Huyen was forced to duck away as the creature thudded against the far wall. With a shriek, it spun again, and this time Yulchar swung, his sword slicing the animal's head completely off. The small head screeched in pain as it splashed into the pool. Huyen was bent over, his hands on his knees.

"Filthy creatures, they spread—"

Zhy yelled and pointed at the pile of entrails.

It moved.

The steaming mess of organs bulged and separated slowly into smaller distinct pieces of filth. Each one moved slowly, almost rolling along the stone ground. A hiss emitted from several of the pieces simultaneously. They little resembled the liver, stomach, kidney, and other innards that had spilled from the rat. Now they glowed with a sheen in the dull blue light, as if covered with a thin reflective material. Zhy's jaw was nearly to the floor as he watched the entrails slowly develop small faces.

Faces of men!

"Demons!" Huyen screamed as his sword flashed. He struck at the creatures in a whirlwind of moves—Yulchar had to jump back to avoid being struck himself. *Clang! Clang!* His sword would strike the stone as he tried to slice the tiny creatures before they grew. They were growing, Zhy noticed—approaching the size of small mice. But their faces—their faces! Men. Huyen grunted as he slashed at the creatures... He seemed to miss more than he struck, for Zhy only heard the sword slice through flesh once or twice. Otherwise, Zhy was jarred with the reverberations of the sound of steel on stone.

A creature flew straight at Zhy and he batted at it like a small biting fly. The thing cried—a high-pitched squeal not unlike an infant's wail—and splattered against the far wall. Zhy's hand came away slimy, as if he had wiped his nose after a fall day at the beach. He wiped it furiously on his trousers and, with effort, pushed down the urge to vomit. He looked up in time to slap away another. And another. Each time his hackles rose, but he smacked them harder, while Huyen slashed furiously at the stone. By this time, Yulchar had danced around Huyen, took a position adjacent to Zhy and was slashing at the creatures with abandon.

The Tunnels filled with splats, splatters, the sound of sword on stone, and a fair amount of cursing. Zhy flung a creature against a stone wall and the sudden silence seemed overwhelming. All that remained of the creatures were dark stains on the stone.

"What—were—those—things?" Zhy panted. *And I bathed in that water*, he thought. He could contain the rise of bile no more and abruptly fell to his knees and vomited loudly onto the rock. He ignored the crushing pain shuddering through his legs, and the deathly, icy chill of the stone as his palm pressed fiercely against it for support.

Huyen snorted and stepped forward a few paces. He made a show of examining the splashes of liquid along the far wall. "Demons."

Yulchar growled low in his throat, much like Zhy had heard another man growl—what was his name again? "Indeed, but how?" The leader uttered a soft curse, but his calm demeanor soon returned. "Sacuan bless us all. I'm sorry, Zhy... Sorry about all of this."

"Ach," Huyen grumbled.

Zhy stood with a groan and spat out the remaining dregs. He stepped a few paces past the slaughter and found some running water in which he could wash off. Thoughts of the rat-like creatures whirled in his head and he nearly lurched forward again, but was able to shake off the thought. Instead, he looked back at the pool, swathed in the light from the off-kilter runes. "But how...?"

"You should have gone to University," Huyen said gruffly.

"What do you mean?"

He only grunted in reply.

"You ask a lot of questions, Zhy," Yulchar said softly. "Huyen, I'm not so sure—"

"Of course that was a demon, Yulchar!" the man snapped. "A rat is never that big—never! And in the Tunnels no less? No, we've already seen one demon in here. Maybe that was the bat! Ever think of that?"

Yulchar bristled. "How could a..."

"And there you go with the how. Listen. Down here"—he gestured roughly— "everything is wrong to begin with. I think our bat transformed, or else..." He cursed and started walking.

The other knight remained quiet and his jaw was set tight. Zhy followed along in silence and didn't dare look back. He thought he heard as slight screech in the far distance, but he shrugged it off.

It wasn't until an hour or more had passed that Zhy bit his lip and re-opened the conversation. "Still... it seems odd that demons would pick a rat of all things, and in the Tunnels..."

"Well, old men and bats might be the standard, but a rat is a fairly mindless creature and could easily be controlled."

"But people kill rats on sight!" Zhy said. Didn't they? Where had he seen rats before? A terrible memory crashed its way through his mind—it was a sudden thought, but it was vivid:

> *Something was tickling his face. He giggled. Perhaps he had taken home the lovely mistress from the inn. But hadn't she poured his ale over his head before she stormed out? And hadn't Kahl demanded he pay for her drinks and meal? Never mind, she may have had second thoughts. She was very pretty. He kept his eyes closed and enjoyed as she ran her many fingers over him, over... he lurched up in the bed, covered in ale and vomit. Through the purple-gray fog of inebriation, he realized he lay near a sewer exit. The "hands" were nothing but a dozen or so rats crawling over him, chewing on the bits of regurgitated food. With a scream, he threw them off and ran stumbling for his home.*

"Great Sacuan's scrotum!" he heard himself say.

"Another memory?" Yulchar asked with a sigh.

"Damned rats."

"Demons are crafty, but they can be short-sighted, Zhy. A rat is a perfect vessel—would have been one, had you been down here alone. You may have fended off the... attackers, we'll call them, but there were so many."

Zhy nodded.

"Maybe if Huyen had simply sliced off the creature's head, we wouldn't have had that problem."

"I did what I did."

And with that veritable snarl, the conversation was closed.

Zhy wondered what other vile creatures they would find in these Tunnels. Was this not supposed to be a shorter and safer route to Gray Gorge?

He looked at the skis longingly. No matter how deep the snow above, at this point he would rather take his chances on those contraptions than face any more creatures from the dark. Yulchar had said they would travel faster in here—faster than normally possible. Whatever magic that was, he did not sense anything. Perhaps he had simply grown accustomed to the pace at which they were traveling, or else the sameness of the blue glowing runes, and their seeming endlessness, made him feel as if he were simply walking in place. Zhy grudgingly admitted facing demonic creatures in the Tunnels was far safer than facing them in the middle of a howling blizzard.

φ

They stopped to bed down for the night, and Zhy asked about the snow above.

"As deep as a man's chest sometimes, even on Crown Road," Yulchar answered.

Zhy whistled softly.

"Getting north of Vronga, to our—well, north of Vronga, in any case, isn't so bad on skis, but once you get farther north of, say, Reldan and the smaller villages, the snow is impossible. Everyone and everything is closed up and hunkered down."

"And we are still going faster than we would over land?"

Huyen snapped, "Of course."

"Indeed," Yulchar agreed. "It doesn't seem like it, but we are probably north of Reldan by now."

Zhy tried to think back on any maps he had seen. There had been one in an inn, he remembered, but the lines and words were blurry.

"Reldan is about here," Yulchar said. He had his palm up, and his finger was pointing at a line a little more than halfway to the beginning of his fingers. "And Gray Gorge is up here," he indicated the middle of his third finger. "And my wrist would be Belden City. Indeed, we have traveled far."

"I see."

The question was answered, but he still felt uncomfortable remaining down here, with...

"Don't worry. Huyen sleeps with one eye open, practically. I'd rather face any number of demons down here than up there." He indicated the invisible ceiling of the Tunnels. "Who knows what creature could rise out of the snow."

"But... it is warmer down here."

"Yes, and?"

"Well, I would think the bats and older men would not do as well in snow."

"Ah, their bodies would not fare well, surely. But the demonic host would drive them to complete destruction—you'd face a blackened creature rising from the snow and would have no time to react."

"Blackened... why?"

"Frostbite, Zhyfrael," Huyen snapped.

"Frost... bite?"

Yulchar answered while Huyen remained silent. "The cold burns your skin—that is the best way to describe it. If it gets bad enough, it turns black and will eventually fall off. It blisters just as it would in a fire. Heat and cold..."

"Are pretty much the same thing," Zhy said softly.

They walked along for several more hours, exchanging only idle talk. Zhy thought again on the miles of rock above his head, and of the deep and frigid powder that surely covered everything in its comforting and devastating blanket.

Chapter 19
Chaos

〰〰
〰〰

Chaos rules. Chaos wins. I am chaos. I have won; there is no need to think any more. Chaos, oh sweet chaos!

Mad Hereald

While many towns in Belden were hunkered down for a long winter, the southern region suffered only from cold rains and dreary skies. The demonic threat in places like Sorang, Vronga, and Belden City was handled easily by the Crown Guard, and by the Knights of the Black Dawn. But as many village leaders, the Holy Elders found, it was hard to restrain the masses from attempting their own type of bounty hunting.

Nestled in the marshy regions south of Port Havren, the village of Moult was no bigger than several dozen houses and a few single-story inns. Beldeners had a running joke that even the smallest hamlet or burgh held no less than three inns and two Temples. But it had been witness to no less than seven suspicious creatures haunting its environs. A gherwza found its death by way of a farmer's arrow, an elderly man climbed up onto a roof, spouted an earful of madness, then promptly walked off the edge of the roof. He was impaled by a fence post. But others had wandered off before the villagers could do anything.

Help from outside was nigh impossible—the heavy rains of late had flooded the single road in, and the marshes were flooded, leaving no overland path. Moult's saving grace was its higher ground, but now that was contributing to its doom, as it was now completely isolated.

Shortly after sundown, a trio of villagers were leaving a popular inn. A light in the distance caught one of their eyes and he stopped his companions. Far out on the marsh, lights were flickering on and off, as if people were swinging lanterns in the dark. But the lights would be so far off the ground that no human could be swinging the lantern.

Had the lights been closer to the water, no one would have paid them any heed, for the marshes provided rice and lily roots for sustenance. In the fall, villagers would take canoes out into the marshes and harvest both natural resources. The rice was used in abundance, and the lily roots were ground into a starchy flour and used for bread and other dough-based foods.

"What are those lights?"

"Demons!" a young man spat.

"No, Tershan, those are not demons," said the only woman of the three. "Mother called them marsh lights. It's part of the swamp."

"Your mother was wrong, Nera."

"Don't call my mother wrong, Will!"

The boy named Will scratched his head. "I don't mean like that. I mean, yeah, sure they are marsh lights. But what causes them?"

"It's just stuff burning out there. Fires can burn for years under the marsh, mother says, so it's not—"

"Demons!" Tershan spat. "Demons. Let's kill 'em!"

"Hold on, hold on," Will said, trying to calm his companions. He was the only one who had not tried the brandy. The stuff could turn his friends into raving fools, and tonight it had done just that. "Let's just wait and see what they do."

"It's probably old Shurden, drunk again."

Shurden was a curly old mage who lived in town and seemed to always have his head in his cups. He liked to use all sorts of strange magic spells when he was drunk, in a vain attempt to scare people. But what would he be doing out on the marsh? "What would he be doing out there?" Nera asked.

Will shrugged. "Let's go."

Arguments continued for some time, but Tershan was able to coax them into returning to the inn for another round of brandies, which he would gladly pay for. It would make them even more irrational, but the warmth of the inn, the sweet sounds of the sutan, and maybe a plate of cheese would do them good. And, hopefully, they would abandon their foolish ideas of what was in the marsh. *It had to be Shurden*, Tershan reminded himself. It had to be.

It had indeed been Shurden out in the marsh, trying to scare the townsfolk. Hearing of demons, he tipped back a few too many brandies and sauntered out onto the marsh to create a display of lights he knew would get the attention of others. With a curse, he watched as the villagers went back into town, and, letting his lights die out, he started back for the inn.

His boot caught in a low section of muck and he tripped, falling face-first into a tuft of cranberry. When at last he pushed himself up, he started walking. A low hiss from behind him startled him, and he turned, his hand coming up to create another orb of light.

The white ball illuminated a row of dripping fangs.

Shurden only had time to gurgle "*gher—*" before the jaws clamped shut over his face. His body thrashed for a few moments; blood poured into the warm and moist earth—it quickly bubbled and boiled before dissipating. The beast moaned with a low, before the beast swallowed him and flew toward the village.

But this was not a gherwza... it was something else. Something far larger and more terrifying.

Whether due to the lush moisture and fertile soil of the swamp, the loss of control by Ar'Zoth, or a combination of other factors, this new horrific savagery of the Dark made a gherwza appear as a small rodent. Shurden saw fangs, fangs that would resemble those of a gherwza, but the enormity of this creature towered high above in the starless sky. Great wings of hardened scale stretched back along its tower-sized back, which itself was covered in a thick, patterned shell, as if leather had been boiled, bent over itself, boiled again, then stretched in odd segments across the muscle. The scales were calcified bone, as hard as granite, and equally impenetrable. Instead of the stubby tail of a bat, this creature's tail slithered out for a few paces, and was covered in the same scales as the body, though they were smaller and pocked with tufts of black, slimy fur. If Shurden had had time to listen, he would have heard the whoosh of the tail as it whipped through the moist air.

As the frightful creature flew toward the village, its large wings swept at the air with a wet, leathery-sounding rush of air. With a deafening screech, it dove down. The screams filled the night, lasting for hours, until the evil beast had devoured every last person... alas no one was there to hear their screams.

A lone merchant made his slow and careful way across the flooded marsh, aided by a canoe and a determination to make at least a little coin this winter. When he saw the beast flying overhead, steaming liquid dripping from its fangs, he paddled as hard as he could in the reverse direction, and raced as fast as he could to Port Havren. The Elders had to know of this!

"That was no gherwza," he said to himself, uttering a prayer to Sacuan.

A Holy Elder at the Temple nodded gravely at the news and took down a dusty tome. "What you saw was a *mulargh*... see this picture?"

"When was that book published?"

"Five hundred years before our current Age, my son. Go. Go now, and pray. Pray to the Light and to all that is good and kind... the end draws near!"

Chapter 20
An Alliance of Sorts

◆

Do not assume that those you fight and those you fear will always be at odds with you. An enemy can become a friend in a time of need.

Prophet Yoz'Hru

On his way out of Belden City, Jafren set a sealed letter into the hands of a drowsy page, who was just arriving for his early shift at the Counsel Headquarters. The boy scuttled off to the High Temple to deliver his message to the Holy Elders. He was not sure the letter would do any good, but someone had to stand up. In the letter, he requested that several Protectors be sent forth through the Tunnels toward the Temple of M'Hzrut.

He made sure to ask that they exit before the normal Temple exit. Just to investigate. That, too, would be a tall order, but he gave it. It was all he could do—give an order, hope someone would see the enormity of the task, and take action.

Jafren hired a horse he hoped could take him close to Vronga, and indeed the animal he chose was fast and road-ready. South of the city, snow had already started to fall, but he was still able to drive the animal far into the northern country before the depth proved too much and he sent the animal back to the nearest village. Strapping on his skis, he started out for the collection of huts that housed the headquarters for the Knights of the Black Dawn.

What a strange alliance, he though as he tramped through the snow to the small building. The Guard for years had denied the very existence of the Dawn and had even gone to lengths to convince people the Dawn was merely the fabrication of a few outcasts who wanted to cause dissention and fear. But now, he needed their help. He needed the help of any organized and armed force he could find.

Everyone, that is, except rowdy bands of villagers bearing pitchforks. The teacher Rhys had been right on that count—but addressing the issue required the inclusion of some very strange bedfellows.

φ

"Well, let's all have a party shall we?" the obese man muttered. "And who might you be? Did you find him?"

"Who?" Jafren was confused. Did he have the right man? He looked back at the small assistant, who returned a nod. And a cocked eyebrow.

"Never mind, never mind! Who are you?"

"I am Grand Counselor Jafren, and I come on official business of Belden," he lied. He had made record time in the snow, but if the Grand Counselor found out he'd come here, he would be hunted down like a rabid dog.

"I see. And do you seek one of my members?" The man's face was placid and Jafren bristled. Even though the Knights were of no government, and no official governance, they should at least have respect for their country's leader! Further, no High Counselor had ever visited the Knights of the Black Dawn, as far as he could recall—many had continued to deny their existence, even given strong evidence to the contrary.

This obese lout seemed not to care a whim that the country's leader stood before him.

"In a way. You see, we have a problem with demons."

"Aye, and you are not the first to say that. Every knight who has come through that door has the same story to tell. And honestly, it worries me, but never fear, we do our job."

"I don't fear that."

Dran'Za scowled. "No?"

The man was insufferably condescending—then again, a man of his size could afford to be. He could squash anyone who went counter to his ideas or opinions. Best to stick to the facts and hope for the best. "No. It appears there is a Keep, far up past Gray Gorge, supposedly inhabited by a warlock—it was supposed to protect the world from demons, much like the Temple. But I fear something has happened—a serious mistake, and there is a dangerous man up there."

"You don't say." He yawned.

"Indeed."

"Well, you're not the first to think something is going on up north. I have—rather—I *had* knights on that very task."

"You'll need more than knights up there, my good man. Do you know of any warlocks?"

"No, but there is a mage in Vronga. Old man. Very powerful."

Jafren sighed. He had skied past Vronga—deliberately avoiding the town.

"How powerful?"

Dran'Za shrugged.

"Listen," Jafren barked. "This is no time to play political games. For years we have been at odds with one another, but now is not the time. The world needs everyone—the Guard, the Holy Elders, Protectors, and the Dawn, if we are to survive this. The man at the Keep is far more dangerous than any of us can possibly imagine."

"My job is simply to make sure the demons are kept at bay by the Knights," the fat man replied. "I do not play politics, and I am not playing games now. I know very little about the mage in Vronga, only that he is said to be the most powerful the University had seen."

Jafren eyed the pile of books with disgust. "Then what are all of these? Children's stories?"

Dran'Za slammed his fist on the books, sending a small pamphlet flying. "I told you what I know," he snapped. "If you have come here asking for help, you are not doing a very good job. This talk of mending past problems is just air. I have lost several members already, and surely you can appreciate what it is like to lose men."

"That is no way to talk to your—"

"I didn't vote for you, so I owe you nothing. My Order keeps the peace here, more often than the Guard."

Jafren nearly coughed and clenched his fists. "As I said, politics should not play into this," he said, clipping each word violently. "We are in danger—we *all* are in danger, unless we work together."

"I don't want to lose any more men, Grand Counselor, is that clear?"

"I can understand that, yes," he snapped through gritted teeth. His jaw hurt from keeping it tightly bound. *How dare this overly-obese man who read books act like this while his soldiers were killed.* A good leader would at least enter the field. Further, this Dran'Za had an air about hem that invited conflict and arguments, and Jafren couldn't help but feel himself get sucked into it. "I—I wish I knew more about the mage, that is all. I skied past Vronga to get here."

"You know more now than had you stopped," the large man replied quietly.

Yes, that much was accurate. He knew now the leader of the "elite" Knights of the Black Dawn was a blubbery, orca-sized glutton with an appetite for pointless reading and mountains of food. The Order was in grave danger indeed if their fat commander cared more about dusty tomes than the lives of his underlings. Jafren felt sorry for knights out in the field—they were most definitely on their own and at risk. Should they be overrun, they would enjoy little help from their leader. But such observations were just that— observations. Jafren had work to do, and there was a very real threat to his country... he had to act.

Though he had sent letters to the elders, he counted them as all but lost and pointless. Not wanting to waste any more time, he buried his loathing and hatred and addressed Dran'Za curtly. "I will return to Vronga. And, so you know, I sent letters for more Protectors to head to the Temple. I'd advise your men not to engage any Protectors or Counsel Guardsmen that they see."

"Unless they have transformed into gherwzas, yes?"

Jafren could have strangled the man. *I should have said nothing and simply left.* The fat oaf had a way of triggering his every nerve ending. "What do you mean?"

"I assume you would want to keep to our mission."

"Of course... I do not want your men killing mine, do you understand?"

"When have we done so?" he asked. His massive double chin wobbled and his puffy eyes had glaze of forced innocence.

"I think you know the answer to that," Jafren replied curtly. He had to push each word out against all instincts to cut the man down where he sat. "But... I will simply repeat the request—do not engage the Protectors or Guardsmen and I will not engage the Knights." He'd heard stories of the Knights and how they had killed Guardsmen before. The men may have been possessed, but Jafren doubted it— overzealous men of the Dawn could cause extreme disruption if given the chance. The Knights of the Black Dawn could easily turn into the pitchfork-bearing villages that Rhys had warned him about.

"We can agree on that."

With another giant effort to restrain himself, Jafren turned and walked from the building.

Chapter 21
Vronga

The pulse of teeming humanity is a thing that can quickly become Dark and twisted into a writhing mass of evil. Men who act as one hardly think at all, and it is easy for the Dark to slip in and take over.

High Cleric Bertrand

Jafren loathed Vronga. He loathed even the slightest thought, loathed the concept of such a sprawling mass, and loathed the very name. The city seemed to him a waste of everything. Far enough away from Belden City, it was a giant festering boil he could not reach. Winter made it worse: more filthy, more... awful.

With the brown slush and dirty streets, the town was worse in winter than in summer, and he hated the thought of having to spend even one hour looking for the mage. Each time he heard updates from the festering sore on the land, the town had grown—and would grow until it covered the entire nation, he thought. Why didn't they build taller buildings instead of low, long, meaningless structures? The smoky fog hung thicker in winter, and everyone seemed to be coughing, Jafren included. He spat up a black wad of phlegm and cursed.

The city bustled with activity, so much that he wondered if anyone knew it was winter and that snow, mud and slime covered every square inch of the place.

His first stop was the University, and he spent perhaps two hours trying to convince a wart-faced director that he was looking for information regarding any mages that had worked there. And after two hours of looking into pale and nearly lifeless eyes, he cursed and turned away. For a brief moment, he thought of using his station as leverage to gain more access, but if this man were anything like Dran'Za, he'd be eating muddy snow. No, if there were answers at the University, he was not going to find them.

As he turned away, a student hurried past him. He quickly turned and called after the young man. "Say, I'm looking for a friend, an old friend. He and I studied here," he lied. "Are you studying to be a mage?"

"No, forestry," the young man replied, his voice cracking. Jafren knew forestry in Vronga was nothing more than the art of slicing down trees to make way for more of this bulbous mass of expanding waste.

"Do you know any mages?"

"No, I only see them in the halls. They keep to themselves. Sorry, I'm late..."

"Do you know where they hang out after class?" he asked as the man started to walk away.

"Down at the Shards," he said over his shoulder. Jafren thought he heard the boy utter "Silly name" before he was down the path and into the dirty street.

The Shards was a dark inn, and it took some asking and wrong turns before he found the nondescript door. Smoke from pipes and a creosote-choked chimney filled the room. Young men sat hunched around tables, sipping tea or small glasses of ale. Many of the men started growing beards and looked rather comical with their stubble and youthful attempts at trying to look like their elders.

For the most part, Jafren received a cold shoulder, but he found an empty chair and dropped himself onto it.

"Good afternoon, gentlemen."

Silence.

He repeated his earlier statements—that he was looking for an old friend, but no one believed him. Each half-bearded face was intent on ignoring him, and each young man either talked quietly with those around him or stared distantly into his cup. He repeated his question, this time softer, but the response was the same. "Do you—" he snapped, but stopped short. *Do you know who I am?* The words were halfway out his mouth but he caught himself. Likely that would attract too much attention, when all he wanted was a little. Curse these fools! With a violent curse, he bolted to his feet and started for the door, when a small voice from a man at the bar stopped him.

"You're not looking for an 'old friend,' are you?"

Jafren scratched his head and turned to face the man. His face was clothed in shadow and he kept a firm grip on his mug of ale. "Not exactly..."

"Sit."

He did as requested. "I am—"

"What are you looking for?"

"I wish I could explain... all I know is I need to find information about mages and warlocks and traveling to the Temple and—"

The stranger whistled. "Quite a lot to know, and why do you need to know it?"

"I have my reasons," Jafren snapped.

"I can see why you have come up empty, my friend. The mages won't talk to you—they are above all of that, and warlocks... well, good luck finding one. Do you seek a particular warlock?"

"No, just a highly-skilled mage. He may have taught at the University. Yes, yes, I've tried there," he said with a wave of his hand. "I couldn't even get in the door."

"I can imagine. A rough-looking man like you, they probably think you're trying to get a mage or a small-man for some other purpose."

Jafren colored at that. It had never entered his mind! Even if he had used his station, they would have thought of that scenario all the more! *Politicians and their little fetishes*, he thought. But that didn't matter, it was what people thought, in any case. "Those are not my intentions," he said softly.

"Aye, but you look up to something. What is it?"

"I told you I seek a mage named—"

The man waved his mug. "Aye, but quietly."

Jafren was confused, but eventually leaned forward. "Wrenflang," he whispered.

"Ah..." A flicker of recognition passed over the stranger's face, but he shook it away. "Never heard of him. It is a he, isn't he?"

"Yes."

"I see..."

"And what do you mean by that?" Jafren said a little too hotly.

The stranger sipped his ale slowly and glanced at him askance. "I don't quite like you, but I see you're desperate. There's not much I do know, but I know a thing or two. Perhaps some small piece of information can get you on your way."

"I would greatly appreciate that."

The man leaned forward. "There's a rock in a hillside— some farm south of town. You'd miss it walking right past, the road is so well hidden. But look if you can... around there is something of interest. A rock in a hillside." The man coughed softly and winked, but Jafren missed it.

Jafren drained his ale and resisted the urge to strike the man with it. A rock in a hillside! He'd wasted a good hour with a worthless stooge, who had nothing to offer.

"I'll keep that mind," he said stiffly, standing with a creak of pine. "Thank you." The last words were clipped, and he walked to the door with his hands at his sides, lest he choke the man, and every last arrogant bastard in the place.

A rock in a hill!

Chapter 22
A Necklace of Skulls

Part of the allure of trinkets is that they extend to the outside world a piece of ourselves. We may not be willing to flaunt our coin, but we will wear a medallion studded with jewels.

Prophet Broundoun

Untrel had been a Counsel Guard for over twenty years. He'd seen everything, or so he thought— the odd drunk in the tavern vomiting blood, a crazed farmer attacking his silo with a scythe, screaming about chickens. There had been fights among women that left both parties hairless, and a fight between a man and a mage that left the attacker stripped of his skin. Then there was Herzan.

"Herzan," he whispered.

Herzan had claimed that he was a descendent of the Wights, and he was a "child of the land," as he called it. The man rarely bathed and took pleasure at shooting arrows into outhouses, preferably when they were occupied. His most disturbing trait, Untrel thought, was his collection of skull necklaces. The skulls were all made of clay, but it did not detract any from the grotesque image the trinket portrayed. For Herzan wore only animal skins, and he was almost entirely covered in hair. He did look like a Wight, or some other-worldly creature, or even a—Untrel stopped before he could utter the word "demon," but it was already at the tip of his tongue.

Herzan had been no demon, and although he had shot an arrow at a man (or so the traveling men had claimed), the action was not entirely out of the realm of possibility for the man. If Untrel had known more of history and culture, he'd easily place Herzan as a savage wilder in Welcfer. But even that categorization was ill-suited.

Herzan was simply Herzan.

And now he was buried in a shallow grave, beneath several feet of snow.

Still, as Untrel set his mug of hot mulled cider atop the bar, he thought back on the day he had come across Herzan. The warrior must have been fast, to outrun an arrow from Herzan. Untrel's arm still ached from the shaft that had stung it. And then the Guard had been thirty pounds lighter, and as quick as a cat, or so his wife had always said. He took another sip of hot cider and nodded to the innkeeper. Untrel's wife peeked out from the kitchen, and yelled unapologetically across the nearly-full common room. "You get half a plate, dear. Until you lose some of that middle of yours. Got to keep fit if you're going to be a Guard!"

Too often she sounded like his mother, but he let it go. She was right. He could barely move at a jog and skis were something he had not touched in years. His wet boots drying by the fire were testament to that fact.

Try as he might the image of Herzan kept floating back to him. He wondered why—that was ages ago. He'd not told anyone, apart from his wife, of the incident, and thought, perhaps, that was his problem.

"Ghoral," Untrel asked the innkeeper. "What do you know of Herzan?"

"The crazy Wight?"

"He was no Wight," he replied, shaking his head. "But he was crazy, that much is true."

"Was?"

"Aye." Untrel set his mug down and sighed. "Before the snows started, I found him dead."

"Dead?"

The words "Herzan" and "dead" seemed to hush the common room. All eyes turned to the Guard. He sensed them and then rose from the stool. Walking to the fire, he set his bulk down on a chair and faced the room.

"For those of you who knew the man, he has passed on." There were a few sighs and a half-smile or two. While it was a relief to know such a savage creature would not be bothering them, the villagers took little pleasure in death. Additionally, many felt Herzan's problems were not of his doing—that he was sick in the head, or even possessed by something. Just not a demon.

Or so he hoped. He was becoming less and less sure. The room seemed to hum as he told his tale, and the walls looked as if they were wobbling slightly. The spicy mulled cider had no alcohol in it, but something warm and inviting was tickling his insides, as if he had drunk a bottle of brandy. The words came out of his mouth too thickly and too forced, but he spat them out anyway.

"I came upon a body in the road, with men standing around it. One was a warrior and one was a small-man. A mage type, I had guessed, but there was no magic being used that day. The road was soaked in blood. Herzan had fired an arrow at the traveling men, and the mercenary— that is what he was, not a true Counsel warrior—had sprinted out to engage him. Herzan had an arrow nocked."

"And the man killed him?" someone asked, his left hand still holding his mug of ale in the air.

"Indeed he did."

The man whistled softly and took a drink. Untrel continued his story, but there wasn't much left to tell. Believing the men, he let them go on their way and buried Herzan in a shallow grave.

"So who did Herzan shoot his arrow at?"

"One of them sleeping against a tree. I saw the arrow, not a few inches from where your head might be. I—I found this on his neck," he said, as he extracted the necklace of clay skulls. His body twitched with a sudden shiver. Where had that come from? His back was against the fire—there was no reason to be cold. For some reason he placed it around his neck and a crooked smile started to form in the corners of his mouth.

"So he shot at the mage or the warrior?" someone asked nervously. Untrel could feel the tension in the room, could hear small murmurs and whispers.

Untrel shook his head. "Neither, some one . . . else." He coughed and phlegm oozed into his mouth. "He was . . ." His lungs burned and he brought up more phlegm. He spat it into the hearth and it hissed loudly in the flames. Someone gasped.

"Are you all right, Untrel?"

"I'm—I'm fine," he lied. His chest burned as if on fire, and the taste of blood filled his mouth. The room was definitely wobbling by this point and the patrons in the inn were shimmering in the glow of the fire. He could see mouths open in alarm and surprise, but he only stared. A round figure in the background clasped a hand over her mouth and then collapsed to the floor as he spat out more blood.

A hand seemed to be crawling up his spine, then across the bottom of his neck. It turned to ice and pinched the inside of his skull. His eyes bulged and his double chin dropped closer to the floor. Untrel twisted in his chair, and the flimsy wood groaned under the weight, but held fast. He tried to focus on the fire, but a wave of red passed across his vision, and the flames blurred into a crimson, liquid wall.

And as quickly as the spell started, it ended. Although when the hand released him, his mind felt blank.

"Maybe—maybe you should put that necklace down, Untrel," the innkeeper said. "I think it's making you sick," he said, his voice shaking. The wrinkled man took a step back and to the side, his eyes never leaving Untrel.

Untrel regarded the innkeeper as if he had never seen the man before. "No," he said quietly, fingering the necklace. "No," he repeated, his voice gritty as if his vocal cords were lined with silt. There were more gasps, but he didn't notice. He needed out of this body. Out!

Standing, his girth knocked over the chair, and he cursed. "I don't need this!" he screamed. A few patrons leapt to their feet and knocked tables and chairs over on their way out. Cold wind blew into the room and he sucked it in through his nostrils.

"I don't need this!" he yelled again, grabbing his large midsection. He turned toward the fire, and there was a loud pop; the fire roared into an inferno and the smell of burning fat filled the common room—rancid, tainted fat burning violently.

As another patron dashed out, he hazarded a glance to the fire—between Untrel's legs a steady stream of yellowed, oily, sour liquid oozed onto the raging inferno, adding to its massive flames. Yellow gouts of fire licked up and out of the hearth, and scorched the rock and mortar with a thick black stain. Heat radiated from the fat-fueled inferno, and bodies that were not already sweating from fear were dripping from the sudden heat wave.

The flames did not touch his body.

Untrel spun, and for a moment, the remaining villagers were frozen. The once-fat man was now a thin wretch. His hair was scorched black, his garments burned entirely away to reveal slick yellow flesh that glimmered in the blazing fire light. The necklace of skulls was charred but intact—small fragments of white were visible along a neck that was suddenly thin and taught.

Tables and chairs crashed as the rest of the inhabitants made a dash for the exit.

"None of that!" he screamed. His figure suddenly lighter, he sprinted to the door to block it. People turned in helpless fear to run in another direction, but his hands were swift hooks, swiping at those trying to flee. With now-bony fingers, he dug into flesh, tearing and rending. His legs swung outward to trip people, as his hands continued their frenzy of rending and tearing.

Blood spat into the air as he tore out throats and hearts and extracted intestines from still-warm stomachs. "I am Gozath!" he screamed. "Gozath of the swirling depths!" The voice sounded strange in his throat, and he knew somewhere deep down that the name was not his. It was never his. But the demon that had held his brain tore that memory out, and Gozath continued in his rage. When at last he stopped, the floor of the common room was covered in offal and body parts. Some men still twitched, but were quickly silenced as the last ounces of fluid drained from them. Untrel scanned the room and smiled. He inhaled deeply of the coppery smell of blood and the earthy smell of intestines. The screams had been the most delicious.

A voice whispered in his ear, and he fed greedily. When at last he had satiated his many lusts, he burst through the door and padded through the deep snow.

North. I must go north.

Chapter 23
The Protectors and Gozath

Fighting the Dark is as much questioning standard ideals and so-called common knowledge. Once we are set in our patterns and our actions are done with little active guidance, we are in danger of being overrun by the Dark.

Cleric Hyun, Order of the Knot

A group of three severe-looking men emerged from the Tunnels into the frozen wasteland. They were days behind Zhy, and were glad to have exited the dark, dank, and blue-tinted catacombs; for they had also battled demonic rats and demons on their journey. The cold did not alleviate any of their suffering, but still the plowed forward, on orders from Jafren.

Jafren had sent for several groups of Protectors, just in case some would ignore his direct orders. Even direct orders could be "lost" in the dead of winter, especially by those who lived on the coastlines and enjoyed figs under palm trees. His decision was fortuitous, given the fact this group of three were the only ones who took him up on his order. If the situation were to worsen, he hoped desperately that the holy Orders would rustle themselves from comfort and take action. Sadly, his hope was more vanity than desperation.

The eldest of the Protectors was perhaps thirty, and the others in their early twenties. His name was Bechten and he was from Belden City and had grown up in a house only a block from the inn Zhy frequented.

The Protectors had obviously spent most of their lives in southern Belden, for they sported rugged tans and chiseled faces. Yet their leader's worn face was not created by gentle southern breezes, but forged in the blinding sun, limb-shattering cold, devastating snows, and the brazen cruelty of both the Spires of Solitude in northern Belden, and the devastatingly isolated mountains in northwestern Welcfer.

While they believed their mission to be noble and just, they still wondered why they were summoned in the middle of winter. This was unheard of. But like many Beldeners, the tales of demons were too many to ignore, and they followed as Bechten hauled them from their homes. Unlike many leaders of Protectors, he was not content to lounge in the sun, and even had relatives in the North—he worried for their safety as well as that of all citizens. While the Temple surely stood, demons were loose in too many numbers.

Davel scowled at the bleak landscape. "If stayed in the Tunnels, we would've reach the safety and warmth of the Temple!"

"No, the Tunnels end right there," Bechten replied.

Davel opened his mouth to protest.

"Listen, Davel," Ulien said softly, but gratingly. He scowled deeply. "This is not about warmth or comfort! This is about a world being overrun by demons! Creatures we have never seen before may be out there. Forget your childish gherwzas and old men bumbling along. Come on!"

Davel grumbled but followed.

Ski tracks that Zhy, Huyen, and Yulchar had left were all but wiped out from the strong winds, but after a few paces, Bechten held up a hand, as an unmistakable depression of parallel grooves was visible in a deeper section of snow. "Ski tracks!"

Davel grumbled but stopped and inspected the tracks as well. "Aye... men, hopefully."

"Hopefully?" Ulien asked.

"Well..." the young Protector trailed off.

"Come on," Bechten said.

They kept skiing.

They passed by a small sea of wintergreen plants, growing against all rhyme or reason in the lee of a stand of stubby balsams. *It should be too cold for the plant to grow here,* Bechten thought. Soft green leaves carpeted the ground, and bright orange-red berries dotted the small clusters. He pondered stopping for wintergreen was indeed a refreshing treat. But he needed to keep the group moving. Crown Road was not far, and there they would find out what their next steps would be, if any. That, and the more breaks and pauses they took, the more chances the Dark had to gain hold and corrupt them.

"What now?" Ulien asked, scanning the snow-covered road.

"Our orders were to come to Crown Road and... well, look for disturbances. Said there was a Keep up here somewhere."

"Is that so?" Davel asked, looking around. All he could see were rocks and the peaks of the Spires in the distance.

"Yes, but I'm not sure, how to—hey, what is that?" Bechten pointed to a figure in the far distance. They were just entering a small canyon—the north side of Gray Gorge— lined on both sides with high, craggy rock. A light wind blew down from above, sending a spray of snow that was as thick as wood smoke. But through the haze, each man could make out a moving shape that lurched across the frozen ground, looking halfway human. It would weave from side to side, dragging a leg behind it.

Davel drew his sword. His companions protested, but he waved them off. "Fine, then, let it kill you."

Ulien sighed loudly, but his hand went to his sword. "You may be an uppity young man, but no one else should have any business up here. After seeing that gherwza and the corpse, I wouldn't trust anyone—or anything."

"You may be right," Bechten said, adding a quiet curse. His sword slid easily from his scabbard. "Whatever this is, whoever it is, doesn't belong here."

The figure shambled ever closer to them, and as it neared, passing through the thin stream of snow, they could see it *was* a human...or had been at one time. The leg it dragged behind itself was twisted and deformed, and flesh hung blackened from an oversized chin. It—he—moved slowly, achingly slowly, toward them.

"I am Gozath, ruler of the swirling depths," he muttered. The snow had nearly blinded him, and frostbite covered nearly every inch of the slick, yellow skin the fire had exposed. He paid no mind to the festering black sores clinging to his body. His nipple itched, and he scratched it, but the cold had worked its way so utterly through the skin that it simply fell off into the snow. Blood trickled from the wound, but quickly froze into a new scab. "Gozath," he repeated, "Gozath... ruler..."

Davel raised his weapon, with Ulien and Bechten following suit. The shambling creature called Gozath was still several paces away, and the Protectors stepped lightly and carefully toward the creature. Bechten tried to coax Davel to remain behind him, but the young Protector had moved to the point position.

Gozath growled loudly, blood trickling from his broken lips, and he leapt. In a single bound, he covered the distance and was atop Davel, his flabby arms working like a windmill as he struck at the Protector. Davel tried to step backward and raise his sword, but Gozath simply reached out and grabbed the blade with a frostbitten hand. Blood streamed from his appendage as the sharp edge cut into it, but he held fast, and pushed the young man backward.

Eyes wide, Davel struggled to keep Gozath at bay, and wildly looked to his companions.

Bechten charged first, his sword outstretched to strike at the demon's midsection, but Gozath's left arm whirled around, and a haze of white light exploded from the nearly blackened hand. It struck Bechten's sword like lightning, and the metal glowed brightly in the dull atmosphere. The leader roared as he was forced to toss the superheated weapon to the snow. It hissed as it plowed into the white powder.

Ulien had already sprinted around to the other side and his sword point was an inch from Gozath's midsection. Gozath still held Davel firm, but in the second before Ulien's sword struck true, Gozath sent forth another bolt of white-hot lightening. This time, the proximity was too close, and the sword melted immediately into molten steel—the heat was so intense it also melted Ulien's hand like a candle. The Protector fell back to the snow and rock, writhing and screaming, holding his stub of a hand in the air. His body twitched like a palace banner in an ocean storm.

Gozath gave a grunt of satisfaction. With another growl, he pushed the sword blade back with such force that Davel could no longer hold the hilt. Blood poured out of the demon's shredded hand, but still he pushed harder, and harder; that the hilt pressed into Davel's midsection. The young Protector tried to take another step backward, but his heel caught a small scrub of balsam and he fell back on the snow. Eyes wide, he screamed as the hilt pushed through his coat and into his midsection with a pop. Gozath finally let go of the blade and shook the blood from his hand, which sprayed out in a shower of red droplets. His boot came up and he stomped full force on the quillon, driving it deeper into Davel's stomach. The young man gurgled and tried to spin away, but Gozath fell upon him, reached into his belly and tore out as much as he could grab. Davel twitched for a moment and was still.

By now, Bechten had retrieved his sword—though it was still quite warm to the touch. With a low growl in his throat, he charged the demon.

Gozath simply stepped back lightly, then let forth a crimson pillar of flame, which bore into Bechten's midsection. The intense pain of the spell set him screaming. The red light glowed intensely while Gozath scowled deeply, his blackened flesh stark against the bleak landscape. The odor of burning flesh was stifling, and Bechten's skin boiled to black, then fell away. Muscle beneath the exposed skin was scorched, and then the Protector's entrails spilled onto the cold stone. He stopped screaming, but somehow remained standing, although his entire body shook. A sickly steam poured from his exposed belly, and a ribbon of intestine swayed in the light wind. For a moment, he regarded his insides that lay scattered on the cold ground, and then gazed up at Gozath.

"You are dead," the demon whispered, but Bechten did not yet believe it. He took a step forward, slipped on his own organs and fell onto the snow-covered rock with a sickening thud. Gozath straddled the body, reached down, and violently tore out the man's throat. Blood gushed in great gouts, running in great rivers along the rock, and turning the snow into a deep-red slush.

Ulien set his jaw and forced himself to rise. Everything hurt, but still he charged—or tried to.

Gozath heard the movement and shuffled to the left just as Ulien stumbled forward. The Protector went sprawling, slipping in the mess of organs that had been Bechten. He roared with fury and spun away, his sword clutched in his remaining hand. His right hand was a melted scab of twisted flesh—small filaments of tendon and vein dangled from the charred stub. The stump still steamed in the cold air, a cloying, sickly odor wafted up from the charred limb and mixed with the fetidness of the mangled corpses littered along the rocks.

Forcing the pain away and trying to focus on the need to destroy the demon, he cursed, and pushed his body into a dead sprint.

The demon let him approach, let the sword come within a hairsbreadth of slicing him open, let Ulien think for a bare moment that he could succeed. In a space of time no longer than it takes a fly's wings to touch, Gozath seemed to *explode* away from Ulien, in a spray of blood-soaked snow. He stood a pace away, his long arms gyrating wildly and spittle running of his face in pestilent streams of rapid-freezing moisture. He muttered in his ocean-bottom voice, "I am Gozath, ruler of the—"

Ulien roared and bounded a forward. Gozath's arms seemed to lengthen inexplicably, stretching outward—away from the sharp edge of the sword—like ropes pulled by a wind. Blackened hands reached out for the sword hilt, encircling Ulien's good hand in their cold, dead grip. The Protector shivered violently as Gozath squeezed. Harder. Harder. Bones crunched and Ulien howled in agony. Gozath squeezed until the entire hand burst in a steamy red and white gelatinous cloud. As the sword fell, Gozath snatched in mid-air, and in one swift motion, sliced Ulien's head away from his body.

Gozath—once known as Untrel—tipped his head back and bayed to the cold sky, crying out in pure ecstasy. Though his hands were bloodied and blackened, he delighted in his victory. As his gaze returned to the gore-splattered ground in front of him, his cracked and bloody lips curled back in a broad smile.

He feasted furiously until his distended stomach burst over with excess. Exhausted, he fell back on the bloody snow and closed his eyes.

A mulargh flew overhead, screeching. He heard the cry and groaned.

"North," he whispered, his voice broken. "My glory lies in the north. I must go north. Farther north." After an hour of walking over the desolate countryside, he started repeating his litany, "Gozath, ruler of the swirling depths. Gozath, ruler of the swirling depths. Gozath, ruler..."

Chapter 24

The Tea and the Leaf

Can you un-bake bread? Can you put the river back into the spring? Once you have steeped your tea, can you put it back into the leaf? Many things that are done, are done with permanency.

Prophet Altyu-M'Zhkara, IV Age

I awoke with a dull roar in my head and a cold wind in my ear. The fire had long since gone to gray ash, and in my fury, I had flung open a window, neglecting to close it as the pain had washed over me. Carefully, I raised my throbbing head and pulled myself to a sitting position, cradling the tender extremity between my hands. My temples throbbed and were hot to the touch. What had she done to me?

As I tried to open my eyes and focus on something, my eye caught the teapot that had rolled to a stop before the soot-covered hearth. Tea would be good for the pounding headache. A nice green tea from far back in the cupboards— the one that looked like it was imported from somewhere beyond the seas. No foreign ship had ever docked in any harbor as far as I—well, as far as Ar'Zoth knew, but that isn't to say someone could not import—

Wait! Tea! Why was I prattling on about tea? With my head pounding, all I could think of was the nice soothing liquid as it sidled down my throat and warmed my spine. But that could wait. Before she had left me writhing in pain, I had almost figured out a possible way to keep her out of my brain. The tea and the leaf. She had seeped into my consciousness like a vile and rotten brew, and there was seemingly no way to get her back into the leaf.

Maybe some tea would help me think through the problem. I stood, wobbly, and strolled unsteadily to the kitchens. The rare tea was buried deep, but I was able to reach back and extract the package. Returning to the living area, I started a fire and filled the teapot with snow from the rampart. I was too worn down to let the fire go to coals, and I simply hung the pot on the hook over the flames and smoke. Perhaps the wood smoke would add a distinctive flavor to the tea. With a curse, I realized I had smashed too many cups, and so another exhausting trip to the kitchens was in order. By the time I returned, the water was boiling.

I threw some leaves into the water, waited the requisite three minutes, poured a cup, and stared into the greenish-brown liquid, hoping for some inspiration.

Only flecks of tea leaf greeted me, some floated lazily to the top, while others hung waterlogged on the bottom of the cup, snug in their near-boiling grave.

"How to get the tea back into the leaf?" I wondered, carefully tipping the cup to my lips. As the hot liquid penetrated my throat, I could feel the pressure abate inside my skull. Instinctively, however, I tensed as the pain lessened. It seemed that each time I felt any type of relief, she would arrive and spin me to the floor. There would be very little time before she returned, I knew, and so it was imperative to figure out how to keep her out of my skull forever!

The tea into the leaf.

How? The question seemed so simple, but the more I thought, the more it remained a mystery. There had to be a way! I had been able to work my way out of impossible situations before—the missing half of the staircase was a reminder of that fact—but something as simple as tea should be no challenge.

Except it wasn't tea. It was my mother! Perhaps there would be a way to—

Hello, Bimb.

I screamed aloud. The teacup fell to the floor, and the expensive liquid oozed onto the carpet. Again, something seemed to clench my stomach and I grimaced. "What do you want now, Mother?"

Having tea? she asked, ignoring my question. *That is nice. I was talking to your friends. They are getting closer.*

"My friends? You mean your friends. It doesn't matter how close they get, does it? There are no stairs, woman! The only way through is over the Spires, and I've blocked the back entrance. If they want to be human flies, they can try to climb up and over the far ravine. But I will surely see them if they tried—"

You will do nothing! she screamed.

"I will do everything, everything—" My protest was choked off as an unseen hand felt as if it were tearing into my midsection. My bowels felt as if someone had pulled them loose, and something warm and sticky ran out from between my—*No!* "No, you did not just make me do that, you vile bitch!" Spittle flew across the room and hissed against the now-roaring hearth. Against the twisting and gripping pain in my stomach, I lurched out to the ramparts to where the chamber pot was stored.

I would need a new outfit.

And Mother would need to die forever.

I am already dead, son.

I growled. "Lyn is gone, the other two companions of his are gone. Gone! And I thought you were too..."

Son—

"Stop calling me that, bitch! I'm not your son. I never was. You fucked the bottle and you got Bimb. Bimb is dead. And you will die too—forever. Whatever place you are in—it is not death. Death is final."

Silence. She was crying, surely. *No, death is not entirely permanent*, she said after a few moments. *I will go on to the final resting place, but not before I see them stop you.*

I padded into the castle and retrieved a new pair of trousers. "And I will get your vile tea back into the leaf and I will destroy your friends the second they take one step toward this castle! I have a horde to control, and you keep interfering with my work!" I was furious. Embarrassed, cold, and quickly reaching the frayed end of my so-called wits. This had to end.

I thought I heard her growl, but that was beneath her— no, it wasn't. It wasn't beneath a bitch to growl. Her anger was a sheet of flame inside my stomach, a boiling river of lead in my veins, and a howling blizzard of broken glass in my skull. I tried to take another step forward, but my legs gave out and I fell to the floor. With a focus of will, I tried to keep my eyes open, to somehow fend off the consuming blackness slowly dropping over my eyes. But I could hold on no longer—she was squeezing tighter and tighter.

"The tea in the..." The thought faded as I slipped away.

φ

"There are spaces between everything," Ar'Zoth *was saying. The image was distorted, but he stood before a room full of students, gesturing with a long wooden rod. "Inside of these spaces are the building blocks of everything. Everything! When you look in water, you see only water. But a trained eye can see the particles of lead, iron, and other minerals. Metals! Small pieces of metal floating in water. And even deeper,* between *the spaces between, you can find the waves and particles that make up everything. You can pull them out, play with them—but be careful! As small as some of the particles are, they make up everything, and as such, can be very powerful. In the event..."*

I awoke with a start. Every muscle in my body seemed to have fallen asleep, and my stomach still ached. The dream about Ar'Zoth was one of many I had been having of late. Perhaps it was his way of visiting me after his death; at least he did not torture me and punish me for nothing. What had he been talking about? I wondered as I straightened myself and sat with my back to a stone wall. Spaces and particles, ever the same lecture time and again. But a phrase he had said countless times struck me.

"You can pull them out, play with them."

Pull them out and play with them!

....Pull them out!

Did that mean I could somehow put the tea back in the leaf? Particle by particle? It was worth a try.

I stood as fast as I could, then paused, listening for her voice. Nothing. Maybe she was off screwing some famous dead person.

With a trembling hand, I grabbed a handful of tea leaves and threw them into the lukewarm water in the kettle. Then I started looking for the spaces and the particles, not looking for anything that would create destruction, but investigating what was there... could anything be deep inside which could help me. Indeed, in the spaces in the water and the leaves, there were tiny particles; solid matter floated in the liquid—Ar'Zoth had taught me well. With painstaking effort, I pulled a tiny piece out of the water and attached it back to the leaf. But soon the particles were drawn out again by the water. I stared for some time, my chin in my hands, before I realized what had to be done.

It was like organizing sand. I would push the water particles to one side, and the tea particles to another, but they would easily flow back together. Upon closer inspection, I could see that even the water particles were made up of other particles... what looked like two little pieces attached to a third—and down and down the building blocks went. I dared not go too far. Carefully, I removed the two pieces of the water particle, and—

The explosion blew me back over the chair, singed my eyebrows and blinded me. I could smell burning fabric and scorched hair. While the room, and indeed the entire Keep, were still intact, I felt a distinct rumble. The very ground seemed to heave upward, shake, and then settle down. I rubbed my eyes furiously until the spots, speckles, and streaks of violet light abated and finally resolved themselves into the hearth and the couch. Cracks became visible along the far wall—very small, but still there. Another shock shuddered through the large castle, but not as intense. I waited for a few moments before I was sure there were no other effects.

Finally, I rose to my feet and began picking apart the pieces of the fire and setting them into the hearth. Pieces of fabric burned and I hurriedly stomped out any smoldering ruins. Ar'Zoth was serious when he had warned me to be careful. Separating pieces of water was not going to make this work—whatever small particles were present in water were powerful enough to destroy everything. Maybe I could use them against her so-called companions? No, the sofa was a charred hulk, and a huge black circle marred the otherwise pristine red carpet—and who knows what that rumbling was. Perhaps a mountain had fallen down somewhere. That kind of power was much too much to handle.

But did it have to be handled?

Did I really have to finish this experiment with the tea? No, all I needed to do was figure out a way to pull my mother apart into little pieces and then stuff her into eternity. Or pull her out of my head and toss her into the fire.

But now I needed a new couch, or at least something to cover up the charred frame. There were thick blankets in a side room, and I tossed them unceremoniously over the sofa, grimacing as clouds of char plumed up into the air. It would have to do. One did not need to waste time on covering furniture when the demonic horde waited and a vile, dead mother was bent on destroying me!

There was an uncomfortable silence, and then a brief— what would I call it? A gust of wind? Not entirely a breeze, but something in my head that clued me into the fact that she was coming.

Hello, Bimb.

"Hello, Mother," I replied as placidly as I could.

What—what are you doing? She sounded worried. My voice was cold.

"I'm putting the tea back into the leaf."

How, what...? This would be difficult. I could *see* the particles in the water, but I could not see anything here! I knew they were there—I could hear her voice, I could sense certain things, but not what I wanted to. The utter lack of any visual reference was maddening. But there was no time; it would not be long before she threw me down onto the ground... If she could grab me, I could grab her. Blindly, I fumbled in the dark void, seeking her voice. *What are you talking about, Bimb?*

There! I had it! Just one little tug here, and then... Yes over here is a particle—

"What, Mother?" I needed her to say something, or I would lose her. Her voice was an anchor.

Bimb, I—

She cried as I pulled the particles out of her voice box and put them into the hearth—into a little urn that sat there. I then pulled apart as much of her as I could and stored it in different locations.

This would not be a permanent solution—dealing with the dead was not dealing with a teapot—but at least I could keep her out of my mind for a short time while I attended to the horde.

Even as I returned my focus to the demonic host, I could sense her trying to pull herself back together again—the spirit world was an utter mystery to me; it wasn't ordered and spaced properly like the building blocks of everything else. It was utter chaos. It flowed and ebbed, came and went, seemingly rudderless.

The demons were loud and grating. To anyone else it would have sounded like gibberish, like the religious zealots who would stand at the Temple altar and spew nonsense from their lips. But to me, it was crystal clear, and it was overwhelming. They were closer, ever closer. One cacophonous, deafening roar—the mix between a prayer and an incantation thundered through my head: *Out, let us out, out we seek the light. Light sweet, dark is death; dark is dying—we are dying! Out, out, to the light, the light, sweet light, to rend and feast and tear and grab and pinch and bite and suck on the sweet human flesh—human flesh, human flesh, so sweet, so nice, so—*

"Stop!" I screamed. The voices were suddenly muted, but they were still there. And farther back in the wall of sound I could hear her putting herself together. I needed to hurry.

But what was I going to do?

Perhaps I should have thought of that before I pulled her apart.

Chapter 25
To Eat a Tree

Ꮸ

We must survive on things other than meat, grains, and fish. The land provides for us a bountiful harvest of berries, leaves, shoots, and roots, which can sustain us in emergency. Learn these well: You do not know when you will be stranded.

From the Knights of the Black Dawn training manual

The blizzard had slackened considerably, leaving Orfel to wonder if the demon had something to do with the weather. But he didn't have time to worry about any of that—his focus was on the dull outline of the Crown Road, and his throbbing ankle. With all the commotion at the reversal, he was unsure which direction he was going. And, although the snow had eased its intensity, the sun was still hidden beneath a thick bank of clouds. He was hungry. His ankle throbbed.

After a long and excruciating mile, he veered off the road and stumbled in the deep snow. The blizzard had ceased, but snow still fell in the crisp air, and he didn't want to chance getting caught in another whiteout. Just feet from the road, a large boulder hunkered against the winter, its eastern side nearly clear of snow. Two spindly pine trees had found purchase in the rock, most likely starting as seedlings within a crevasse, now their roots burrowed deep into the solid stone. Nearby, a much larger white pine stretched high into the snow-filled air, its long branches providing a welcome protection from the snow. Even with the huge snowfall from the blizzard, the area under the pine was fairly clean and covered with brown needles. Orfel sat with a sigh and leaned against the rock.

He was beyond hungry. His stomach growled and rumbled. A mouthful of snow from the rock face only seemed to make him thirstier, and he grimaced. Having left in such a hurry, he had forgotten to pack any type of nourishment. Normally a careful and well-prepared person, his drive to find the boys had overtaken his usual rational thinking. And so he was stranded in the far north with nothing to eat. There may be deer and smaller animals in this area, but he'd made such noise in getting to this spot, it would be hours before any would chance by.

During his training, he had read several books and texts that dealt with surviving on edible wild plants, but unfortunately, many of those were written for every season *except* winter. The winter survival guides never seemed to mention food—as if assuming that one would have the foresight to have something on hand. But there had been one book that provided at least a couple of options, although neither would be appetizing or easy on the stomach.

Still, he would die if he did not make an attempt to save himself. He pushed himself away from the rock and then hoisted himself to his knees, scanning the surface with a deep scrutiny.

There. It looks very appealing, he thought bitterly. He swept more snow away from the rock to reveal a think, fuzzy moss that covered the gray surface. It was Reindeer Moss, and while somewhat slimy and gelatinous, it would certainly serve as sustenance in an emergency. Which this was. He pulled a handful off the rock, added some snow to it, and started chewing. The thick moss nearly jolted back up his throat, but he forced more down and clamped his jaw shut.

The inner bark of the pine would be another starchy option. He wasn't sure his stomach could digest any of it, but the moss was starting to stick to the roof of his mouth, and each time he flicked his tongue to chew on it, the flavors of rot and decay filled his mouth. He had to press a hand under his chin to keep himself from vomiting. With another groan and protest from his ankle, he rose and stumbled to the pine tree. He extracted his knife and peeled away the outer bark, and then carefully sliced slivers from the interior. While he loved the scent of pine and the taste of piñons in the spring, the bark was stringy and downright foul. Still, he forced himself to eat until his belly was partially full. The starch would need to sustain him a little longer.

In all of his training, he never thought he would have to eat a tree.

φ

He skied for several days, camping at night in makeshift snow houses and surviving on moss and some berries he found buried in the snow.

When he arrived at a collection of huts, he decided he would have to make a difficult decision. Those who lived this far north would surely have put away plenty food stores, but only in amounts necessary to feed their own families. It was doubtful that anyone would have food to spare a wandering Knight of the Black Dawn. But he would have to try.

No one answered the knock at the first hut, nor at the second. But the third door opened slowly to reveal a bearded man wrapped in a wolf's pelt. His face was round and his skin strangely dark for this time of year. A pudgy nose sat awkwardly on his puffy face, and he seemed to have no facial expressions—his eyes were dull and his lips set in a straight line.

"Yes?" If he was concerned over Orfel's sword, he paid no mind. The skis, propped up in the snow, likewise garnered little reaction.

"Greetings. I am a representative of the Holy Orders—" at that there was a very light raising of an eyebrow, which quickly returned to its usual state—"and I am in desperate need of food. I had a run-in with a... shady character who found it necessary to steal all of my food. I've been living on moss and tree bark."

The man stared, his eyes nearly glassy. *Maybe he sits and drinks Zor'Tarak all winter*, Orfel thought. He nearly turned away when a husky voice answered him. "I don't have much to spare, but you may have some. If I give too much, I may not..."

"I understand. I would not take more than necessary. In fact, I have to go north for only a short time, and then I will be able to return and bring supplies with me." That last bit was nearly a lie, but Orfel intended to fill a large pack or two, perhaps a sled, once he had dealt with the boys. If it meant a return to Vronga, and then another ski back here, he would do it. That was assuming that he would return alive.

"Is that so?"

Orfel nodded. "As long as you had your supplies within two weeks—three at the most, would you be able to spare a little more?"

"How much can you carry?" That at least was a partial yes. Orfel wanted to jump with excitement.

"I can carry a lot in this large pack, but even more if I had a sled."

"A sled I can't afford to give you," the man replied. "But I have salt pork, dried rabbit, jars of beans, and even a little tea. Wait here."

The door closed and Orfel was left to ponder the ragged grooves in the dried-out structure. After a few moments, he thought the man had left him to freeze, but the door opened after a while. The man beckoned him inside and he followed into the gloom.

Inside, the hut was almost completely dark, except for dull filtered light from an unseen window or opening. It was cold, but the smell of wood smoke clung to everything—no doubt a fire would be roaring once the sun descended. In one corner was a bed, and in another a small table, piled with wrapped bundles and a couple of jars.

"There you are," the man said quietly.

Orfel thanked him profusely and packed his bag with the goods. He would normally offer money, but a coin would not feed this man.

"Be sure to return, as you promised."

"I will at that, I will," Orfel said, extending his hand. The stranger gripped it fiercely and then returned to his hovel.

Orfel strapped on his skis and shouldered the pack. His stomach still felt flat and empty, and the very thought of a hunk of salt pork set his mouth watering. But he still had many miles to go, and the sun would soon be gone. As he climbed ever northward, the hours of sunlight would be less and less, until the entire day would be dark. He had to be quick.

There was no time.

As he skied, he thought back upon the man's hovel, and the strange collection of bundles and jars. No doubt much was food, but a small handle had poked out from one of the bags, and to anyone else, it would look like an ordinary stick. But Orfel recognized it—they had such an artifact in the Knights' headquarters. It was a rod for summoning creatures from the underworld. Demons. Orfel spat.

Orfel should have cut him down in his home, but he had greater problems to attend to. And, seeing the rod gave him other ideas, mainly about the boys. He remembered a lesson from his education as a Knight—it was obscure and most likely meaningless, but the teacher had said that laymen used such rods, often with no outcome. A warlock, however, would be able to call forth any number of demons using such a device. As such, any knight was instructed to confiscate and destroy such a device.

Times had changed, and Orfel had less concern over a simple man trying to summon demons—*he probably only does so to ask for more food, or strength to survive the winter.*

No, what caught in Orfel's mind was the word "warlock." The innkeeper had mentioned that the boys were going north, but insisted they were not going to the Temple. But what if... What if they were going there? There, as in the obscure area north and west of Gray Gorge? Orfel had only heard of it when he had been listening in on a conversation between Dran'Za and another man, many years ago, when the obese leader only had one chin. The consensus was that there was a large castle in that area, inhabited some a recluse warlock, either drained of power, carefully warded, or simply in retirement. No one could ever trace any malice or evil deeds to the place, and so it was forgotten.

But what if the boys had found out the warlock was there? What if they had such a rod and wanted instruction on how to use it? Or had they already caused the release of all the demons and were trying to get to the warlock for help? No, in a time like this, with everyone having gone insane as a collective society, demons loose and more powerful than ever, and secluded northern men with the summoning rods, the chances that the boys were innocent were less than zero.

Chapter 26
Strange Voices

There is so much that you can hear, if you only open your ears and close off the rush of daily thoughts. Birds, trees, leaves, and grass whistling in the wind. All of this is missed with our mind's constant rattling.

Cleric Archean, Order of the Knot

The voices of the underworld were loud this morning. I dared only to listen passively at their murmuring. If I answered them, she would surely hear me. And so I lay on the long couch with my head cradled in my arm and stared at the fire. The flames were muted and licked lazily over a single remaining log—if I didn't add more fuel soon, it would go out. But I didn't care. I lay there listening to the horde with my eyes half closed.

That will be excellent, yes, I am on my way.

I started at the voice. Was I dreaming or still awake? Who had said that?

"Who's there?" I asked.

Silence. Strange, that. I rose and added a log to the fire. After a few minutes, I hung a kettle over the fire and waited patiently for the water to boil. She was going to visit me again, I knew, but the moments of respite seemed to be growing longer. How long would that last? I was able to pull her apart—to put the leaf back into the tea—but I could feel she had already put herself back together. That was the danger when dealing with the dead; they could be slippery and conniving.

Perhaps I could just keep tearing her apart and putting her in different places; that would gain some time for me to work with the horde. But that was only a temporary solution, and I did not have the energy to waste on such diversions.

I'm trying to reach you, but you are not there... Another strange voice faded into the distance. Or was that the same one? What was happening beneath the miles of stone? I was sure the demons were much closer to the surface now, and they needed me. I stood to retrieve the kettle when a litany of voices, one atop the other, whirred through my head.

> *There is a place—*
> *Coming to see them—no, that won't work—*
> *Yes, you must come here I need you—*
> *Don't waste more—never—it is beyond—*
> *Gray—dying—failing in the light—*
> *Failing in the—*

"Enough!" I roared. Forgetting the tea, I leapt to my feet and burst out onto the ramparts. Snow stung my face but I ignored it and plowed forward to the courtyard. I hadn't bothered to don a coat, and the cold soon dug into my skin. Yet the voices hummed in their strange chorus, and I could not help but fall to the snow-covered stone and press an ear to the icy rock.

The voices continued, and I realized with a sudden revelation that they could easily be used to subdue her.

How is that?

"No!" I screamed.

The hand started to tighten, but I quickly reached out to try to pull her down into the voices. It worked. But for how long would it work? Slowly, slowly, I could feel her start to sink into the undulating throng, and with it a slight gurgling. Perhaps she could drown!

It was all I could hope for.

Chapter 27
"Holy" Orders

.... And we shall have the authority to declare war on any entity we deem to be a threat to the Light, to our Order, to any Holy Elder, or Cleric, or the teachings we hold as self-evident. Our enemies will die once by our Holy hands, but will burn eternally in a lake of molten fire.

High Cleric Hael'Morsha, II Age

He liked to think of himself as the High Cleric of *all* Holy Orders, though the philosophies of the more popular Order of the Knot had by now been absorbed into the catechism and adopted by nearly every Elder from the smallest hovel to Belden City. And that "only" two hundred years ago or so. He, High Cleric Gorand IV, was going to hold to the old ways, even if they were gathering dust on the minds of men.

Sighing, he opened the envelope from Jafren. It wasn't often the High Cleric received missives from the Grand Counsel Guard. Then again, he had heard the rumors of demons, but surely the Pillars were safe and the excitement was just that. Worry and fear over something the populace deserved.

The pillars. No, the Pillars, he thought, *the name must be honored.*

And Jafren threatened everything by claiming that the Temple was in the wrong place! The Temple of M'Hzrut was in the right place, always. In the middle of Welcfer, the breeding pit of all demons; every last one, he was convinced, had come from Welcfer.

Filth, he thought. *A vast pit of filth. What demonic leader is up there, in his skin-covered hut, breeding more demons.*

Gorand shook his head, trying to clear it. *Jafren, you err, and poorly. No, the Temple stands, we are not in danger from demons.* "We are in danger from ourselves, from our own sin! Sin!" This last he screamed.

The secretary popped in, brushing down his uniform.

"I'm fine, I'm fine," Gorand snapped, waving the boy away. A briny smell wafted into the room. *Is he at the olives again?*

The High Cleric read the letter again.

"You dare question the location of the Temple? You dare question my Holy Protectors? You dare *ask* for help from those who protect people from sin. You are a fool."

He pushed the letter aside.

"Fool." Gorand took a sip from his leaded cup. "And you are damned."

Chapter 28
A Bottle

A bottle can be a river. When filled with milk and given to a babe, it is a river of sustenance. When filled with brandy and given to a man, it can be a river to damnation.

High Cleric Gorand

They had made it through Gray Gorge, through the dark tunnel, and a half-dozen miles along the winding path that led to Ar'Zoth. Exhaustion settled quickly in their tired limbs, as the sun faded over the western ridges.

Yulchar threw a blanket down on the snow. He and Zhy sat with their backs against the steep incline along the trail. It felt good to sit. Leaning back his head, Zhy took a deep breath and exhaled in a cloud of warm steam. Yulchar rustled in his large pack and extracted something with a sigh. Zhy's eyes remained closed, but a familiar pop—*was it familiar?*—echoed in the small valley.

"Would you like some of this?" Yulchar asked.

His eyes fluttered open. The knight sat there, a bottle of some sort in his right hand, the small cork pinched between the fingers of his left. When the man glanced at the bottle, it was as if he were regarding a most beautiful woman. There was no label on the bottle.

"What is it?" Zhy asked.

Instead of answering, Yulchar brought the bottle slowly to his lips and tipped it back. Zhy could see a faint stream of reddish liquid trickle out of the bottle. The knight swallowed, and proffered the drink to Zhy. A look of ecstasy crossed Yulchar's face as he held out the spirit.

Zhy reached out with a shaking hand and took the bottle. *You don't want to do that*, he thought he heard a voice say, but it sounded much like his own. Why? What would the harm be? He'd never had anything like this before, had he? *You have had more than you can possibly bear*, the voice replied. If it was his voice, why was it talking like that?

Yulchar eyed the container hungrily, but Zhy held it steady. "It is a type of brandy. Thick, almost like syrup, especially in the cold. Normally it is a very dangerous brandy, but we have been exposed to the cold for long enough that I'm sure it can't do any harm. Zor'Tarak, they call it. Though I've heard it called darkdreams before as well."

Zhy knew what brandy was, didn't he? A memory of a dung heap leapt to the fore, and he nearly gagged. "I-I don't think I can, I'm sorry. I seem to remember that I had a problem with that at one time."

"Well..." Yulchar said, reaching slowly for the bottle. "If you don't mind?" Zhy shook his head slightly. The knight took another large drink, then surprisingly, he handed the bottle back to Zhy, but Zhy shook his head and put his hands on his knees.

"I thought the Knights didn't drink any spirits?" Zhy asked.

"Where would you have gotten that impression?"

Where, indeed? "Well, since you are from a Holy Order..."

Yulchar laughed. "No, no."

"You are not of a Holy—?"

"Oh, yes, yes," he coughed. "We are, but I mean, no, there are no restrictions on drinking. Within reason, anyway." He looked at Zhy with an eyebrow cocked.

"Sorry, I didn't know."

"It's no bother," Yulchar replied and again proffered the bottle.

Zhy shook his head. *Is he trying to get me drunk?*

Drunk. *Drunk!* That word sparked something. The image of a dung heap flashed again, but then others came with it, each alternating with the other. Horror against comfort. Pain against pleasure. There were visions of long and pleasant conversations into the night, a view of a man falling headlong down a flight of stairs, the taste of cold ale on a hot day, vomit streaming from a distended stomach, replete with rivulets of blood, a beautiful woman opening her legs, a toothless hag smiling at him in the morning, red wine at sunset, and maggots crawling over the mouth of a bottle he had just tipped his lips to. "No!" he screamed, waving his hands violently, forcing the images away.

Yulchar stared. "Maybe you shouldn't have this stuff."

Zhy looked at the bottle dumbly. And again, images flashed, each one conflicting with the next. He reached a hand out, but something seemed to push his arm down. *What in Sacuan's name...?* He reached out again, and again, his arm felt as if a weight were attached to it. Finally, he forced his arm upward and snatched the bottle, careful not to spill any of the liquid.

Images spun faster, colliding and contradicting, whirling and bending. He nearly lurched forward, but was able to plant a foot on the ground. His hand was white from gripping the bottle. With an effort, he raised it to his lips and let the liquid slide down his throat.

The sensation was like none other—or was it a much too familiar feeling? A warm, thick liquid oozed down into his stomach; he felt almost as if his insides were burning. He suddenly felt as if spiders were crawling back up his spine, along the back of his neck, and into his head. A low hum started in his ears, and his vision became dull. Once-white snow was gray, and the sky above a dark purple where it had once been bright blue. A numbness descended to his legs, and he feared he would not be able to stand up. But this fear was quickly replaced by a wave if giddiness and fulfillment that he had never felt (or had he felt it before? He wasn't sure). His head lolled and he handed the bottle back to Yulchar, but with effort—he stared after it with a sort of lust. It would please him to no end if he could just tip the bottle back and drain the entire thing. And then drink more. And more, and more!

Suddenly, he tipped over sideways onto the snow. A small hand seemed to reach up from his insides and grab the bottom of his tongue. It squeezed slightly, and he found himself vomiting noisily onto the snow, thankfully away from the blanket. He rolled back, away from the vomit, and lay face-up, his mind blank.

He was vaguely aware of voices and sounds near him, but he could only stare at the purple sky and hope he did not sick up any more. Why was the sky purple? What were those white things floating by? They seemed to wobble and shimmer, and he had to close his eyes.

Eventually the sky stopped moving and resolved back into a dull blue. He tried to stand, but his legs gave out and he collapsed again. Someone grabbed him underneath his arm and pulled him violently to his feet, and he swayed.

"Why did you let him drink it?" a gruff voice barked.

"I thought—I thought he could handle it!"

"Ach, you have no idea!" the man snapped. *Huyen*, Zhy thought dully, *the man's name is Huyen. He's mean. Yulchar is the other one... but what is* my *name?*

"What do you mean?"

"For Sacuan's sake, Yulchar!" the man spat. "Don't you know this man was a drunk before, a raving, bottle-a-day drunk? You just opened the floodgates, and I'm not sure we can get him back. She said we needed him! As much as I detest the man, we need him to battle Ar'Zoth. What have you done?" The last was merely a whisper.

"I-I only wanted to offer him a little. I did not realize, did not know..."

"You knew! Of course you knew! Did you not see his house in Belden? Was that not enough for you? You, who won't act without seventeen different varieties of proof, you give a bottle of Zor'Tarak to a raving drunk?"

"He was dead before, I thought—"

"No, Yulchar, once a drunk, always a drunk! You can't give a man like that a drink, *especially* Zor'Tarak, for Sacuan's sake! What were you thinking?"

"I—I guess I did not, I am sorry. I honestly thought it would not be as deadly, seeing as he was dead, and given the cold."

Huyen sighed. "Well now you know."

"Now I know," the knight said softly.

"I..." Zhy started, but clamped his mouth shut as his hackles rose. He swayed a few seconds, then spoke again. "I think I'm going to be all right. I—" The world spun again and went black.

Chapter 29
Into the Void Once More

Should you decide to stick your head into the mouth of a wild beast, I trust you have good reason. Should you do so again, I trust you are insane.

Prophet Z'Hara

"What do you want me to do, drag him along on the ground? I could bundle him in the blanket and pull him with my skis."

Zhy heard their voices through a dense fog, as if they were miles away. His head throbbed and his eyes burned, and he wanted to open them, but he could feel the sunlight through his lids and kept them closed.

"No, no, we should wait for him to wake up."

"We cannot! We have wasted enough time already with this!"

"It has only been an hour... How much did he have?"

"Not much."

"How can only a small amount possibly—"

Zhy groaned and then forced his eyes open. "I'm better now," he said hoarsely.

"You do not look it," Huyen snapped. He shot an angry glance to Yulchar.

"I—No, really, I'll be fine. I'm sorry," he added hastily. Rising to his feet was a chore, but once he stood, he found he didn't wobble or sway. His head throbbed slightly, and he had a vile taste in his mouth, but otherwise, he felt refreshed.

"No, it is I who am sorry," Yulchar replied softly. "I did not know that—I—" he stammered. "I should not have given you that drink. I apologize."

Zhy shook his head sadly. "No, you are not to blame. There are things in my past I should've known would not go away. Even with death." *Even when I'm dead, I will not be free from it,* he thought bitterly. His grand visions of the afterlife—rooms of bottles and plates of food—endless drinking and carousing. None of that would come to pass. Eternal torture had little appeal. He nearly threw up again, but his stomach was empty.

"I should have known better."

Huyen sighed loudly. "Are we done with our pity party? Good. I have inspected the opening. No traps that I can see—they must have been tripped already. There's nothing in there, though. Hopefully we don't fall into a bottomless hole, or walk around in the dark forever." He said everything in a complete monotone and then briskly walked toward the black opening.

"The tunnel opens into the valley," Zhy said. *How did I know that?*

"Good," Yulchar said over his shoulder. "Come on then. Bring all the gear. We'll need the skis on the other side."

φ

With Huyen in the lead once more, Zhy followed behind Yulchar and stepped into the pit of black. He had done this before, but a second pass through did not make it any less disconcerting. A quick look behind him showed nothing, and there was no indication that two men walked ahead of him. He could hear the man muttering in the darkness, but the knight's voice sounded disconnected and faint. Zhy wanted to offer a kind word, but their next steps took them back into the blinding, snow-covered landscape.

Zhy looked out over the familiar landscape with sadness. The vast cavern ahead, the sheer rise of stoic pines, and the thick and comforting blanket of snow, should've provided a sense of calm and awe. It had awed him before, but now everything seemed gray and dull. His stomach felt as if something were slowly turning it into a knot. But the overwhelming emotion was no longer fear—it was a crushing sadness. *Bruce, Darrell...* When he looked along the trail, he swore he could still see the indentations of their footprints, although they would have been long since buried by snow. There had been a snowstorm, hadn't there? Images flickered before him: The burly warrior bounding through the snow, searching for something, and the small-man furiously trying to keep himself from being buried. There had definitely been a blizzard. And his throat caught as he realized that those men lay crushed at the bottom of the valley.

The clack and rattle of skis falling to the snow shook Zhy from his reverie. Huyen grunted and tossed the skis unceremoniously atop the snow. "We had better hurry," was all he said. Indeed, the shadows were lengthening quickly, and the once-bright light, even muted by thick clouds, was fading.

After Zhy strapped his boots into his skis and straightened, he looked to his left. He had not noticed the large clearing before. "I missed that before," he said, using a ski pole to point at the fallen trees.

"What?" Yulchar asked.

"That area there... It would've made a good shelter in a storm."

"We need to move north," Huyen said flatly. He was already skiing ahead along the narrow trail.

"Huyen..." Zhy began, but followed glumly. Their skis were going to become useless very soon, but Zhy let him ski forward. He remembered walking along a path no wider than a pair of boots, and this path did not stretch nicely through flat balsam-covered ground. A misstep meant death. Skis would be too unwieldy.

The path along the valley was familiar. The cave was familiar, though much colder with Huyen instead of Bruce, Yulchar instead of Darrell. Sleep was hard to find, and worse to experience.

Chapter 30
Unwanted Answers

We often ask questions, but we refuse to accept the answers. If you do not want to know the truth, do not ask the question. But take solace in your ignorance now, for later it may doom you.

Cleric Hrozon

Zhy awoke with a start. His nose felt like a block of ice. The Tunnels had been warm, if not cramped and damp. But the cave offered only a small respite from the cold and the wind. All that remained of their fire was a small, glowing chunk of charcoal, a small orange-red flicker. He pushed his face down into his pillow and tried to return to sleep; he had taken one small step over the precipice between the waking world and dreamless oblivion, when her voice shook him. He wasn't sure if he was still awake or if he had fallen into sleep when she spoke.

Hello, Zhy.

"Am I awake?" His voice sounded detached and hollow.

You always ask me that, but each time it is the same. No, you are not awake. I may soon be able to reach you when you are awake, but not yet.

"What do you mean?"

Silence.

"Cerease?"

I'm here. Are you getting closer?

"Yes, why can't you see me?"

Something is happening. He is trying to get rid of me, and he sometimes succeeds.

"Gets... rid of you... How?"

It is hard to explain, but he is trying to send me to the final death, the final place. He can't quite get it worked out, but he has come close. I recently had to put myself back together again—he'd pulled me apart.

"Pulled you apart how?"

He thought he heard a laugh. *Well, when you're dead, a few things are quite different, obviously. Somehow, he got ahold of me and put little pieces of me all over the castle...but once I realized that was no more than a strange dream, and not reality, I got myself back together again.*

"How...?"

I wish that you were dreaming. That act of his was harmless... If he can figure out how to send me to the final death, we are doomed. You are doomed. You need to get here as soon as you can. I wish this was over. My son is evil—evil beyond anything you can imagine. I am glad you are helping. There will be much more that you have to do.

"What can I possibly do? Yulchar and—"

They will do what they do, but you are the key, even if you do nothing.

"How can I be the key, if I do nothing?"

You will have to wait a little longer... Please stick with your companions and heed their advice. They are the experts.

"Experts in what?"

Do I have to answer that? He could sense the deep sigh. *Would you have survived without them?*

"No, I—" He stopped. There had been a previous journey, as well, where he would never have survived without the help of others. If he was so dependent on others for help, why was she trying to cast him as the hero?

Zhy, listen. Bimb has become more and more unstable. He wants to release the demons from the earth, and it is all I can do to stop him. I will not be able to hold him off much longer. Not only has he mastered magical arts, he has learned a few things about this world—this area between death and the great darkness. He will spit me out sooner than late. I would rather go on my own terms.

Suddenly, the voice was no longer tainted with the pleading, helpless whine that he had heard in it before. Now she sounded determined. There was a hint of desperation and fear. *How could the dead have any fear?* Zhy wondered, but those were small slivers compared to the grit and willpower he could sense from her. She had decided that her own son was a threat, and that he needed to die.

The steel had returned. *I have an idea of what you are thinking, but you do not understand.*

"I guess I don't," he snapped.

There was another sigh. *I don't do this lightly, Zhy. Sacrifice is difficult, especially when it is your own blood— but this blood has soured, has been overtaken by the demon Ar'Zoth, and we—you—must act. You will never see another sunset if you fail.*

"Because I'll be dead," he replied with a vein of sarcasm. "I'm already dead, so what does it matter?"

You are not *dead! I have taken you away from here, from the true death. Listen, Zhy, if we fail,* nobody *will see another sunset, Zhy.* Zhy sighed. The cliché was getting old. *If Bimb survives, everything will fall under the weight of the demonic horde. I've sensed it—I've seen it, Zhy, and it beyond what you could ever picture in your mind. Great armies of the underworld will destroy everyone.*

"But why?" That was a question long unanswered. What purpose did the demonic underworld have for destroying Belden and Welcfer?

There is no reason, Zhy. None. I have tried to seek it, but the only emotions that Bimb displays are hatred and a lust for destruction. They only want to destroy and consume.

"But how are these knights going to defeat Bimb?"

They will know what to do, and you will help them.

Zhy rolled his head on the pillow. "So far Yulchar is the only one who seems to have a care. Huyen would rather I die—I don't know why he stays with us."

He remains because he is dedicated to his Order, and he knows that without you, they fail. You will never hear it from him, perhaps, but it is the truth.

"And how would you know what Huyen thinks?"

I know from how you describe him... My husband, Fanlas, talked often of men tough and bitter, who never offer thanks or a kind word. But in the dark, they cry over lost animals and past pain. Men are weak...

Zhy suppressed a chuckle. She was right, as sad as it was... Men were weak, and he was the weakest. "If he— Huyen—succeeds, how am I to be sure he won't kill me?"

He won't. It is above his Order and his training to do so. He may leave you to your own devices, but he will not kill you... I would not worry about any of that, now, Zhy. Your focus should be on Bimb. And—another sigh—*on how to destroy him.*

Zhy let out a sigh of his own. "Cerease, you owe me an answer," he said, his mind quickly changing to a different subject. An icy draft of air burst through the small cave, and his tears froze to his face.

And what would that be?

"I want you to answer me, or I will not go any farther from this cave." He could almost feel her tense. But he had asked the question before, and the answer was less than satisfactory. No, it was not an answer. It was worse than no answer at all. He had to know. "Am I dreaming, or am I dead?"

You are neither dreaming nor dead, Zhyfrael. He tensed at the use of his full name. *Zhyfrael Lynnheard. Does that make you uncomfortable?*

"A little... yes. How did you know...?"

I just... know. If you find it difficult to hear your full name, then you will not want me to answer your question. Take comfort in the fact—

"No! No, I will not take comfort in ignorance! I need to know... As bad as it is, or as bad as you think it is for me to know, I need to know." He thought he sounded as if he were whining, a child looking for an escape, threating to sit down in the trail and cry until his daddy picked up him and carried him. That was not his intent. He wanted answers— not just information regarding Bimb.

She hesitated. *Zhy, the answer... The answer will trouble you.*

"Am I dead?"

You were dead—you were where I am, but I was able to bring you back. I had to take a few chances. It was my only chance. You were the only one who knew anything. Her voice was cold and hard.

"What was your only chance?"

Zhy, do not fear, nothing has transferred to you. You are clean.

"Transfer? What could—?" A flicker of a memory caught him, but he let her continue.

I needed to call on the help of others to move your body. And of a magic—the only type—that could push you back out into the world. I was too weak—and who knew where my body was? Perhaps underground already? No, I could not go back, but you could. You knew everything... everything. I'm sorry, but... other—creatures—that you may have an aversion to—helped me.

"What creatures—?" Before the words were out of his mouth, he knew. With a rising flood of bile in his throat, he knew. He turned his head to the side and dry-heaved. No. "No!"

Yes, Zhy, there was not a way to move your body back to Belden, where I knew it would be safe. Bimb had tried to wrench your soul from your body, as he did the others. But I caught it. He sensed something, I'm sure, but I caught it. Once he had let go, I put it back, but I had to send you home. There was no other way. There was no way I could let you wake up in a strange place and still leave you halfway coherent. In the snow and ice, you would have died within minutes, anyway, and you barely survived as it was...

"But..." His tongue was a thick wad of tissue, and it clung to the roof of his mouth. Words came out like tar. "But, how...?"

I needed a gherwza, vile creatures that they are. No other animal would let me in. But a gherwza easily accepted me, thinking that dead women can do no harm...

Zhy shivered.

You were carried gently back to your home in the night— the door was open, and I used the animal to drag you upstairs. After you were deposited, I flew the animal out across the Opal Sea and left it.

"But, if the animal had—"

Don't worry, nothing transferred, Zhy. There is nothing evil in you... nothing demonic. We all have our good sides and our bad sides, but you are clean. I assure you.

"I assure you." The shock was overwhelming. It was crushing and devastating. No matter her assurances, one never knew what strange magic demons possessed. Could something have transferred to him? If so, how would he know? Would he awake suddenly and find himself covered in the blood of Yulchar and Huyen? Or would he suddenly be able to cast magical spells? A demon—a demon had carried his body the thousand or more miles! A demon! He dry-heaved again, and his mind raced through a hundred different images of fire, death, pain, suffering, and dripping fangs. The cascade of horrific images overwhelmed him, and he finally fell completely off the precipice and into a dreamless sleep.

Chapter 31
A Bitter Road

We must live with our choices, however bitter the path that they set. Such is the consequence of working with the knots of mankind, and of living in this world. No decision creates an easy road.

Cleric Bertrand

*O**dd-looking rock in a hillside? That will not help me at all.***

He thought of returning to the Dawn's headquarters, but that seemed just as futile. If he saw Dran'Za again, he would surely murder him. A black wall of despair seemed to be falling upon him. Jafren, the Grand Counselor, stymied at every turn, every wall was made of solid rock, and every man was a blank slate of worthlessness.

There was a smaller inn down the street, and he watched idly as a few small-people entered it. He shrugged and followed, sloshing through the thick, dirty snow. He would give one last attempt at finding information. One more try. Jafren paid for his room and swiftly began diving into the brandy.

"Are ye sure ye would like another brandy, sir? Ye've had 'bout five too many," the innkeeper asked after an hour or two. Time seemed to have stopped.

He was iron. He was steel. *I am a failure.* "I need one more."

The innkeeper grumbled, but poured the brandy and took the coin. The small-people were having a heated conversation and even through the cloud of inebriation, he could hear everything. Leaning his head to the side, he had to put a hand up to stabilize the heaviness.

"I'm telling you, Strenflag, he is nowhere in this town! He's flat-out disappeared!"

"The most—he was a very popular man, he was, I tell ye!"

"Powerful—popular, yes, he was. More powerful than any of us combined!"

"Excuse me," Jafren drawled, turning in his chair to address the small-people. The room shifted mightily and he clasped a hand on the arm of the chair. "Are you talking about a mage?"

The one called Strenflag buried his face in his mug, and the other turned away, muttering.

"Yes, yes you were, don't lie to me. Do you know who I am?" he tried to sound stern, but every word rolled forth with an awkward slur.

Each man shook his head.

"I'm the Sacuan-blasted leader of the Sacuan-blasted Counsel, and I could have you tossed right out of here and back to your land without so much as a thought!" He tried to hop off his stool to reproach the men, but he stumbled and nearly toppled to the floor.

"You look drunk to me, whoever you are," Strenflag said flatly.

"Aye," Jafren agreed, swaying. "But, I—" He broke off, ready to unleash another torrent, and perhaps draw his sword, but a small voice in his head stayed him. He had to be better than this! What was he coming to, the Grand Counselor, drunk in a dusty inn in Vronga, yelling at small-men? "But you *were* talking about a mage. Who was he?"

"Why do ye want to know?"

"I'm looking for one. I need help."

"You won't get it from him or me," came the snide remark. "If that's the type of 'help' you are trying to seek!" He made a face and turned to watch the sutan player.

Jafren colored briefly. But he was above that. *I'm steel. I'm steel.* "I have no interest in that. I need a mage for some work up north."

"What kind of work?"

"That is Counsel business."

"Then telling you who he is, is none of ours."

"You don't know where he is, I know that, but who is he, and where did you last see him?"

The unnamed mage opened his mouth for a retort, but Strenflag had been studying Jafren's face and put up a hand. He set his mug down. "You seem honest. Drunk, but honest. All right. His name is Darrell and he's a kind of runaway."

"So, he's not with the University here?" Jafren's face fell, and he stumbled. *Lost. All is lost.*

"No. He thinks they're going to put him back into service, if you know what I mean, and so he's run off. But we need him to help with the battles—he's too good a mage."

Jafren remembered reading of the battles. The Archives held a few accounts of the Welcferian savages and their constant assault on civilization. Indeed, any type of mage would be beneficial against them, since they were so often described as naked men carrying nothing but spears. In one horrific account, they had attacked an entire battalion barehanded, and the well-armed men had incurred severe casualties.

He nodded slowly, and the room wobbled. "I'm sorry to have bothered you."

"It's no bother," Strenflag said, his focus already on the sutan player. "But if you see him, tell him we are looking for him."

"I will," he replied sadly, returning to his bench. He ordered one more brandy and stumbled upstairs to his room.

Darrell. Whoever you are, you are meaningless to me... Run while you can. His thoughts were disjointed as he attempted to start a fire in his room. He couldn't seem to get the flint to work, and he burned his fingers more than he started the dry tinder. At last, he gave up and collapsed on the bed in his full outfit.

Darrell might have been adequate, but not worth the trouble. He could find ten men like him at the University, but only one man like Wrenflang. Or was it Strenflag? No, he was the man downstairs. These Welcferian names were confusing and all sounded the same to him. Wrenflang was nowhere to be found, either. Maybe they were running together.

In any case, all was lost. He had sent his men, sent for Protectors, talked with the Black Dawn. But no amount of armed force would be able to protect the world from the coming demonic invasion. No amount. He needed Wrenflang. That was their only hope, and he had lost him.

A rock in the hill. If the bed weren't slowly spinning around the room, he would have leapt up, hunted that man down, and sliced him from neck to anus, just for saying something so inane. Instead, Jafren willed himself not to vomit and lay staring into the dark.

I am iron. I am steel. He tried to repeat the litany, but it sounded hollow.

"I am a failure," he whispered to the dark.

According to thousands of years of teaching, the untying of one's own knot was a grave sin and sent one into the dark regions between life and final peace. The Elders had admonished countless numbers of the sick and infirm because they were better served suffering agonizing torment, rather than loosen their own worn threads and be left undone.

Jafren thought upon this ingrained thought and shook it off. It would be far better to step aside now than to face the horrors that were bound to come. He had done what he could do. He had tried. He had put forth his best effort.

It wasn't good enough.

I am a coward. Was he a coward? Was he simply saving himself a far worse punishment? Or was he plunging the world into a vile darkness that it could never escape?

"There was nothing more I could do," he whispered to the dark. The dark did not answer. Jafren put a palm over his forehead, and the hand slowly moved to his eyes to wipe away the steady stream of tears. *I have failed.*

His own knot was useless upon the world. There was no good that it could possibly do—he had served honorably in the Guard and protected citizens from street criminals and hucksters. He had risen to Grand Counselor by a nearly unanimous vote because of his tenure and service. But now, he could not save anyone from a real threat—he couldn't even complete a simple task.

"For Sacuan's sake, I couldn't even find a warlock. Just a bunch of drunken Welcferians who are going to be as dead as everyone soon." Images of death and horror passed through his mind. It would be his fault. His! Whether demons or angry villagers killed him, he would pay for his failure. No, it was far better to untie the knot and to pass on.

The bed creaked as he pulled himself to a sitting position.

I have failed. I have failed. I have failed.

"Sacuan preserve me, and Sacuan preserve the world." Reaching into his jerkin, he retrieved a small dagger and gripped it tightly.

As his life flowed forth from the wound in his arm, the darkness slowly grew deeper. His knot slowly unraveled to pool in the knotty pine boards of the room, and he collapsed silently. One last thought flittered through his mind—and his eyes shot open. But there was no time to act, for they opened wide, and remained that way.

In the seconds before death, the mind can race through countless images and memories, as Zhy would be quick to point out. Jafren's mind raced through his visit to the Archives, and latched upon a faded document to which he had neglected to attach any importance. It described the Tunnels in a little more detail, and their entrance near Vronga. Had he thought through the information completely, he would have realized that the stone slab in the hill was significant. His trail for the warlock may have gone from ice-cold to warm. Alas, these thoughts came too fast—and too late.

Jafren's knot had come undone.

Chapter 32
To Remember Dying

We do not remember birth. We should not remember our deaths.

Prophet Hourzan

When they arrived at the base of the stairs, each man stumbled to a clumsy stop.

Where did they go? Zhy wondered. He did not remember any event where such a momentous explosion had taken place—it had been an explosion. Hadn't it? Thinking on the sheer power of Ar'Zoth, it was not outside of his ability to completely destroy several tons of masonry and stone with a single blast—but Zhy remembered none of this.

"What in Sacuan's...?" Yulchar breathed. "How...? Why...?"

The scene before them presented a hundred different questions. To the newcomers, the very existence of the giant castle was one of wonder. Zhy thought he remembered having many questions himself, but now he just stared dumbly at the huge black void that had been a massive stone staircase. The bottom third of the stairway remained, but it had been thrust violently up at an odd angle. The top eighth remained, and there was no reason that it should still cling to the castle, but it did. Between the two sections, there was nothing. Each man stood there, chests heaving as they stared wide-eyed at their predicament.

What happened here? Zhy wondered. Was that how he fell to his death? Or did Darrell or Ar'Zoth do this? "I wonder if that is where I fell...?" he said quietly.

"Perhaps. Do you remember any of that?"

Zhy shook his head. "I only remember falling."

Huyen whistled softly.

"Whatever magic did this, it was powerful. I can still hear a buzz, like the small biting insects down south. Do you hear it, Huyen?"

The gruff knight nodded.

"Indeed. I can't conjure up any spell with near enough force to do something like this."

For a few moments, they stared dumbly at the devastated staircase, breath cascading out in steamy clouds. Zhy thought briefly on the moment he had met Bruce, and the odd sensation of finding a strange body in his usual stool. A light breeze floated across the disfigured stone, and suddenly Zhy felt as if were being watched. The feeling seemed to pass through each man, as they turned in unison to glance around nervously, but no other being could be seen.

He can't see you. I have him otherwise occupied.

"Sacuan's scrotum!" Zhy blurted, then realized he'd spoken aloud. His left thumb and forefinger were furiously rubbing his earlobe.

Yulchar and Huyen turned, their faces flat. What counted for alarm in these knights? "Yes?" asked Yulchar calmly.

"I—I heard the voice!"

"Her voice?"

Zhy nodded slowly. He grimaced, not wanted to hear it again. "She's never contacted me in the daylight."

"Maybe she's close to us."

"She said that he, whoever that is, can't see us. She has him 'occupied,' she said." Zhy's hand came away slowly from his ear.

Yulchar bobbed his head. "Yes, she must be here then. Or at least, somehow keeping whoever is in there"—he pointed up at the castle—"busy. Whatever that means."

Huyen turned away, disinterested, and shifted his gaze to the northeast, intently studying the sheer rise and the towering pines, looking closely for some sort of pathway. It seemed hopeless.

"You aren't thinking of—" Zhy began.

"I am, Zhyfrael," the knight snapped. "I am. It looks bad, but we will have to do it. Unless she has taught you how to fly?" The question was punctuated with a sneer.

An image of a drooling, snarling gherwza flitted across Zhy's mind. He shook his head. *You would surely kill me if you knew.*

"Well, then, that is the only way. I don't think we could go down into the canyon—" Huyen walked gingerly to the edge of the great ravine and looked down with a scowl. His glance darted south, then north. "There looks to be a trail far off, but I don't see how we get down there... unless we back-tracked to the beginning."

"That would be just as wasteful," Yulchar said. In the cold, his voice had taken on a gravelly edge, and he scowled briefly.

Huyen grumbled. "Well, then that's it. I've got a rope, but I think we'll just have to go slow and use it where we can. There are lots of rocks, roots, and branches—who knows how far we will go. This will take some time."

"It must be done," Yulchar said flatly.

Zhy was sent up between Yulchar and Huyen, but he felt little comfort. Each step was arduous and wrought with fear. A boot would slip, and one would have to quickly grab at something—anything—to remain upright.

There was no opportunity to look at the gaping chasm behind them and to their left. They simply climbed, inch after agonizing inch. Yulchar's rope came in handy a few times, when he was able to hook it over a solid branch or a jagged rock. Zhy feared the rope would give under one man's weight, let alone three who used it to pull up to a good resting point.

Not that any of the ground was flat. There were, however, sections that were less steep than others, and the men could rest leaning slightly forward without fear of being toppled backward. A couple of tall pines provided shelter at their roots, for the snow had not settled as deep around the massive trunks. Zhy and the knights were able to find two trees under which they could rest—each man leaning against a section of tree. Instead of thick snow directly beneath the tree, they were happy to sit atop a bed of brown pine needles. The bed was damp but serviceable, and they shared a quick meal of dried meat before climbing farther.

"And are you sure he cannot see or hear us?" Yulchar asked, peering around the massive tree. They were positioned such that the castle was out of view, and their vision was filled with snow and snow-laden boughs of the large trees.

Zhy shook his head. "That's all I she said. I've heard nothing since."

"I see."

"If you are lying, Zhyfrael, I will—"

Yulchar held up a hand. "Enough of that. This is why he is here with us. We have to trust him now."

"But—"

"No, Huyen, no." Yulchar's voice was soft but stern. He smiled slightly, a smile with no humor or concern. "It is time."

Zhy looked up the steep rise they still had to climb. "This is going to take a very long time," he muttered to himself.

It took until dusk of the following day to climb the rest of the way. As they ascended, they remarked with a few groans and curses that several areas near them would have provided an easier climb. But to get over to the flat spots, handholds, and conveniently shaped rocks would have put them all at risk. Huyen noted that they at least had a better path to follow on the way down. Zhy scowled, then a deep sadness flooded him; he was not sure he would go back down again. Yulchar only laughed.

At last, they collapsed onto a level patch of ground. In the fading light, Zhy looked again upon the great stone castle that clutched to the mountainside, and beyond was an ocean of snow-capped mountain peaks that stretched into the dark beyond. He thought he could see small animals moving in the far distance, but when he tried to re-focus, they were no longer visible. Above them, balsams stretched into the dusk, and a few snowflakes fell from the upper branches carried by an imperceptible wind.

When darkness fell, they didn't dare start a fire, but instead hunkered down beneath a large white pine. The ground was nearly level, but still uneven, and Zhy had a constant sense of sliding. Sleeping was going to be a challenge, but they needed rest for what was to come. Days were so short here that it was not worth trying to deal with Bimb today.

Thoughts danced and paraded through his mind, and he thought back on how he had first met Bruce. He relived their conversations, but an image of Kahl floated through, and his mind jumped even further back in time, to a story Kahl had told about visiting a small town, but the name flittered away. Zhy wasn't sure why he was remembering a small piece of miscellany, but somehow it stuck—perhaps since the innkeeper never traveled. Ever. And here he had even taken time off to visit some village south of Moult. In the dream, the conversation was almost as strange as it had been in reality. Zhy thought perhaps the innkeeper had been sampling his wares too much.

"Where had you gone?" Zhy asked.

"Little village a few hundred miles south of Moult," Kahl replied.

"Is that so, why?"

"I found—I have family there." He coughed and took a drink of brandy. Brandy! The man never drank anything while working. Why was he—?

"Who lives there?"

The dream suddenly flickered and went to black. When he awoke, there was a light snow falling. It had snowed overnight—when he looked back along the trail, he could see a fresh coating that had buried their tracks, although in their shelter of the enormous pines, only a thin dusting lay on the ground and their gear. He was thankful for that, for even evidence of their slow trek up the hillside had been erased.

Chapter 33
Dawn Has Broken

CƷ

When brother fights brother with swords, the end is nigh. As the dawn breaks for the final hour, we will see families torn asunder, communities ripped apart, and demons will walk freely among us.

Cleric Archean

Like most everyone who had gone through the passage in Gray Gorge, Orfel followed the narrow path to the right. The scenery before him nearly caught his breath and he gazed out with wonder at the massive trees and the spreading valley below. He had only moved forward a ski length when a familiar, grating, and arrogant voice burst into the chill air; the sound of a human voice shocked him into a daze and his skis nearly slid out from underneath him.

"Hello, there, Orfel!"

Leaning on his poles, he swiveled his head around. Tralen stood there, skis planted in the snow. With a curse, he realized he was at a distinct disadvantage. Whatever had brought Tralen this far in the north in the heart of winter was not pleasant. He had not come here to deliver Dran'Za's famous spiced cake.

"What are you doing here?" Orfel growled. How had he covered his tracks? There was no indication that the man had skied through here.

"Killing you." The arrogant face was wind-burned and chapped, but his voice was smooth.

"Why would you—?" Orfel started to turn his skis around to face the man, but the confined space made it difficult. He only hoped he could face the right direction before the fool did something stupid.

"I would ask you the same question, Orfel. What are you doing here? Returning to your master now you have slaughtered the innocent and four Knights of the Black Dawn? Four!"

"What makes you think I—"

"Silence, demon!" Tralen spat.

He tried to reach down to unfasten his skis. If only he had had the more advanced bindings, he could simply loop the tip of his ski pole inside and simply pop out the ski boot. But with these older bindings, he had to physically reach down and untie the strap—which he had purposely tightened for the deep snow. And Tralen knew that.

As soon as Orfel bent down to loosen the small leather strap, something shoved him hard, and he fell to the snow. He expected it, but he had to take a chance sooner rather than later—he couldn't fight this man strapped into skis. With the long skis still attached to his boots, he collapsed like a tree, landing on his side. The skis popped out of the powder, wrenching his already swollen ankle.

"I never thought that you were one to use magic," he spat into the snow. *How had he done it?* Orfel wondered. He could feel the thin chain of the medallion around his neck, and the metal of the trinket pressed against his chest— perhaps it was too buried in his thick clothing that it had no effect. *That* was *magic*, he thought with a sickening feeling.

Tralen's shadow loomed over him. "Magic?" came the condescending reply. "Magic? No, I think the Light simply struck you down. Demon!" he shouted again.

He's crazy. He always was a little imbalanced, but the snow must have... His thought was shattered as a thick-toed boot collided with his midsection. Black spots danced before his eyes, and he tried to take a deep breath, but the boot struck his head and he wound up inhaling a wad of snow. Lifting his head quickly, he gasped for air. He could hear

Tralen breathing behind him and could sense the man smiling his off-kilter smile, that he often used to address people he loathed, which was just about everyone.

We'll see how smug you really are, Orfel thought. If the man had just kicked him, it meant he was close. And Tralen was nowhere near the skier that Orfel was—though he had somehow made it this far. *He could never do this*, Orfel thought.

With his skis in the air, parallel to his body and each other, he looked utterly helpless. But with his experience, he was much faster than Tralen expected. In one fluid motion, he swung his skis down to the ground and set them as flat as he could, and then used all of the strength of his lower body to swing himself up to a standing position. He shoved away the screaming pain that his ankle brought, and instead focused on Tralen. In another split-second, he had one ski shoved forward between the knight's legs, then jumped with both skis and spun counter-clockwise. The spinning ski tangled Tralen's legs and he went tumbling into the snow. In that second, Orfel reached down and tore off the scrap of leather bound to his boot. As Tralen writhed on the ground, Orfel had his sword out.

"Tell me again that wasn't magic!" Orfel spat. "For a man who believes all mages and warlocks are demons, what exactly was the point of that?"

Tralen spat snow from his mouth and stood, his own sword coming free of its sheath. A tuft of snow fell lazily off the handle. Orfel noticed briefly that the sword was old— and most definitely not any sword issued by the Knights of the Black Dawn. What had happened? Had he been...? No, he... *what if he killed...* the thoughts were fast and many, but Orfel didn't have time to wonder.

"I told you—the Light must have struck you. You killed four Knights of the Black Dawn. For that you deserve to die!"

"You said that before. I'd like to know why you think that." Orfel had heard of knights falling into a blindness of sorts—every other person in the world was a demon, except for them, and anything not in their narrow range of acceptance was discarded as Dark. Tralen had fallen into it, but dangerously so. To have traveled this far through the cold and snow, just to attack another knight belied a profound sickness.

The two men stared at each other, swords drawn. It would not be long before Tralen charged. Orfel was not going to move an inch until the other knight did. The man was delusional and insane.

"You are a demon. Do I need to say more?"

"Other than you are an inbred fool?"

With that, Tralen lurched forward, snow pluming up from his boots as he plowed through the deep snow. He swung his sword in an arc, but Orfel easily blocked it.

Tralen growled.

Fighting in the deep snow was painfully slow. Like chasing someone through a small creek or running through the ocean, the faster you ran, the slower you felt you were going. But whatever magic Tralen knew, he thankfully didn't know how to walk on air. Still, the fighting was slow, though the swords flashed like spinning diamonds. Boots would catch on rocks or infant trees, and as much energy was spent on staying upright as attacking the opponent.

Tralen barely blocked a thrust from Orfel's sword, and with his left elbow, he shoved the knight backward. Orfel's boot caught a small rock and he went sprawling into the cold powder. Instinct told him to roll to his right, and again he was rewarded for quick thought, for something hot sizzled past him. The snow boiled. He came to his knees in a flash, sword still in hand.

His focus locked on Tralen and time stopped.

White light danced between the knight's fingers. With the hue of white already dominating the landscape, the tendrils seemed to become invisible, then re-emerge. *The bastard... the utter, hypocritical—no, no time now—I have to be fast.* The thought was barely formulated when Orfel pulled back his sword arm. At nearly the same moment, Tralen raised his hands to the sky.

In a single tick of a clock, molten energy went streaking across the small space between the men, and a curved sword flew with deadly accuracy toward its target. Tralen had kept his eyes on his magical spell, and his eyes did not register the glinting steel spiraling toward him.

Perhaps the sight seemed so out-of-place that he ignored it, for his entire focus was on Orfel. He wanted to watch as his magic incinerated the murdering Knight of the Black Dawn. One who thought Tralen would never use magic. The absurdity! Magic was demonic for a Knight of the Black Dawn. But Tralen was no longer a knight. Now he was a hero. He had taken on the true enemy of the world and won. If only—

His thoughts were severed as the steel blade sliced cleanly through his Adam's apple and back through his neck. The hilt punched his chin with a crack, nearly shattering the bone beneath his stubble. He tried to speak, but merely gurgled. The world suddenly grew much taller, he thought briefly, before realizing he was on his knees. Blood streamed from his neck and slowly started to cover the landscape in a slowly oozing velvet carpet. As his life streamed onto the snow, hissing as the warm liquid melted the white powder, he was able to see the effect of the magical spell. The white bolt struck Orfel—well, it didn't quite hit him fully; for some reason the trinket worked a little better this time, but the few tendrils that found their mark were effective.

Orfel was sent sprawling over the ravine, arms flailing.

φ

Orfel awoke with a splitting headache and an ankle the size of a stump. He lay wedged between two large boulders. With an agonizing slowness, he rolled to his stomach and looked up at the sheer rise before him. There was no easy way out. And the drop-off to the bottom of the ravine was worse—he was lucky to have simply wedged himself into these rocks. To the right was a trail no wider than a man's foot—it could have been a deer trail, but seemed smaller than that. Perhaps an arctic fox had made a trail to some food source. *If I don't get out of here, I'm going to be a source of food for some animal.*

He pushed himself up with agonizing slowness. The swollen ankle nearly gave out, but he threw an arm out and found purchase on a small rock. Just a few feet away, the beginnings of a white pine offered a tentative handhold, and he made his way slowly up the slope, hoping the small tree could hold his weight. It bent, but it held. *Only the strong survive here, including the trees,* he mused. The roots of the small pine would be nearly as strong as a southern tree half its size. With the incredibly short growing season and the rocky soil, trees took hundreds of years to grow only a few feet.

With a glance up at the towering white pines along the western slope, he shook his head. Except for those. He almost laughed, except his chest burned when he took a deep breath—he was exerting intense physical energy simply to keep himself from falling backward to his death. *Perhaps the soil is richer there or... or something else keeps them tall. Nothing to worry about now.*

He reached for another small pine and pulled himself upward with a grunt, and found himself panting. Still, as he inched ever upward, he let his thoughts drift back to the encounter he had barely survived.

How did that magic work? Against the demon, his trinket was the only thing apart from his wits that had saved him. Now it seemed useless. The arrogance of Tralen was astounding—perhaps he'd found some other way to get through those trinkets. After all, the man had acted as if he knew the last word on everything. Additionally, the trinket had done some good—after all, if the spell hadn't shattered, he would be dead.

Dead. All dead, every last person, would be dead. And Tralen thought *Orfel* had been the demon? Perhaps the knight was a demon himself... or had gone over to worship things of the Dark.

Where had the sword come from? That question returned to the fore and he paused in his effort to think. The sword was not issued by the Dawn, and it was definitely past its prime—something someone would likely hang up over a mantle. Tralen could have lost his sword in a fight or in the snows, but Orfel doubted that. Something had happened that he had it removed. Perhaps Dran'Za had finally booted him from the Order, but of course, Tralen had still been alive, so that theory didn't make sense.

What if the Order had finally broken? It was a sickening thought, but the world was definitely undergoing an upheaval. A hundred things could have happened to disrupt the Order: The Guard, bands of villagers thinking the secret order was somehow full of demons, a new and crazed High Cleric. Or simply dissention. Any of these could have doomed the Order and brought on its collapse.

But did it matter? He looked up at the gray sky and wondered. No matter if the Dawn was whole or not, he had demons to deal with. More than he alone could bear, but he would have to try.

There was another small rock before the narrow trail leveled out. He took a deep breath and heaved himself forward. Once on somewhat level ground, he rolled onto his back and propped his ankle on a rock. *I thought cold was supposed to help these things*, he thought darkly.

As he lay back, the sun poked out from behind the leaden sky, and he was reassured that it had not drifted too far to the west. Somewhat comfortable, with the sun beating down on his face, he dozed. He felt a little fluttering in his stomach, as if he had been drinking, but he attributed that to his cracked skull. At least he wasn't seeing double. As he drifted off to sleep, however, he thought he heard bees buzzing again, but the sound faded with unconsciousness.

After a few moments, he awoke again and continued forward.

And thus Orfel made the mind-numbing climb to the top—exerting great effort to cling to rocks and infant trees, and resting on semi-level portions of the trail. He nearly panicked when the trail ended abruptly, but he realized that he had arrived at the top. With a grunt and a curse over his twisted ankle, he hurled himself up and over the lip of the ravine, landing face-first in the snow. After the exertion, it actually felt good, until his teeth felt as if they would crack from the cold.

He shuffled to his feet and walked over to the massive blanket of red snow. Tralen lay face down in the snow. Orfel didn't spare any words or thoughts on the man—he simply found his skis and strapped them on.

Ankle be damned, he thought as he skid a few paces away. As long as he forced his skis to be straight and didn't move the ankle from side to side, he hoped it would heal faster. But by Sacuan it throbbed! Orfel grabbed his temples as a sudden, sharp pain wracked his skull. *I'm probably hungry,* he thought. *Pine bark and reindeer moss can't be enough.* For a few moments, a slim ray of sun peeked through a thin break in the heavy cloud cover, and he decided on a direction. With a glance at the muted sunlight, he set off down the trail.

Chapter 34
Dead Spaces

The things unseen are the things that will surely doom us. For the unknown is a knot unto itself; a dark, shifting, malicious thing.

Prophet Broundoun III, IV Age

There were only three—no, make that two—men out there. Yes. Only two. I had destroyed the staircase with my reversal of the Bolt of Sacuan, yet there were men there, climbing along the treacherous ridge along the mountainside. One misstep and they would be of no concern to me. Perhaps if I cast a small—

I doubled over with a scream as the unseen hand again clutched my stomach and twisted it into a knot. How was she doing this? She was dead! The pain was unbelievably excruciating and each time I tried to bend my torso back up to look at the interlopers, the invisible hand would grab me again and spin me down to the hard stone. This stomach tightening was getting old. If only I could figure out how to get out of it. "I won't—I won't—" I could not breathe. I started to rise, but again I was thrown down. There was a crack that I hoped was only a joint, and black blotches danced before my eyes. I lay there, glassy-eyed, looking at the stone pavers as the black spots grew. My mind was slowly starting to fade, but I tried to keep my bearings. The combination of the black spots and the paving stones presented a distorted image of blotches, whorls, grooves, and straight lines that resembled a child's first artistic drawing. Lines would intersect, covered by a black dot that moved slowly to reveal random patterns in the stone. Slowly, slowly, the black spots grew and took up more of the picture.

Spaces.

Dead spaces.

These were spaces where nothing was nor could be. Magic encompassed harnessing the living spaces between things, but these—spaces, if one could give them a name— were empty. Somehow, my mother was using them to punish me. To push me down and rub my face into the excrement. If I could divine a way out of here, I would, if only I could get at the live spaces! But all that I could see was black.

And as the spaces slowly coalesced into a solid wall, I suddenly realized that even though the spaces were dead, they were still spaces. This was not putting the tea back into the leaf, this was a much more volatile and important effort. I could get her out, once and for all.

I had it!

While Ar'Zoth found it quaint to wax poetic about the little pieces that could be extracted from the greater structure that was everything, he missed the larger picture. Was not the world just a piece unto itself? A small chunk in something larger and more encompassing? Magic's focus was too often the miniscule—on particles and waves and beams of light and energy. Why couldn't one step back, up, away—whatever term fit. Stop focusing on the tiny and move to the *BIG?* There of course would be a limit to such work—I could not move the castle or the mountains since were far heavier and bulkier. I could, however, take them both apart piece by piece. But then that brings everything back into the whole discussion on small particles. When it came to the dead, however, rules changed. The black wall that my vile mother was slowly driving toward me could be moved. It was only a chunk in a larger space. I didn't need to dive in. I needed to step back!

Instead of trying to push the wall away, I turned my focus to the spaces beyond the wall—specifically above it. With a great mental effort, I forced my focus above the wall. It was like leaping in a dream in which you could jump higher and run faster than normal. In this case I "jumped" above the wall, and I could see the space around it.

Many spaces!

There were souls everywhere! The countless souls of the dead—those who were stuck between the death Lyn had been in, and the final darkness. Each was in a contained space, and each space was bordered by a black wall that exactly mirrored the one that Mother had been pushing at me. The walls were solid, as thick as a man was tall, but the edges shimmered in a smoky haze; miniscule tendrils floated from the tops and sides of the walls, and they drifted in the void I suddenly found myself swimming in.

So that's how they do it.

Lyn and my mother had not visited the living. They had simply pulled the living into their space—into their black box in the afterworld. I looked at several boxes, but they only housed the dead. Perhaps no one else knew how to pull in the living. Or they needed to have special abilities. Music had been the draw for Lyn.

Shaking myself from my reverie, I turned my focus to the box I had leapt out of. Mother.

She looked up to see me and her soft face fell. Her image was wobbly and unstable, but it was her face. A double-image was there, if but for a brief moment—it seemed like someone else was there, but then vanished. How was that possible? Or was that simply a consequence of my presence here? Her sad, drawn, pathetic excuse for a face. A face of a woman who had destroyed her only son. Who was trying even in death to destroy him. I had no time to wonder how to destroy her in this position, but I knew that escaping this place would free me of her. And then I would be free to work with the demons.

As soon as I dealt with these pesky intruders.

I started to rise, but she was quicker than I had been. As usual. The walls were rising! I had tried to push myself up and out of the collection of souls, but somehow she was extending the boxes that surround each person. The higher I climbed, the higher the smoky black walls crept. How high could they possibly go?

Into forever, I swore I heard her say, but that may have been my own projection of her voice. There was no end to the height to which she could push these walls. Upward, upward they rose as she pushed. I panicked, but realized with a sudden sense of calm that I was still playing her game, by her rules, in her field. This had to stop!

I had to stop thinking like my enemies. They brought with them their own weapons, their own trinkets, and their own styles of fighting. For so long I had been the meek and timid member of society, relegated to the edges, to the shadows. I had spent nearly half a lifetime bowing and scraping to others. Bimb was a pushover. Bimb could be cajoled and coerced.

But Ar'Zoth could not! Ar'Zoth fought on his terms!

Why was I not fighting on mine?

So she was going to push me to the edge of eternity, was she? She wanted me to go up, up, until I expired. I made a feint, and I swore I could hear her chuckle. My eyes rolled back in my head and I began to fall. She may have smiled for a brief moment. That is, until I pushed myself down, like an orca diving deep into the sea. I dove as fast as I could in this barren world between life and death, between dream and lucidity. She cursed—I heard it clearly as I zipped past her, and down. Ever downward.

I heard no more as I crashed through and "landed" on the hard stone ground. To an observer, my eyes simply snapped open to reveal my whites as wide as the Opal Sea, and my knees as they knocked together. There was a very brief thought of Sacuan himself—if only I had had time, I could have dealt with him... but there was a greater, and much more immediate need. I stumbled a step and then arched my back. A roar began in my throat and echoed across the valley.

And with that roar, I raised my hands and hurled *Light of M'Hzrut* at the mountainside.

ф

The trees above exploded in flame.

"Sacuan's scrotum!" Zhy screamed. He slipped and fell face forward in the snow. Yulchar and Huyen wasted no time and leapt forward, crossing the distance between the hillside and the castle in a single bound. At the castle door stood a man. A young man, from what Zhy could see through the snow. Suddenly, another bolt raced forward, shattering the snow above him. A wall of thick white powder fell onto him in a great cold heap.

Zhy looked down to see Yulchar and Huyen engage the man at the Keep.

I have seen this before, he thought to himself. He tried to stand, but he slipped on the uneven ground and flew face-first into the snow. His boot had become wedged between two rocks, and if he moved any more, his ankle would be snapped like a dry twig. With much effort, he reached down into the powder, loosened the laces, and extracted his foot from the boot. Then he wrenched the boot free, shook out the snow, and jammed his foot back in. A few flakes of snow had blown in, and he shivered as his foot touched the cold wet liquid. At last, he looked up, expecting another magical bolt to come flying at him, but the men hardly noticed him struggling—as if he didn't exist. He grinned briefly, and made his way slowly through the snow, trying to stay behind trees when he could, and at the same time remain upright, for the slope was impossibly steep. How had Yulchar and Huyen moved so deftly?

ф

"You and your blasted trinkets!" I screamed as every spell bounced off the men. I had only enough time to trap one, but the other still charged, his sword drawn. With a desperate effort, I flung a spell to knock the sword away.

"The only way to ensure you don't kill us all," the man barked. He stopped, however, as I spun away to face him. The reversal of Bolt of Sacuan was looking more and more attractive.

"Is that so? Do you see that hole there in the stairs? A man stood there once, when the staircase was full—a man who wore the same exact trinket you do."

Horror played across the man's face for a second, quickly replaced by anger.

"One of you, I see. You never give up, do you? Tell me, how were you able to drag my dead mother into this? I thought you fought black magic."

"Your dead... mother?" His feigned innocence was maddening. His companion growled behind his invisible cage.

"Yes, that bitch. She trapped me here until you could arrive. Now I see it all. I see everything. But I have had the last laugh, you see. I have trapped her! Trapped her in the dead spaces." Their stares of terror were delicious.

ф

The man was talking to Huyen, and Yulchar stood stock still and fumed. Why wasn't he moving, and where had Huyen's sword gone? The wind started swirling with more intensity, as it usually did. *How do I remember that?* With the muted howl in his ears, Zhy only caught bits and pieces of the conversation, but he swore he heard the word "mother" come from the man's lips. Huyen looked ready to vomit.

Cerease!

"Cerease!" he called out loud, but a gust caught the sound and flung it into the tall trees.

Nothing.

"Leave it to the dead," he muttered dejectedly. "Drag you a thousand miles and then leave you to fend for yourself."

I'm not... came a strangled voice in his head, and then it was gone, as if pulled down into a pool of muddy water.

Zhy tried to step forward, but slipped, caught himself, and hugged the tree trunk. Small chunks of pine bark broke free and floated lazily into the gaping void. His chest was heaving and his heart hammered—he would not float so easily.

ф

Huyen had had just about enough of this. So this was Ar'Zoth or Bimb. A madman, true, but a madman with enough power to decimate half of the world. The knight swore he could hear buzzing and scratching deep below the earth and worried briefly that the madness was part of this castle. He got the better of his senses and realized the buzzing was probably the demonic horde. Such a buzzing would drive anyone mad over time. This was a very dangerous place.

"Please, you must understand. We did not know about your mother," he said, extending his hands outward, palms up. He tried to paint his face with his best look of fear, but the anger kept building beneath the surface and his words sounded forced and rough-edged.

The man—warlock? What was he, anyway? The warlock laughed, wiping spittle away from his lower lip. "You lie poorly. Now. First, there were three men who came here to play with Ar'Zoth. But he killed them. Then came the Knight of the Black Dawn." He pointed at the gaping chasm. "He's passed on. And now you." The man looked up and Huyen swore he was looking in the eyes of a child.

Which, he was, if what Zhy had said about him were true. Rather, what Bimb's dead mother had told Zhy about her son. True, the man had undergone a marked transformation from the innocent, simple-minded boy, but yet strangely the eyes retained a disconcerting look—a mask of a child's eyes, covering a great rolling tempest of madness. A great shudder rippled through his body.

So that is what happened to Gryn, he realized. A countless amount of stone and rock was obliterated, literally wiped from the face of the world, all in an effort to kill one man. Gryn had been brash and insubordinate, and deserved to be put in his place, but not like that. Huyen felt the smallest twinge of sadness before red-hot rage boiled over. This man had destroyed an enormous structure in order to kill only one man? The knight could feel the veins in his neck as they bulged and pressed hard against his skin, throbbing relentlessly as he fumed.

He could stand it no more, and in a heartbeat, he grasped several threads of energy at once and flung them at Bimb.

φ

The bastard had the gall to use magic! I had no time to consider the utterly vile and base perversion that such an action indicated. Knights of the Black Dawn had no magical ability! This was known! And here, he dared to unleash a spell on me? Were these men really demons in disguise? If so, how could my own horde turn on me?

I only had time to dive sideways to the left, thank whatever demonic god there was, for the black void was only feet away to the right. My knee jolted against the edge of a paving stone and I nearly screamed in pain, but I had no time to worry about superficial wounds.

As I rolled over on the stone, my hands came up and a purple ball of devastation leapt from my hands. Being this far away, I knew it was only a diversion, a feeble attempt at self-preservation, since the Sacuan-blasted knight's ridiculous medallion would save him.

But then I realized something. Something tickled the back of my mind, and I realized that those medallions were supposed to prevent the wearer from using magic, as well! If he could cast a spell, that meant he wasn't wearing it, or it was too far away to do any good! I could destroy him easily.

Wait! No, that could not be—my spells had bounced off *both* men and now he was casting? How? Or were his spells so mundane that it was a meaningless gambit anyway. That had to be it. I didn't recognize anything he was throwing at me, because it was all lights, sound, and fury—nothing that could have hurt me. He was trying to get me to react, to launch myself into the cavern!

The bastard.

"This is going to hurt," I whispered. *Tendril of Doom* flickered off my index finger, and rocketed across the space between us, striking the still-gaping knight in the chest. He was lifted off the ground a scant foot, and his boots flailed.

"This won't kill you," I said. "But it *is* going to hurt." Already he was screaming in agony as the red-hot finger of light burned his skin and slowly etched into muscle. The acrid stench of burning hair and skin filled the small square and I snorted in disgust... He stank even in his burning! I backed off the intensity—it was easy to reduce the number of heat particles and replace them with the chilled air; even snow would do nicely to calm the fire before I increased its heat. I could stand here for hours and slowly melt the man's heart, while his companion bellowed inside of his invisible cage.

φ

Huyen's chest blazed with fire. The magical beam was burning his muscle! Soon it would burn into his heart and he would die. But the madman was keeping everything in check somehow—he was penetrating and releasing the energy such that the world wobbled and spun. He emptied the contents of his stomach, and the action inflamed the pain all the greater.

Yulchar still writhed within the confines of his invisible cage, but the madman only laughed. The trapped knight glared at Bimb and scowled at Huyen.

"He can't help you now. In fact..." Bimb stole a glance at Yulchar in his cage and nodded slowly. "In fact, he will ensure that the pain is all the greater, is that not right?"

To Huyen's horror, Yulchar nodded back.

If his stomach were not already empty, he would have emptied it again. Huyen's barrier had been released. But why? Eyes wide from pain and shock, Huyen gaped as Yulchar stepped forward, grinning dumbly. The knight shared another brief, conspiring look with the warlock, and smiled.

Bimb's smile faded to confusion for a moment and then his lips quickly returned to a flat line of apathy. He regarded Huyen with those madness-filled child's eyes of his and shrugged.

Yulchar slowly drew his sword.

Chapter 35
Drastic Measures

∿∿
∿∿

When good deeds fail to keep the Dark at bay, when prayer fails, and when Evil seems to win regardless of the kind deeds we do, we must rely on our own strength to guide us and to protect us. Faith must come with action.

High Cleric Gorand

Forshen burned. Gherwza and mulargh flew overhead, screeching their awful cacophony of demonic terror. The fire of the mages spells missed their targets more often than they hit, and buildings suffered as a result, sending the innocent out into the cold air with little to warm them. Counsel Guards ran around trying to deal with rickety men who were bent on tearing faces and eating flesh... and the flying bats.

"Where in Sacuan's great harem is Jafren?" the Counselor screamed.

Gheren put his palms on the table and shook his head sadly. "I wish I knew, Horesh, my friend, I wish I knew. Last I saw him, he was headed to the Archives."

"He went where?"

"The Archive—"

The word went unfinished as the Counselor spun and raced off down the corridor.

He burst through the Keeper's chambers. "Where is he? Jafren. Where did he go? Tell me now!"

The Keeper was just waking, and he coughed. "Horesh, I—"

"Tell me, old man. Tell me now." He gritted his teeth, wishing that the words had not come out so harsh and demanding.

"Then it has started," the old man whispered.

"It has started," the Counselor confirmed, scowling. "Where did he go?"

The Keeper sighed. "The Dawn. He went to find the Dawn."

"Sacuan be damned!"

He flew back down the long halls and returned to Gheren, who was reading another report. He didn't have to ask as to the contents. It would be more news of the demons.

"The Temple has fallen, there is no other explanation!"

Gheren turned, his eyes red. "I believe it has."

"Jafren went to see the Dawn, it appears. Perhaps they are working together, or this so-called secret Order has murdered him, but we've heard nothing in days."

"Any word from the High Cleric?"

"No, why?"

"Well..." Gheren started. "I have a note indicating they were to marshal Protectors. Surely, those orders came from Jafren. The Holy Elders would never send anyone north this time of year unless it were an emergency."

"I see," Horesh said, biting his lip. "Well, we need more than that. Get everyone you can. Everyone. Rouse them where they live if you must, but we need the entire Guard on this."

Gheren's horrified gaze went to the map on the table. "We do not have enough soldiers," he whispered.

"What?"

"Look... Look! And this huge pile of papers arrived only a few minutes ago. It is too much, Counselor Horesh, it is too much."

"We do what we can. Send orders out to every town we can reach—any messenger who can ski is to be sent to the north. The others will scour the south. I still have twenty thousand stationed just east of here for winter exercises, and I'm sure they have some in Vronga. Who knows how many. It's an all-out war now, Gheren... It's war. War against the demons, and a war to protect the Temple. If the place still stands..."

Gheren sighed. "How could something like this happen?"

"I wish I knew the answer to that, but right now there is no time to try and find out. Whatever Jafren was searching for, he may have found it. It could explain the Knights of the Black Dawn."

"It makes sense," Gheren replied. "After all, they supposedly fight demons. If he can rally them behind us, we may have a chance."

"We have very few chances left," Horesh said with a grimace. "We need everything, and everyone, and it won't be long before we start pulling strong men from their beds and handing them swords. It is reaching that point. I will try a plea with the High Cleric, but I'm not sure I can hope for much."

"No?"

Horesh shook his head sadly. "No, but I will try. It is all I can do." At that, he turned to walk from the room. Pausing, he turned to Gheren. His face was scribbled with worry and his eyes were exhausted dark pools. "And keep trying to find Jafren."

φ

The High Cleric was in a sour mood, and being asked to send double the Protectors only set him bristling even more. Mentioning the Knights of the Black Dawn nearly set him over the edge.

"I believe what you say about the demons, Horesh, but this is nonsense. The Knights of the Black Dawn do not exist."

"With all respect," Horesh began, leaning forward in his seat, "we need to cease with this charade. Jafren has already met with them." If he could gain support of the Holy

Elders and their vaunted Protectors, he would have several hundred more troops. He needed thousands—tens of thousands, if all the reports were true. But marshaling the Protectors could persuade ordinary citizens to join the fight, and those men he could surely use. "They do exist, and we must combine our efforts."

The High Cleric shook his head. "Sadly, the Knights are a figment of yours, and of Jafren's, collective imagination. But—" He held up a placating hand. "But, I will offer assistance. I can send for the Protectors we have and they will join your forces. As soon as the thaw—"

"No!" He slammed a fist down on the table, heedless of whatever reaction the holy man would have. Damn him! "No, villages are burning. Demons are loose... Do you not care that the very Temple may have been compromised?"

"I highly doubt that."

Horesh stared. "You are blind," he finally spat.

The man leaned forward, his voice dangerous. "Would you like my assistance or not? I can easily decline your offer and let you deal with your imaginary problems on your own."

"Imaginary!"

"Yes, your so-called Knights of the Black Dawn and the preposterous notion that the Temple has fallen. We both stand here, and that is testimony to the fact the Temple, in fact, stands whole. Yes, I have heard of demons flying, and of these new, awful creatures they call the mulargh, but that does not mean the Temple has fallen."

"What does it mean? Would you enlighten me on that?" He pinched out the last question between teeth that wanted nothing more than to tear at this purported holy man's throat.

"It means our world has entered a time of sin and of sadness. We must repent that we do not be overcome by the dark. Your demons may be beaten by fire and sword, but they will continue until the world turns away from its Darkened ways."

Horesh colored and clenched his fists. "Are you saying that... prayer... *prayer!* will move us away from the precipice?"

"That is what I am saying," the High Cleric said, folding his hands.

"I can't begin to tell you what is wrong with that sentiment. But I will count on your troops—come the spring thaw." The man nodded slightly. "And I will have to deal with this in my own way." Horesh stood.

"We all must pray and meditate—"

Horesh slammed the door.

φ

"Curse the Holy Elders!"

"What did they do now?"

"Nothing!" Horesh screamed. "Nothing. Are my men on the move? Have you given the order?"

Gheren nodded. "As soon as you left. We will have the Guard out in force, starting south and moving northward. I have sent messages to Vronga. Mages are going to be stationed with each unit—as many as we have, that is. We'll see if this force can handle the demons."

"Good. No hope for the Protectors."

"No?"

"Not until the thaw. Cursed High Cleric, he said all of this was because we were not pious enough— didn't pray enough. Curse him forever!"

Gheren looked stunned. "How could they...?"

"Because they don't want to move from their soft cushions, that's why. Never a lift a finger to—"

"But the Temple—?"

"He said it still stood... arrogant bastard. Claimed that things would be much worse. Worse! How could they get any worse?" he veritably squealed in frustration. "We are standing at the precipice of a great disaster. Look around you!" He gestured again to the map and the stack of papers. The Counselor clenched and unclenched his fists and fumed for a few moments before sucking in a deep lungful of air. "So..." he said as he exhaled, an approached the map, "what do we do? If Jafren is trying to align us with the Knights, we may have hope yet. The Protectors are lost."

There was a soft scuffling of feet in the doorway. "I think I may have some ideas to help you."

Each man spun at the refined voice behind them.

"You..." Gheren said softly. He nodded at the newcomer and forced a welcoming smile that came out flat and lifeless. "This... this man in Rhys—he alerted me to the issue. Well, he alerted us to the scope of the problem, and what could happen if we did not take action."

"I see," Horesh said, stepping quickly across the room to grip the man's hand. "Normally we don't take any advice from anyone of, well, of certain positions." He took a breath to say more, but closed his mouth. Given the situation, he cared not a whit as to how the man entered the Counsel Headquarters—if this was one of those citizens who could rise up and protect his homeland, then he'd welcome him, even if he came through in an unorthodox manner. Damn the clerics and all holy men of the land!

"I understand," Rhys said.

"So, Rhys," Gheren said, "I have not had any reports of villagers on the rampage or attacking fellow citizens. It seems like the fight is now against the demons."

"For now," Rhys said quietly. "That will change. Their hearts are now on fire and they itch to slaughter every last demon. In villages like mine, once they clear the demons, they will turn and look at each other and wonder who will transform next. Which aging citizen will suddenly grow long fingers and start attacking everyone? And then it will be a bloodbath." He hung his head. "Excuse me, I have already told you this..."

"You haven't told me," Horesh said evenly. "It's good to know and it makes sense when you think about it. I'm too angry right now to think straight... these holy..." He trailed off, balling his fists. "So, we will do what we can."

"I thank you."

"Rhys," Gheren said, "you said you have more information?"

"Not more information, just something to offer. If you already know this, I'll leave."

"What is it?"

"Warlocks," Rhys said softly, barely above a whisper.

"Warlocks?" Gheren asked, his brows raised.

"Yes. I could not help but overhear that you plan on sending the Guard, and even the Knights—this Jafren is going to get—but this demonic influx is far greater than I think the army can handle. Not that they aren't... I apologize if I offend."

"No, no," Horesh said briskly. "Now, what about warlocks?"

"You need them, I think, to destroy or otherwise compel these demons." Rhys was nearly flabbergasted that such an idea had not been thought of—it seemed so obvious. And he was doubly surprised that these two high-ranking men had not thrown him bodily out of the building.

Gheren straightened, but kept his gaze on the map. "He is right, Horesh. Look, I know of a couple of warlocks here—" He pointed to a town southeast of Vronga. "And even some over here by Port Havren. Yes, we could do that—I will send notices immediately." He ran for the bell to fetch for a messenger.

"And..." Rhys cleared his throat softly. "And the exiled ones." If he had been traipsing along delicate ground before, he was now out over the paper-thin ice—he winced internally, expected a shout, a curse, or even a boot to his behind as they flung him from the building.

At that, Gheren's glance became ice and his face drained of color. "What did you just say?" He seemed frozen in place.

Rhys drew air. "I think the exiled warlocks must be involved as well. I know some are farther south on the islands, but we may need them, too. Who knows how far this has gone?"

Horesh shook his head. "That is too dangerous."

Rhys didn't answer, but walked to the map. He still expected to be expelled or put down, but so far, the men had listened. Perhaps he could convince them fully. *Stay smart, stay strong.* "I—I hope we won't need them, but it was a thought. I agree... dangerous." He scanned the red-speckled map, and pointed to a few towns. "Now, the ones I know of, at least from what I could gather as from rumors at inns and the like—are here—" He pointed to southern Belden, not far from Belden City. "And I'm sure a few are farther out in the islands. They will be hard to reach, but best send some boats out now so they can come ashore and move quickly."

Gheren nodded slowly. "It may take more skilled people away from battle to retrieve them."

"You will be gaining far more power as a result," Rhys added.

"Wait a minute... Just how do you know this much about warlocks?" Horesh asked.

It was the teacher's turn to color. He spread his hands out, palms up. "I have been very busy, going from inn to inn and tavern to tavern. Asking questions—carefully, mind you. I hear there is a vast archive here, but I was only able to view a few documents that were deemed fit for public use. But the people do know a lot, once you take out the exaggerations and outright lies—once I have heard a story several times by people who don't know each other, I can assume it is at least partially true."

A messenger arrived, panting, and Gheren shoved a note into his hand. "Go, run. Run!" The boy flew down the hall, his feet clattering noisily before they faded.

Horesh cleared his throat. "Rhys, stick around here, would you? We may have more work for you."

φ

Chaos continued.

The marshaled armies of the Guard moved northward, covering ground slowly but deliberately. Archers shot down the great flying beasts while mages ignited the shambling men. Care was taken to avoid the corpses of the beasts, and when time permitted, the mages would set them afire. Too often the fire bolts would go astray, or overshoot their intended targets and houses would burn, which displaced the poor citizens and created overcrowding at inns and other dwellings.

A warlock, grizzled and scowling, rode his horse to the point position of a large platoon of Guardsmen and two mages. They were just approaching a large village that lay due south form Moult, on the far southern edge of the great marsh. Flames were visible from several buildings, and a mulargh was alighting from the roof of what appeared to be the inn.

Red flame arched out from the warlock's hands and arced toward the beast, igniting him in a strange glow. A second light, this one bright green, followed, and enveloped the beast in a type of net.

A mage started to conjure up fire, but the warlock growled at him. "No, you think you can kill these things with fire, but they only come back. Gherwza and the men, yes, you can handle, but not these." The mage bristled, but stood down, focusing instead on a figure sprinting toward them—a gray-haired figure with too-long fingers and blood dripping from seemingly every orifice. A bolt of fire struck it in the chest as an arrow pierced its throat. The thing stumbled forward a few steps before collapsing on the hard ground.

With his arms raised, the warlock held the energy, and the mulargh, in the air.

"Now what?" the mage whispered.

"Now, it dies."

A tendril of red light burst forth and bored into the creatures large eyes. The warlock seemed to stumble for a second, as if slapped on the forehead, but he recovered, and kept his beam targeted. "There..." He grunted. "Got you." The beast suddenly exploded in a huge spray of flesh and bone. Men ducked instinctively as pieces of the animal fell around them.

"What did you do?"

"I had to control the demon first," the warlock replied, as if he were describing how to tie a simple knot. "It had to think I was in control of it, and then I blew it up." He rubbed his temples with a grimace. "I just hope I can keep this up. if I show any weakness, the control will reverse itself and I'll find myself at *its* command, not mine."

"And then what?"

"Then we fail."

Chapter 36
Wreckage

Ships can be wrecked upon the great reefs along the shore. Without a light to guide them, they flounder. So, too, can we be wreckage upon the world. Our souls require light for guidance—without it we are doomed.

Cleric Hyun

The tendril suddenly released and Huyen fell to the stone in a heap. Yulchar approached him, a look of utter loathing etched on his once calm and understanding face. Where a smile was easy, now a twisted scowl had been carved, where twinkling eyes gleamed now were only pits of demonic blackness. "You pathetic worm, Huyen. You worm!" He raised the sword as if to sever the man's head when Bimb's voice stopped him.

"Not yet, my friend. Not yet."

Yulchar spun. "Why not?" His look of disgust for his companion suddenly switched to Bimb, who stood there, his eyes almost glazed in the cold.

"Because—stop him!" In the brief second that Yulchar had taken to turn to look at Bimb, Huyen was rolling away. He leapt to his feet and sprinted as fast as the snow would allow. Hands raised quickly to cast a spell, but he ran a hundred more paces before spinning and turning to face Bimb and Yulchar.

Bimb tried to let loose with another web of lights, but Huyen was prepared now. As the green energy flowed from Bimb's hand, a purple bolt of lightning severed it in midair. A violent explosion ripped in the space between the men and shook the air. Yulchar went tumbling, and when he finally stood, Huyen was out of sight. Footprints were clear in the snow, leading down and away from the castle.

Without waiting, Bimb unleashed a bolt of fire toward the footprints. The spiraling ball rocketed toward the east, then dipped below sight and exploded against something with an enormous retort. There was a horrific scream followed by the sound of boiling water.

Was it snow boiling, or blood? Zhy wondered.

"You should have let me kill him," the knight hissed. Yulchar's voice had taken on a deeper and more sinister timbre. His sneer was carved out of ice and hatred.

"I was going to, you worthless excuse." The man looked and sounded like a ten-year-old bully. "We still needed more information about my mother."

"Your... She never talked to any of us. She talked to him," he said, gesturing in Zhy's direction.

φ

Zhy ducked back behind the pine tree. Had he been seen? He cringed, anticipating the inevitable explosion, but nothing happened. *Of all the horrible things to happen*, he thought. He should be incensed. He should be shocked. He should throw up in the snow. Something, anything! *Why do I have no feelings?* Yulchar had been the one who had led him along this journey, who had been kind when Huyen was gruff, and who had protected all of them against things of the demonic underworld. And yet... there he was, cavorting with Bimb.

Why would I expect anything different?

And why should he? Watching Bimb torture Huyen and then release Yulchar, Zhy thought back on a day when two men attacked, blindly and without provocation, a powerful warlock. *On those very stairs.* He should have expected a twist, a change, an evil outcome—there had been no reason, then, for Darrell to attack Ar'Zoth, and now there seemed little reason as to why Yulchar had so quickly snapped. But that is why he should have expected something after being brought back from the dead by Bimb's mother, carried in the jaws of a gherwza and then hauled back a thousand miles to the very place of his death. Why should he face any other fate than the exact same one?

I can't beat it twice, he thought.

And though he remained cowered behind the tree, he knew he was simply wasting time, waiting for either Bimb or Yulchar, or both, to destroy him with magic or cleave him with a sword.

φ

"Yulchar, my friend, I thought I commanded you to keep order among the demons that are loose. I did not expect to see you at my home. While a nice surprise, it is definitely a surprise!"

Behind his cover, could hear boots shuffle lightly on the stone. What was Bimb talking about? *Yulchar* had been responsible for the demons? But he had seen the man kill one in the Tunnels.

Sacuan bless us all...

He started at her voice. "Are you...?" he whispered softly.

I'm trying, Zhy, I'm trying... He could hear her voice catch. The steel was weakening as she realized, as Zhy had, that they had been betrayed.

"I-I decided it best not to follow your advice."

"What?"

"You see, I did quite a bit of thinking on the way here. We had been sent to find the boy Zhy—well, it was really Huyen who figured out the cryptic message. I went along because you had contacted me—"

"I had contacted you?" He sounded confused. "Me?"

What manner of madness is this?

"Of course... Wait, didn't you just say that you...?"

"Yes?"

"Is everything... is everything well with you?" Yulchar asked, in that sympathetic voice he had often used with Zhy.

But the voice trembled slightly as the knight realized he was dealing with someone immeasurably unstable.

"Everything is perfect. When did I contact you?"

"How else would you know my name?" the man veritably screamed. Bimb had addressed him by name and had given him specifics on a command and now he didn't remember?

"I'm sorry. I must have gotten confused there. And you are?"

"My name is Yulchar! Yulchar! You only just called me that. Are—why are you twitching?"

There was a long pause. "I'm not twitching, I have an itch. Perhaps... Yulchar, is it?"

Zhy pictured the man nodding. A needle fell from the fir tree. Zhy put it in his mouth and nibbled on it. The taste of pine brought back a pleasant memory of trotting through a forest with the two men who lay shattered in the ravine far below.

"Ah, perhaps my... ah... perhaps—"

"You look as white as the snow,"

"She was in my head. In my head! And now she has used me to contact you!"

"I don't f—"

"No, of course you don't!" he snapped. "Death!" He spat on the snow. "So that was your voice?"

"My voice?"

"Yes, you said you were coming. And... she must have done it! Oh, the pain. The pain she has caused me all these years, and now she drags you into it. So what is it that you are doing?"

"As I said," Yulchar continued, his voice wary and faded, "I have decided to come here. I've also taken the liberty of letting some demons out into the world."

"Some?"

"Some," he repeated. "The Tunnels of Woe are an interesting phenomenon," he said, and as he spoke, Zhy's heart fell to his frozen buttocks. "Yes, for centuries people have thought that demons were kept in check by the Temple of M'Hzrut. Right here we sit atop a great many demons. But there are lines that stretch from east to west, and they are easy to access from within the Tunnels."

Sacuan help us... Cerease repeated.

All hope had sunk or been smashed upon the rocks completely. It was a mass of wreckage upon the shores of the world. The demons would be let loose, Bimb would win, and he would die. Again. Zhy had heard a story once, of a ship that had crashed to shore far to the northeast on a desolate coastline inaccessible by normal means, for a massive cliff stood between the shore and sea. A man out exploring the area noticed the shape of a ship listing in the sea, and when he raised his spyglass to look, he ran away in horror. On every square inch of the ship, from the top mast to the rudder at the stern, along the bow, across all decking, and clinging to tattered sails, were rats. Rats. Red-eyed, slimly, mangy rats. Zhy thought briefly of their encounter with the enormous rat in the Tunnels and shuddered. Cold— a cold borne of wind, fear, and hopelessness, descended upon him and he nearly wept, for Belden and Welcfer were now that ship, crawling with rats.

Zhy, I am so sorry...

He had heard that before.

"Lines?"

"Yes, ley lines they call them, although they are just small rifts atop the underworld. They are quite harmless, and only a few demons really escape from there. Although 'escape' is not the word I would like to use, but... in any case. When inside the Tunnels, there are certain access points that can be used to open wider shafts in the ley lines. Unfortunately, they only stay open for as long as you are near the access point. We only camped next to a few, but still, I think I've achieved my goal."

"And that is?" The man's voice sounded very dark.

"Well, aren't you supposed to be guarding the demons? Keeping them at bay?"

"No! No, I'm going to release them! But she keeps stopping me." His voice was now that of a child or of a simple man who had been fighting against and unseen foe in desperation.

"Oh," the knight replied mockingly. "Then I guess I have arrived in time to help you."

"Help... me? I don't understand."

"Help you release them. I brought a present for you, something you might enjoy as a plaything."

Zhy's stomach turned to ice.

"Is that so?" Bimb asked.

"Yes, and in fact, I thought I could have brought him here dead already. If he hadn't keeled over from a small drop of the stuff, he'd be nicely wrapped in a bundle for you."

Zhy clenched his fists. So that was it. Yulchar *knew* Zhy could not handle liquor, and he deliberately forced it upon him, hoping he'd die from it.

"But he's hiding, yes he is. If you want, I can get him—"

"I'm sorry, but I am tired." The voice did indeed sound tired, as much as a lunatic would sound tired, but it was laced with an edge of calculating maliciousness: a boy with one hand feeding the cat and the other holding the knife.

"Yes, but, my gift." The pitch of Yulchar's voice changed such that Zhy knew he was turning to glance back at his hiding spot. Before, he had simply shut down and gone numb...now he waited with anticipation, the pine needle smashed in his teeth, and his fists clenched.

"You waste my time. You waste it utterly."

"I'm afraid I don't—"

"So how would these demons even get out of the Tunnels, can you answer that? I think you lie."

He could almost see Yulchar shrugging. "Some get out, some don't. We had to kill one just to keep up the disguise— and one turned out to be a giant rat, which would have done no good in the world. They got out by returning to the entrance near Vronga, or through the small springs and holes that are all over the place. Now that they are loose, however," he said with a deep breath, "once we release the demons from this point, the world will drown!"

It was Bimb's turn to sigh. "Listen, Yulchain, or whatever your name is... Listen to me! You are too late—I have won, I have removed her from my head, and now I am free. There are only a few steps left before I overrun the world with demons. There is nothing you can do, and further, I do not want your help. You think it was I who contacted you, but it was her. She fooled you and she fooled me, and now she will die."

"I have a plaything—something you would want to—" he repeated. Zhy hunkered deeper into his curled position against the tree.

"I have many toys here. I don't care what you brought. I think you lie just to save yourself."

"But I—" His voice was pleading and desperate.

"No, this ends now!"

There was a sudden movement in the snow, and Zhy could hear feet shuffling, followed by a grunt. He thought he heard another fire burning, but that was replaced by a scream that echoed across the valley. With inexorable slowness, he inched his face closer to the rock, daring only to expose an eighth of his eyeball as he peered gingerly at the scene below.

He nearly threw himself backward at the sight, but he feared any sudden noise would alert Bimb. Instead, his one eye throbbed as it took in the horror in the courtyard below. Yulchar was burning. Trapped in rivers and ribbons of yellow flame, he stood rooted in place, with only his arms flailing out among the inferno. Acrid smoke eventually reached Zhy's nostrils and this time bile lurched in his throat, and he had to spin back behind his cover, noise be damned. He forced the bile back down his throat with a grimace and then scooped a handful of snow into his mouth, following with several more pine needles.

φ

I looked at him with sadness as he burned. Even that fire I could control—every so often, I would remove particles from the fire, starve it of air, and then re-ignite it, just as I had done with the other knight. It was too bad. He had come a long way to die. And how dare he let the demons loose before I had my chance! Letting the demons loose was a waste. And to claim he had another companion—there were only two of them. Only two.

"Letting the demons out will ruin my plans!" I screamed at him. "If you even let out a small trickle, you have created a flood you can't stop. Don't you get it?"

He screamed louder.

"Stop screaming!" I pulled the fire away at the same time I threw up another invisible barrier. He still moaned, so I slapped his mouth shut. Ar'Zoth had taught me much, and not only magical spells. He had taught me not to suffer fools. Anyone who wanted to be a friend would stab you in the dark, and anyone who thought he was working with you was surely against you. If you should ever face them, he had said, give them what they don't want, and deny them what they need. And then kill them. In any case, this Yulchar was not here to help—he was another of mother's tools.

Was she still in her little box? There was a faint tugging, but I had escaped the trap she had laid—she did not expect me to react, she expected me to be ignorant when it came to the dead. I was a quick learner. If she had ever listened to me play the sutan, she would know this. She would know that a ten-year-old boy does not immediately pick up a ten-stringed instrument and play like a virtuoso. Did she care? No, she sat by the fire, drank her Sacuan-blasted spicy drink, and cried. She cried. Why not raise the monster you created, rather than moan about it? At least Fa loved me.

I waited a moment longer, but the tugging was gone. It must have been only a part of my imagination—I'd let my thoughts run to things I was trying to bury. Mother may not be gone forever, but she was of no concern now. Yulchar— Yulchain? What was his name...? In any case, he should be my focus. And whoever else was out there. Was there anyone? No, no I'd taken care of the other knight. ... And Yulchar thought he was working for me, did he?

There was no plaything, there couldn't be. He was a bad liar. True, he had betrayed his companions in an effort to assist me, but by releasing the demons, he'd made a mess of things. Now the soldiers would fight—the Black Dawn would fight, would be ready. They could not hold back the full force of the horde, but they would be ready, and giving the worthless citizens of Belden even the smallest opportunity to defend themselves was disturbing. Now they had warning, now they could prepare! I did not want my invasion to be wasted.

It was surely Mother who was behind this—only she would cloud men's minds, and goad them into joining her twisted vision of reality.

He looked like he wanted to speak, the vile worm. "Yes, you want to say something?"

The clamp across his mouth loosened and he coughed blood onto the snow. I looked at the bloodstain in despair—such a waste of the beautiful snow. "Or—" He coughed again. How irritating! "You will eventually find that the villagers will go on a great big"—another cough – "demon hunt and wind up killing each other."

"You bore me." I started the fire and let him scream. It was comforting to hear a man die in agony, especially against the backdrop of snow and rock, and the occasional green tree. Large snowflakes started to fall from the thick sky, and I opened my mouth to catch a few. I smiled as the man's screams turned to gurgles. Eventually the gurgling was replaced by hissing snow as the charred corpse collapsed to the ground. "Good day," I said, turning my back to the dead man. It was time for some honeyed chestnuts before I tore off the slab of rock beneath the courtyard. It had taken far too long for me to release the horde... far too long.

ф

Stand up, Zhy. Do it! Go to him!

"He'll kill me." Zhy's gaze had gone out of focus and he stared blankly ahead. His response was automatic.

No, I don't think he will, I think—

"He will kill me."

Zhy, listen, you have to something now. Now!

"Don't you get it?" he whispered, breaking from the trance. His words were clipped and spittle flew out into the chill air. "He will kill me. Just as Ar'Zoth had." Zhy shivered as a massive spasm of cold, rage, and terror shook his frame. *I'm not going to die again!*

Yulchar's screams were execrable—they echoed across the valley, careening off seemingly every mountaintop in the near distance. The smell of boiling flesh and muscle was overpowering, and as his body was consumed by fire, the knight's bellows became louder instead of tapering with death.

He is torturing him! Cerease was crying, but it was not the timid, meek cry. It was the cry of anger and bitterness. Zhy could sense her steel hardening. *You need to get out there now. He will soon be dead, and you need to face Bimb.*

"NO!" Zhy screamed and smashed a fist into the cold snow. It plowed straight through and landed on tuft of moss. With a curse, he flung the small pieces of green material into the woods. "He's going to kill me! Do you understand?"

He will not kill you, Zhy, she stated matter-of-factly. Her voice was again hard, and the emotions from before were completely erased. *We need time.*

"Time for what?"

I wish I knew. Once you step out there and confront him, I will be able to decide on an effective course of action. If he reacts as I expect, we will succeed. Do you still have the small knife?

Numbly, he reached back and felt his pocket for the miniscule bulge that was a small knife—nothing more than an instrument for peeling fruit. "What Sacuan-blasted good will that do?" He wanted to add, as he cast a sidelong glance at the ruined staircase, "*Against a man who can melt miles of stone?*"

You've killed with it before.

"That was dumb luck."

If you say so. Maybe we can rely on dumb luck one more time.

"I've used up my chances, Cerease. I don't want to die."

So you say.

"What is that supposed to mean?" He was tiring of this. If she had been able to summon a gherwza to help her drag his body a thousand miles, she could deal with Bimb. Let her save the world. Not Zhy.

I have been released from Bimb, Zhy. I don't know how he did it, but he has pushed me out. I am no longer as powerful as I used to be. You have to act.

"I—I'm not a hero." He was tiring of repeating that. He wasn't a hero in any sense of the word. Never. He never would be.

No, and I'm not asking you to be one. Heroes don't save the world, Zhy. Heroes stand on ledges and rescue people from fires, or pull them from the sea. Those who save the world have no name. No one knows your name. No one knows the names of the Protectors at the Temple, and no one knows Bimb. If the world can be destroyed by a nameless man who once was simple-minded, who once was my—she caught on the word—*son, then it can be saved by the town drunk. Now get up!*

Yulchar's gurgles were diminishing, though the smell still hung thickly in the air. Zhy rolled out from behind the rock and stood, his legs shaking. "I'm only doing this because you brought be back from the dead. From a death I didn't deserve. I only regret you didn't bring back Bruce and Darrell."

I could not reach them in time, she answered sadly. *No, Zhy, you do this because it is the right thing to do. Now, walk... as quickly as you can.*

Zhy stumbled and slid, cursing. Bimb paid him no mind. It was as if the man did not see him shuffling down the slope to the front ledge in front of the massive Keep. Zhy glanced up in time to notice the man quickly turning away—had he been looking right at Zhy? If he had, he gave no indication that he had heard anything, which was all the more disconcerting. Cerease's words echoed in his mind: *He won't see you. He won't see you.* He shook his head slowly, trying to convince himself that were true, but he still could not believe that a stumbling, nearly falling man would garner no attention. Soon he found his feet upon the snow-covered stone.

With effort, Zhy avoided looking at the charred hulk that was Yulchar. Bimb had turned away and started walking toward the door of the castle.

φ

Say his name, he swore he heard Cerease say, but her voice was faded and strained, as if she were fighting something.

Bimb twitched as if he heard, too. He was three or four paces from the lintel above the massive door when Zhy spoke, his breath coming out in a strangely thin and translucent plume of steam.

"Bimb," he whispered.

He had said it barely under his breath, but it could have been a shout. The man who now called himself Ar'Zoth turned slowly to face him. Zhy clenched his teeth and balled his fists, expecting... something. Something violent. He expected the flash of a sword, a burst of light, or even *Bolt of Sacuan* to come flying from the man's fingers. At least that would bring a quick end to everything.

But the look on the boyish face was one of utter horror. Now paler than any Welcferian, he was as tall as Zhy, if with thicker legs and a trimmer mid-section. Brown hair jutted in all directions, much like the unkempt black mass Zhy vaguely remembered seeing on Ar'Zoth. And normally demure eyes were wide in terror. There was a catch in Zhy's throat as he looked at the boy's eyes; they were nothing he had expected. Not the eyes of an idiot child, not the eyes of a raving madman, but a grayish blue that chilled better than the air atop the Spires of Solitude, and a piercing twinkle that belied a nearly bottomless well of intelligence.

He remembered wetting himself while facing Ar'Zoth. That memory was suddenly painfully clear—his own piss freezing to his leg as he hung above the canyon. And Ar'Zoth stood there, laughing, while Bimb...while Bimb ate a honeyed chestnut! He nearly drove at Bimb with the knife. *He ate a chestnut while I was murdered!* But those cold eyes of Bimb's held him, for the barest of seconds, and he swore he was still looking into the eyes of Ar'Zoth. Zhy froze in terror. *Don't be afraid, Zhy, don't—*

Some unseen hand seemed to push him forward and he nearly stumbled the two steps he took toward Bimb. Bimb likewise stumbled backward himself, his child-like eyes narrowed slightly before growing into wide pools of white.

"No..."

Chapter 37
It is Still Unknown

This world is a mess. It is so simple and backward that it has become a complex knot that one could call demonic. If there were not good people in the world, I would say it was a swirling pit of demonic energy that needed to be purged.

Unknown, IV age

The bodies lay scattered in the icy fields. Many were twisted by spears and arrows, others simply smashed remains against the unforgiving rocks, and countless others lay facedown from Sacuan-knew-what, limbs twisted into odd shapes, pools of blood coagulating in the cold, and skulls crushed by swords and maces. There had been no mage this time, he was thankful for that—too often these Welcferians brought their powerful magic-dealers and all that was remained were charred husks of men.

He often invoked the name of the Beldener prophet—a name he'd heard once from someone traveling in the northern wastes. The man had been nearly blind from the snow, and was en route to some holy temple or other, and he had called upon Sacuan to help him. In fact, he kept screaming the name as his sword cut the man in two. Hjor's underlings often wondered who Sacuan was, but he refused to tell them. If he could hold something over others, knowledge only he possessed, he would remain in control.

"Hjor"

Hjor. Both his name and the name of his clan. He wore both with vicious pride.

He looked over the scene. Red clouded his vision and he wiped the river from his eyes—a sword had nearly cleaved his scalp from his skull, but still he stood, if shaky. He stumbled through the field of dead bodies, every so often finishing with his sword what would have taken hours to finish, and grimacing each time. This battle was the worst he had seen in many years.

And there had been no mages! He shuddered.

Welcferian forces were getting stronger, and his tribes seemed to be getting weaker. That would have to change before next summer, or they would be wiped out completely. He thought back on that temple the strange Beldener was trying to find. The man had never said in which direction, but Hjor guessed south. Maybe there was better land to the south? Now was not the time to be considering a move, but he would have to, for already the deep winter was going to kill a thousand more. Added to the casualties he had taken today, and there would be no spring for the Hjor.

The forces moved away, and with a sickening feeling, Hjor noticed one of the men stop and look back... his look one of loathing. Hjor was a target in the open, ready to be plucked. Slowly, he raised his spear into the air, in a gesture of respect to the enemy—saying, *you have won, you may do as you please.*

But the small-man rode off. Hjor sagged, sighing deeply. *South, we must go south,* he thought, stumbling back to his small collection of huts.

They had a long winter and spring ahead of them—they needed to stay out of the way of the Welcferians, at least until late summer. The change in plans would definitely rile the elders, and many of the tribes, but it had to be done. He had a plan.

But this has nothing to do with the main story and can again be abandoned.

For now.

Chapter 38
You are a Piece of Wax

I am a bee, I am a bird, I am wax, and I am the flame.

Mad Hereald

I reached desperately for the spaces between all matter, but found only searing pain. Where tendrils and particles had once existed, now there were empty, blank, lifeless, dead spaces! How had she done that? Or had she? Was this Zhy—this man who Ar'Zoth had killed—doing something? Or was I simply frozen... by what? Fear? Where had Zhy come from? He was dead! He *is* dead! He was the drunk! The aimless, wild-haired, pointless piece of existence and he had been flung deservedly off a cliff onto jagged rocks. And he was dead!

Wasn't he?

Yet he stood before me. But why did he look as terrified as I felt?

I had removed the tea from the water, put it back in the leaf, yet I was powerless. My stomach was no longer tied in a ball, my head was clean and free, but there was nothing there! Nothing I could grasp—as with the first so-called Knight of the Black Dawn, I had reached out and found nothing.

He took another step toward me. I backed away, fearful of falling backward. Why would I fear that? I was the most powerful warlock in the history of the world! Why was I afraid of a dead man?

ɸ

"You." He pointed with a shaking finger. "You. You are dead. Dead. Dead," he repeated. He was as mad as Ar'Zoth. Wait, no. *He* was *Ar'Zoth*, Zhy reminded himself.

Now.

Zhy shrugged.

"You are dead and an apparition. I saw Ar'Zoth throw you off the cliff myself. I watched, back there." He pointed in a general direction but did not move his gaze from Zhy. "I was eating a chestnut."

Zhy nearly lunged at him with his bare hands, but he would be match no for this man, as crazy as he was. *Ate a chestnut while we all were murdered!* Cerease was right! But he'd learned the first time. No, better to play the opossum now. Somewhere far back in his mind, he remembered hearing that it was better to play dead when everything else had failed. And so, resisting the urge to wet his pants again, he remained silent and stared into those cold and lifeless eyes.

Do not say anything.

Of course he would not say anything, as terrified as he was of stepping out in front of a monster. Bimb was in every way a mirror of Ar'Zoth, his facial feature excepting, but he carried himself like a true madman.

ɸ

He shimmered in the cold, like the apparition that he was. Or was I just cold? He seemed like he was not there... He could not be there. He *should* not be there. There was no way a man could survive such a fall—I had looked at the body! It was smashed beyond all recognition. But... it had been whole. In one piece... Was there any way that he had...? No, that could not be. His companions were destroyed by the fall, and I knew nothing could survive such a fast plummet to those rocks. I had even felt his soul—I think that is what it was—as it hung outside of his body. He was dead.

"You are dead," I repeated, a little stronger this time.

The man stared—stared with lifeless eyes. If he spoke, would that mean he was alive? Or could the dead talk? Was this some trick of mother's?

ϕ

Zhy took another step forward and Bimb took another backward. He could not believe that such a dangerous man was backing away from him, as if he were truly an apparition. *He thinks you are dead. Say nothing, keeping walking slowly, maybe he will fall back off the cliff.*

Zhy moved forward. One step. Then another.

ϕ

I was going to end up falling backward off the cliff. But the dead man kept walking. Step after painful step, he approached me. If he was dead, I could run right through him easily were he truly an apparition. Unless...

"You want me to die. You want me to back up and finally fall."

Silence. Cold, dead eyes.

"Do you want me to run through you? Do you think I could?"

Nothing.

"Answer me! Answer me, you pathetic worm!"

If this was all an illusion that mother had designed, I should be able to walk right through him. She'd want me to fall back of the cliff to my death—she would want to see me perish in a most horrible way. Of course. But I would not give her that.

I took a deep breath, and then sprinted straight toward him.

 φ

Don't move! Whatever you do, don't move! He will go around you.

It took all of Zhy's willpower to stand stock still. He remembered being a child, and standing still to avoid a small swarm of bees—as long as he did not move a single inch, he would be safe. But this man was far more deadly than a couple of honeybees. Bimb was going to run into him—he was going to knock him back over the cliff, and he was going to fall to his death. Again.

No, he will not. Stand still!

φ

He wasn't moving! He was not going to move! What if he was solid? Would I bounce off him and fall into the canyon below? Or would I run right through him? I didn't want to take the chance that something could touch me, something from him, that would hurt me.

She was up to something. I knew it. She was gone, and with her, the tight grip on my stomach, but now she was here. Thankfully, she left my insides alone, but still I could smell her stench. I could smell brandy—even in death, she wanted a drink!

That bitch was going to die!

Somehow.

I reached the massive oak door and spun to face the man. He stood there, staring ahead in the same direction as before. Slowly, he turned, his lifeless eyes upon me. So deep, so vibrant, so cold, and yet... so lifeless. There was no spark of magic, no glitter that told of a hero, no scarring of a warrior. He was as a baby would be—blank, empty, without focus. He *was* dead.

"No! No, you cannot! You cannot stand here!" I yelled. He was most likely not there—something Mother had done, but I could sense nothing. I had cast her out. He could not be real. I shook my head as it filled with a loud buzzing sound.

I was desperate. Another spell like the *Bolt of Sacuan* reversal would surely destroy everything, but that was the only choice I had. The familiar bits of energy were there, swimming between everything else, and I started to string them together.

If I killed myself in the process, I would leave the horde unattended and not be able to see the fruits of my hard work. But that was the sacrifice, that was the price I was going to have to pay to be rid of her. To kill a dead man. To kill someone who had already been killed. No, it was not fair! It was baseless and putrid! I squeezed back the tears that were forming in my eyes, tears of frustration and hatred. This was far worse than having my bowels unplugged, worse by far. *Mother, how dare you! How dare you deny me my victory!*

But it had to be done. He was going to kill me. He was dead.

φ

He's going to—get out the knife, Zhy, it is time to take matters into your hands. Kill him. Strike at the stomach, and then the throat. Cut his—cut whatever you can cut, but be fast. He will try to retaliate, but he's starting to cast a spell, and it will be devastating.

Zhy pulled the knife out with a trembling hand. He could see the small flickers of light dance between Bimb's fingers and then swirl together into a ball. The blade of the small knife caught a glimmer of light that had dared poke through the leaden clouds. There was a brief flash the cold air. Bimb's head snapped to Zhy, who returned quickly to his frozen state. His knife, however, was clutched in his right hand and Bimb noticed it with wide eyes.

φ

He moved! The bastard moved! He was not dead...so, what had she done? Was she directing his body, like she had done with mine? If she could twist my stomach into a horrible knot, surely she could make a dead man hold a knife. No matter, the spell was almost ready. He was going to attack me, was he? With a small little knife that could barely cut through a piece of soft cheese? Yes, he could charge me, he could sprint, for all I cared—it would only take a brief second more before I destroyed everything within a square mile.

I was not scared of a small knife, not with the power that was soon going to destroy this entire valley. If only I could be sure it would not destroy the castle—no, no such thoughts could be had. This had to end now.

This was going to end in a spectacular way, whether I survived or not.

φ

Zhy sprinted at Bimb. At least, he at attempted to sprint, but he was filled with a sickening, nervous nausea, and his steps were sluggish and stumbling, like walking through a nightmare. He expected to die now. The ball of energy would strike him and destroy him in a quick burst of light— unless Bimb intended to burn him alive, as he did Yulchar. Zhy would have vomited again had his head not been filed with the constant urging of Cerease.

Now! Run, run, run! Drive the knife deep into—

The knife came up to slash Bimb's throat at the same time the man stretched his right arm back. A swirling, shimmering ball of purple and black flame danced along his palm. Small blue and green sinuous tendrils of light arced up from the surface of the ball and skittered along his fingertips, tripping tiny flecks to the snow. Where they touched the ground, miniscule holes opened in the ground— holes that had no bottom.

Suddenly his back arched, his mouth open in a rigid grimace, followed by an ear-splitting scream that echoed across the wide-open expanse around the castle. His hands flew upward as his torso flipped back awkwardly, and the purple ball leapt nearly straight into the air—to the south and west. The whirling ball of energy streaked across the gray landscape, rising in an arc until it vanished in the cloud cover. Where it passed through the sky, coal-fire orange flames burned in snaking ringlets, and the clouds glowed ominously purple for a brief moment. There was a roar as the ball careened back down on its arc and ignited violently against a snow-capped peak in the far distance. Of the mountain, nothing remained but a boiling cloud of smoke, ash, and steam—a cloud shaped much like a woodland fungus as it billowed into the far horizon.

ϕ

As I started to hurl my energy, a sudden, searing sensation pierced my spine, forcing me to curl back in an unrelenting agony. Cold metal bored into my back, just above my buttocks, and I screamed aloud—the pain was overpowering and smothering, and at the same time pointed and full of a million tiny needles as they poked my entire body. My legs felt made of water and I wobbled on the stones as I slowly lost any connection to my appendages. Contact with the ground was lost and I felt nothing. The devastating spell went astray, and violently so, but I was blinded by pain.

I tried to reach back and remove the metal implement from my back, but the sword had pierced where I couldn't reach and I flailed like a cockroach on its back. My legs tingled for a second, and there was a dull pain, numb and shocked with electricity. I had fallen. My right cheek fell hard against the stone and I could only see the large castle in front of me and the dead man's legs. Pain had been replaced by a numbness, and the world began to dull and fade—I could no longer focus on anything. The castle slowly turned to a blurry, waterlogged blur before fading to the background, and the dead man's legs vanished completely. Soon there was nothing but blackness.

And a tired voice... no, a once-tired voice, a voice that had once been weak and pleading. The voice was now kind. Yet there was an edge of sadness, a vein of something I could not quite describe... but twined within sympathy was a hard edge of steel.

I told you I would stop you.

φ

Zhy spun and watched with a gaping mouth at the form of Huyen. His sword hung loose in his hands and it clattered point-first to the cold stone, and he leaned heavily upon it. His legs shook noticeably through the thick leggings, and his torso swayed slightly. The surly Knight of the Black Dawn was covered in snow, his face a mess of scrapes and scratches. His coat flung open and snow-covered fur flaps swung slowly in the light breeze. Huyen stumbled slightly as he tried to take a step forward, and he rested a moment. After a heavy sigh, he heaved his sword up, sheathed it, and slowly approached Zhy, his scowl deep and dark. The knight took another step forward, but finally collapsed to the stone.

Repressing the instinct to rush and save the man, Zhy forced himself to wait a moment before acting. This could be a trap, to bait him into helping before Huyen finally killed him outright.

"Zhy..." He heard the man whisper. "I'm... I'm not going to hurt... you."

"Why should I believe that?" Zhy asked, standing still.

Huyen coughed, and Zhy could see a plume of steam up into the air as he struggled to bring himself back to a standing position. "Could you...?" he asked.

Zhy didn't move.

"So be it." The knight cursed as he wobbled and swayed on the snow-covered stone. "I thought perhaps you'd be thankful for me saving you, and..." He pointed out to the landscape. "And all of this."

"The masses thank you, I'm sure," Zhy said. He still clutched the small knife in his hand and stared at it dumbly. What good would it be against Huyen or anyone? What good had it ever done him?

Huyen noticed and nodded slowly. "They should thank you too, Zhyfrael."

He didn't bristle at the name and instead looked up at Huyen. His eyes seemed misty. Perhaps it was the cold.

"You have done a great deed today. I thank you. I also understand your mistrust." He coughed suddenly and moved a hand to his chest, but winced sharply as the hand pressed against the roasted flesh.

"Seeing as Yulchar led us to this awful place only to kill us, I don't trust anyone at the moment."

Huyen bent down with a groan and looked at Bimb's body. "Such a waste...such a Sacuan-blessed waste. I'm afraid I've only made things worse by doing that."

"Worse, how?" Zhy backed away a step. What was he rambling about? Was he turning like Yulchar had?

"No." He shook his head. "I know what you are thinking. Yulchar, he... I can't believe it." Huyen shook his head again sadly. "No, by killing this—demon—we've left something unguarded, something vile and dangerous. I can hear them, buzzing like flies, as I'm sure you can."

Zhy took another step back.

Huyen attempt a chuckle, but the grimace returned. "Or perhaps not. In any case, there is something horrible and destructive right beneath our feet, or at least close by. That means something quite horrible."

"And what would that be?"

"The Temple of M'Hzrut is in the wrong place!"

"Wrong... place?"

"Yes, listen. I know you can't hear any of the buzzing, but try. Surely anyone with any spark of ability could hear it."

Zhy strained to listen, to see if he could hear something— instead only the light rustle of wind through mighty balsams floated across the valley. He shook his head slowly.

Huyen nodded. "Well, there is a buzzing, and beneath that a scratching, like so many termites or beetles, or..."

"Demons," Zhy whispered.

"And he was going to unleash them... but what if they still find their own way out? I think they will. That confirms that the Temple serves little purpose where it is." He looked up and to the east, his mind's eye trying to picture the Temple of M'Hzrut those many miles away across a trackless wasteland. "Ar'Zoth and Bimb kept them at bay, even though they were going to release them anyway. But now... now what?"

Zhy sighed. Had they only made it worse? "So let me understand. A mix-up in paperwork is what got Ar'Zoth here in the first place, and his scheming, no doubt, brought Bimb here." He spat into the cold air. "And now the demons are completely unguided. All of the demons! The Temple in the wrong place, and... and..." His face fell into an expression of hopelessness.

Huyen gazed sadly at the destruction around him and coughed again. His hand drifted to his chest, but he let it drop. "There's not much that can be done now, except try to get word out. Get to the Temple, get someone here." They stood for some time, gazing dumbly into a bleak world. Zhy felt as if they had accomplished little or nothing in killing Bimb. Things had only worsened.

"Is there nothing you can do?" Zhy's tone was almost pleading. They had just beaten perhaps the most powerful warlock in existence, a man who could reduce an entire mountain to a mushroom-shaped cloud, and now they stood powerless in the cold, while a throbbing mass of demons pulsed beneath them, scratching inexorably toward the surface.

"No, my magic is not strong enough to keep a horde of demons at bay—not a horde that size, anyway. It's overwhelming."

"Did you hear Yulchar?" Zhy asked quietly. Small flakes started to fall from the sky and fluttered languidly on the slight breeze.

Huyen's face was grim. "I heard enough. I hope there are enough Knights to deal with whatever he has created. I suppose we'll need someone down in the Tunnels, too, to seal off the openings."

There was a tense silence, and steam slowly filled the space between the men as they stared glumly at everything and nothing. "I fear we've done no good," Zhy said sadly.

"We have done what we came to do—there is more yet to do, and we are nearing the end of this chapter."

Zhy's head snapped up at that as a sudden gust of air whipped through the enormous trees. "What did you just say?"

Huyen's look was blank. "I'm sorry. It happened again... I said something, didn't I? As if someone were using my lips..."

"No matter, but you're right. I hope I wake up from this, but it feels less and less like a dream. Just one question, though... Why didn't you use magic back there?" Zhy asked as they surveyed their surroundings. The black void pulled their collective gazes toward it, as if it were the only thing around. Zhy shook his head and forced himself to look out across the sprawling countryside, and finally back at the twisted corpse of Bimb.

"Do you mean when I attacked Bimb?"

"Yes."

"He would have sensed it, I'm sure... would have fired one of his spells that melted the stairs, and you'd be dead."

"I already am dead." He wished he had the words back as soon as he uttered them.

"No you are not. Stop saying that."

"I'm sorry. I feel that I still am—especially with him. Bimb, that is. He acted like I were an apparition—a ghost. Why would he act that way?"

"He expected you to be dead, so he fully believed it. Only you and I—and Yulchar, curse his dead soul—knew that you were not fully deceased. And so"—another cough—"you were able to at least detain him until I could do something."

"I thought he killed you. That blast—"

"That blast went over my head, thankfully. I rolled off down into a snow bank. As soon as I saw the fire, I screamed as loud as I could, to make it sound as if I were dying."

Zhy shook his head and looked down at the steep rise, and out along the valley. *I should be happy that monster is dead,* he thought, but there was little to celebrate. The death of a mad warlock would not save the world from the demons—they needed help, help from people who knew what they were doing. These Protectors, as he had heard them called, they needed to be here. Perhaps even another warlock. He shivered at that thought. Well, at least one saner than Bimb or Ar'Zoth.

But as he stared out at the frozen landscape, he couldn't help the feeling of despondency and loss wash over him. They had only scored a very minor victory.

Chapter 39

... An End is a Beginning

After a strenuous task, a respite is important. But do not dither too long, for well-deserved rest can turn into idleness and sloth.

Cleric Hyun

It was much harder to descend the steep slope than to ascend it, now that only two of them remained.

They rooted around the castle and found a few bricks and some pieces of wood. Huyen took a few moments to investigate inside the castle, but there was nothing of interest that he could find, apart from a collection of smashed teacups, a new coat to replace his burned one, and some clean cloth, which he could affix to his wound.

Once they had some bricks and other useful materials, they set to work in the fading daylight. It was a dangerous task, placing bricks into the nearly sheer rise. They brought their packs and had to be careful to shift the gear inch by inch. The knight coughed often, a dangerous, wheezing cough, and every so often spat out a pinkish liquid, but he continued working.

Huyen had set a large brick into the hillside, and found he could stand safely on it. Grabbing a thick pine branch, he swung his body around to face the staircase. From their vantage point, they were looking down on the remains of the great stone structure.

Huyen hung precariously from a tree branch, and swung his arm down in order to slide a brick to Zhy, who caught it before it flew off the edge of the world. At an urging from the knight, he turned himself onto his belly and crawled face-first down the extreme slope. He set the stone a few feet below the other one. When he had gathered enough courage to turn his gaze away from the mountainside, he stretched to view the hole.

He expected at least to see a pile of rubble at the bottom of the pit, perhaps a few shattered pieces of stone, and piles of fresh snow. But there was nothing. *Nothing.* But that word did not do any justice to what he was looking at—as if the crater somehow sucked light from the very air. Zhy had the feeling that his gaze was being pulled down into the void. Along the edges of the pit, he swore he saw swirling tendrils of white light, but that could have been an illusion from the stark white snow against a black that was darker than any starless night. Zhy shivered and took another tentative step onto a block.

And thus they made their painful way to the base of the trail. At the bottom, Zhy and Huyen paused for a rest.

"I must thank you."

"Why?" the gruff knight replied.

"For saving my life."

"Don't thank me, Zhyfrael. You did most of the work. And she, too, of course."

Zhy stopped and listened, but heard nothing apart from the light hush of the wind. Where had Cerease gone? "I think she's gone... So, you aren't going to kill me now that you have the chance?"

Huyen's laugh was out of place in the cold air. He laughed easy and free, his scowl all but vanished, and his normally pinched eyes turned upward. "No, Zhy... Zhy, I am not."

Tears welled in his eyes, and for a moment, he wanted to hug the man. After the previous ordeal, he would've thrown himself off the cliff had the knight been as rude and scurrilous as he had been on the journey. "I don't—"

"Do not think I have not thought of it before... before we found out who Yulchar really was. I always suspected him, and you, of course, but you have proven yourself. But remember, if you show any signs—" His hand went to his sword.

Zhy nodded slowly. *A gherwza, its fangs surely dripping, carried my body those thousand miles to my home... If I show any signs, I'd be glad if you killed me.*

Without a word, Huyen turned to retrieve their skis where they had left them. "And these"—he grunted, hefting Yulchar's skis—"can be tossed." The wooden implements fluttered end over end, as Huyen heaved as hard as he could. Zhy listened, and after a few moments, heard them land with a soft crack.

Zhy and Huyen skied slowly along the trail, sharing idle talk for a few moments, before turning their full attention to the trail.

Zhy, I must go now. He needs to—

And she was gone.

φ

"Great Sacuan's scrotum!" Zhy exclaimed.

"Will you please stop saying that?" Huyen barked. "It's getting very old."

"I—"

"Never mind, never mind. I am sorry," he said, recovering himself. "I was deep in thought there. What—what is it?"

Zhy pointed.

They had stumbled upon the body of Tralen, a stiff blue corpse prostrate in a field of bloody snow. Huyen reached down and flipped the man over, and uttered his own curse. "Tralen," he muttered and glanced around.

"Another demon?" Zhy asked.

"No!" the knight spat. "One of us. A Knight. His name is—was Tralen. The most arrogant fool I had ever met." He stared at the body, his jaw set. "They are after us, too, Zhy. You can be sure of that now."

By now, Zhy had seen so many bodies he barely paid any mind to the blood-soaked snow. Small tracks of some small animal covered the snow, and small droplets of blood led every which way, as they were carried by the animals.

"Why would they be after us?"

"Because we left the Order to find you. Yulchar didn't want Gryn to off on his own, but once we figured things out—about Ar'Zoth and all that—and the strange encounter in Vronga, we went our own way. I am sure they were out to kill us, remove us if you will. And surely Tralen here would volunteer for that task."

"But why, if you were going after a warlock like Ar'Zoth?"

"Because of you."

"Me?"

Huyen nodded. "You and your companions. Look, we were not far behind you when Gryn took off. He thought you were in league with the warlock and went to kill you. Ah, don't worry. It all worked out. In any case, once we made our discoveries, we figured perhaps that was not true, but we knew for sure that Ar'Zoth was very dangerous. But you could never explain that to someone like Dran'Za or Tralen."

"Dran'Za...?"

"Our fat leader with little sense of anything except how to make cake," Huyen answered absently. He was still furiously searching the terrain for something. "Look over here," he said finally, pointing to the edge of the cliff. "It looks like someone took a fall. And ski tracks all over the place. I didn't know Tralen knew how to ski. The bastard knew everything. Everything!"

"Someone fell?" Zhy asked. He was confused.

"Yes, over there. But why is the snow melted here?" Huyen pointed to the barren ground. He peered over the edge, where he could see the impressions left by the falling body.

But where had it gone?

φ

The trip back to the Tunnels and then to the Temple was uneventful—the corpses of the Protectors lay only feet from where Zhy and Huyen walked, but the snow had buried every last trace of the slaughter. And by now, Gozath had shambled farther north.

When they at last emerged from the Tunnels, Zhy was so exhausted he kept his head down and walked forward with painful steps, missing the beautiful scenery around him. A deeper layer of snow covered the birch and fir trees, and the piles around the Temple nearly reached the small stained-glass windows.

After curt introductions, someone ushered him to a cot and he fell asleep.

"He looks dead," another man said.

"Oh, stop saying that!" he heard a familiar voice complain.

I'm not dead. No, not this time. Thankfully. But, you never—

The thought was cut off as Zhy's loud snores filled the room.

Epilogue

... And though the world may be random, confused, chaotic, and senseless, there are those who do good for the cause of good. There are those who save others who need saving, and damn those who need damning.
Often they know not what they do.
Great warriors of the Light often lurk in darkened corners and simply lend a hand when needed, while the loudest voices who profess the Light are themselves darkened shells.
This world is not guarded by men bearing arms, or men who pray the loudest. Nay, it is saved and served by those who have no name...
And by those who may be dead.

Prophet Altyu-M'Zhkara, IV Age

Fanlas tossed restlessly.
Fa?
A child's voice floated through the dark void of dreams. He almost smiled, remembering Bimb.
Fa? The voice repeated.
Was that Bimb? Could it be? How?
"Bimb?" he whispered in his sleep. Just a dream. Just a dream.
Fa, I am sorry. Very sorry. I did something very bad.
Tears started welling in his eyes. He wanted to wake up, to get away, to ignore the voice. It had to be a nightmare. There were still months left of his watch. But something seemed to tug at him, another voice, a deeper, sadder, and softer voice, and it told him to remain as we was.
You are not dreaming.

"I understand, son. You are in the north as well?" He wanted to hope against hope. But he knew. He knew.

I... was. I am gone now. I am sorry.

Rivers flowed freely from his eyes.

Fa, a bad man got hold of me. A very bad man. I went to the north. I killed people. Lyn wanted me to kill the bad man, but I didn't kill him until he killed others.

"Bimb, I know you are not simple anymore. I know..."

No, but I'm going back. Back. I don't want to forget things... Please write them down.

"But if I wake up, you will go away..."

I can hold on a little. I'll keep it simple—Fanlas thought he heard a laugh at that—*and you fill in the gaps later.*

Sobbing, Fanlas opened his eyes and then lit a candle. From the side desk in the room, he retrieved a sheaf of paper and quill. And he wrote furiously as Bimb relayed his version of events, from the first meeting of Ar'Zoth in his mind to Zhy's father, and finally, to his end at the hands of Zhy and Huyen.

Not soon after he had relayed the last piece of information, Bimb stopped. Fanlas could almost hear the sigh, and he heaved one himself. He felt as if he had let every last drop of emotion flow down his cheeks, and there was nothing left but to sigh, offer a smile for his son, and put down the pen.

Fa, I have to go now. Ma is here. Plus, I have to—

Suddenly, the voice was gone.

Fanlas stared at the ceiling. No sense in striking out now—there was work to do. He rose and started rousing the others. Sleep was to be a memory for now, for the work was still not finished.

"It is never finished," he whispered.

ϕ

In Belden City, a burly innkeeper wiped the bar with a clean rag. The shadows were long and the cold rainy days of winter would soon bring with them an influx of customers. He stared for a long moment at a polished stool, and shook his head sadly. Almost as an afterthought, he opened the front door and scanned the street, but there was nothing of concern. With another slow shake of his head, he returned to the murky inn.

φ

In Welcfer, a weary father rose early and marshaled his troops. The army was smaller, but they could pick up fresh recruits on the way. Thankfully, the freezing rain had stopped and a few days of brilliant sunlight had melted enough ice that passage to the east was difficult, but not impossible. Drunplug scowled as he left Foltrag, scowled at the sun, at his troops, and at that pulling at his heart. Wherever Darrell had gone, he was most likely not coming back—he hoped the next battle would be short, but he knew it would be bloody. Without the help of his son, this war would never end.

φ

Zhy awoke in a darkened room. A dull light flickered, and he smelled wood smoke. For a moment, he thought his house was on fire. His eyes jerked open and he tried to focus on his surroundings, but nothing made sense. He had expected to awake in his home in Belden—wasn't someone supposed to be pounding on the door?

But no, he was in a small, dusty room. It looked almost like a temple of sorts with the altar, the stained-glass windows, the fireplace, and—

He shot upright, and the cot creaked loudly with his movement.

Huyen was eating from a bowl; steam wafted up, bringing with it the sweet smell of apples. Another man sat before the fire. He turned to look at Zhy, and the resemblance to Bimb nearly knocked Zhy over. "You—" he started, but Huyen waved him off.

"Well, good morning, Zhy."

"Good... Wait, I... How did we—did we?"

"Did we what?" Huyen asked around a mouthful of porridge. "Oh, did we make it back across? Yes, you don't remember? Ah, you must have slept hard. Remember our trek back to the Tunnels, and then north?"

Slowly he remembered their journey back from Ar'Zoth's castle. It was still fuzzy, but he knew this time it was due to exhaustion. It had to be. Everything was crisp and clear. "At least I'm not back in Belden City," he said softly.

Huyen laughed. It was strange to hear the surly knight laugh. But much had changed. Too much. "Aye, but this time you didn't die!"

"I didn't at that," Zhy said, managing a chuckle. "So, now what?"

"Fanlas here has agreed to help us move the Temple. I'm hoping you'll decide to help—the danger should be over now, at least in this part of the world. I don't think we can take the full altar, but we may get the main pieces onto sleds. When new Protectors arrive, they can send a couple more men over, but basically, we have to pack this up and get it over to Ar'Zoth's—I hate saying that. What do we call it?" he wondered.

"How about what it is," the man named Fanlas said. He really did look like Bimb. "The Temple of M'Hzrut."

"Aye, we shall. So, Zhy," the knight said, "will you join us?"

What else was there to do? He had been dead and brought back to life, but his only real contribution in defeating Bimb was the fact that the man had thought he really was dead. Maybe Zhy really was dead himself, and he was just dreaming a dream within a dream. If he wasn't, there was nothing to go back to in Belden. Kahl would be bitter he was losing money, but—

Kahl! Memories flooded back, in full this time. Every last image was sharp and clear, and Zhy let his mind race across his first journey to the north. Even the scowl on Kahl's face, and his smirks and smiles were fresh in his mind. He could picture every nuance of Bruce and Darrell, and sadly, each detail of their horrible demise. He held his head in his hands and trembled slightly.

"I'm no hero," he said softly, at last raising his head.

Huyen stopped in mid bite. "No one is asking you to be one. You have become quite a good skier of late, and we need all the men we can take to move this place. The faster the better. There is no time."

"I've been hearing that a lot lately."

"That is because it is true. Look, Zhy, there is a demonic horde out there. You know that now. With Ar'Zoth, Bimb, gone"—he chanced a look at Fanlas, who winced—"everything is out of control."

"Who can control them?" Zhy asked. How could the death of one man disrupt an entire horde?

"I will let the old mage explain on the way. I am sure he is coming."

"Indeed I am," the gray-bearded man replied as he emerged from behind the altar. Had he been there the whole time? "Zhy, you may not think yourself as part of all of this, but you are. We would like your help for the final task. I am going to need help. Even though I can keep the demons back, I cannot do it alone. Look at this place." He gestured to the Temple.

"I never said I wouldn't go," he said hotly. These religious types always seemed to make him nervous. "I'll go. I'll go."

www.ingramcontent.com/pod-product-compliance
Lightning Source LLC
Chambersburg PA
CBHW062122170626
46813CB00002B/536